Cauldrons and Cat Tails

Cover illustration and design by Žana Arnautović

Chapter header and page break images by Etheric Designs

✿ Formatted with Vellum

Cauldrons and Cat Tails

MOONVALE MATCHES
BOOK TWO

HAILEY BLACKWOOD

THE REALM
OF
ALDOVA
Dragonspear Mountains
Tidegrove
Ash Hills
Rockward
Sunhaven
Willowvalley
River of Wishes
Kingston
Oakhollow
The Barren Lands
River of Hope
River of Souls
Starshore
Moonvale
Greenwood

For my readers seeking escape in stories.

Welcome back to Moonvale.

Author's Note

I want to make sure everyone is FULLY aware: ***Cauldrons and Cat Tails***, while cozy and stress-free, does contain themes that might be upsetting to some readers.

You can expect:

- Adult Language
- Explicit Sexual Content
- Very Mild Injury/Blood
- Alcohol
- Accidental Ingestion of Behavior-Altering Substances
- Intentional Ingestion of Behavior-Altering Substances

You may proceed. (:

CHAPTER 1
Kizzi

"**O**ld Gods spare me," I grumbled through clenched teeth as I fought to yank my arms out of my cauldron.

Brown tar-like sludge clung to my fingers and splattered onto my worktable as I tried to extract my hands from another failed cauldron concoction. I was elbow-deep in the monstrosity, and it was holding onto me for dear life.

Something went terribly awry. Again.

Gods damned sprites.

Sprites had been making my life a living Hell's Realm for months. Years, really. Almost my whole life. The wretched, tiny creatures ruined *everything* for me.

I'd done anything I could think of to try to get them to leave me alone. I performed rituals. I set up salt barricades. I brewed repellent tonics. I called in other witches for help.

Nothing worked. They always came back.

The supposed-to-be-energizing-potion refused to release me even after I yanked my arms free from the cauldron, sticking to my skin like it wanted to swallow me whole. I dunked my hands in a bucket of steaming water, scrubbing my skin raw with my strongest cleansing soap.

My forearms burned like the heat of Aldova's dual suns, but the slime slowly dissolved. The bucket of water turned murky, like a stagnant, smelly swamp. It was gag worthy, truly.

A long-fingered hand flitted into my field of view, startling me from my efforts. I flinched so hard my heart nearly stopped, probably shaving a few days off my lifespan.

"You've got a little something there..." The finger swiped across my forehead, gathered a chunk of the sludge. "You're lucky your hair is tied back today, or it would be a mess. I bet we would have to cut it off."

Fiella, my best friend and the local vampire trinket shop owner, examined her sludgey finger with a grimace, her fangs gleaming in the warm enchanted light illuminating from the ceiling sconce. "What is this? It's disgusting." She wiped her finger on a cloth, and then wiped again—harder this time. Only some of the substance came off onto the fabric. She glowered at it.

Her vibrant blue hair (that I had made possible, you're welcome, Fiella) was twisted back into a loose braid that flowed over her shoulder like water. A few strands escaped and hung by her face and the nape of her neck. Her long, lean figure was draped in a comfy-looking tunic and trousers and short black boots adorned her feet. The soles must've been enchanted or something because they didn't make a *peep* when she walked in.

"Gods! You're as quiet as a wraith, make a noise next

time." I resisted the urge to clutch my thundering heart—this tunic was too cute to ruin with slimy cauldron remnants.

"You just have bad hearing. I walked in here like a normal folk," she grumbled.

"Whatever. You seem freakishly sneaky to me." I glanced at Fiella as she stepped around my worktable. "Wait—no, don't touch that!" I swatted her hand away from the basket she was about to pull off a stool.

She froze, the color draining from her already pale cheeks. "Kizziah Cedarton, what is in this basket?" She leaned over hesitantly, trying to glance inside. "It better not be what I think it is."

"You're using my full name right now? It's not that serious." I snatched the basket and shoved it under a cubby, my wet hands leaving a trail of water in their wake. The grasshoppers inside chirped loudly.

"Ugh, bugs!" Fiella visibly shivered. "I hate those fucking things."

"I know you do, you big blood-sucking baby. They're gone now. You can sit. Just... don't touch anything." I resumed my station before my cauldron, considering my options. The massive bowl was half-full of roiling, twitching brown sludge. It was somewhere between a liquid and a solid and seemed to have a mind of its own. Considering how aggressively it had clung to my skin, it would be *impossible* to clean up.

I crossed my arms over my chest, tapping my foot in frustration.

Paper rustled behind me; the scent of caramelized sugar bloomed in the air. My mood lifted immediately.

"You really are a good friend." I whirled around, reaching a hand out expectantly.

Fiella paused mid chew. "You think these are for you?" She snorted. "These are mine. Get your own." Sugar fell from her (still somewhat messy) fingers and settled onto her lap. She brushed it off absentmindedly. The particles settled on the floor like a fine dusting of snow.

My jaw dropped. "You come into *my* shop to chow down on pastries and don't bring me any? You're the–" She pulled out another pouch with a low chuckle and tossed it in my direction.

"I was just messing with you. I would never—I am not a demon." She chuckled darkly. "Lemon scones today. They're incredible."

I caught the pouch and yanked it open, inhaling the delectable fumes. "Thank the Gods. I almost cast a curse on you."

I looked around for a clean cloth—I would be damned if I ate anything my grimy hands touched. Sure, I had scrubbed them hard enough to draw blood, but they still felt tainted. A small white handkerchief came to my rescue.

The scone was still warm, perfectly crispy with a tangy bite of citrus. I groaned around my mouthful. "Did Mitz make this one?" Mitz ran the bakery in town, and that alone made her one of my favorite folk in the entire realm.

Fiella nodded, swallowing heavily and taking a swig from her steaming mug before speaking. "Of course. You think these angelic creations came from the coffee shop? Nope, that's good old fashioned fae handiwork."

"She's Old Gods blessed." I shoved the rest of the scone in

my mouth with a happy hum, tucking the handkerchief into my tunic.

"So, care to explain the situation in the corner over there?" The vampire pointed to the cauldron steaming menacingly, mocking me. I glared at it.

"Those damned sprites again. I was trying to brew up a large batch of energizing potions, they must've snuck some extra ingredients in when I wasn't looking. I don't even know what it's become at this point, but it makes me nervous. And it's going to be a nightmare to clean up."

A large bubble rose to the surface and popped, splattering miniscule specks of liquid onto every nearby surface. I stuck my tongue out at it while flipping it my middle finger.

Fiella smoothed her hands over her arms and shivered. "I can feel a lot of magic in here. More than usual. Did you put extra oomph into it or something?"

I shrugged. "I might've. It was a big batch—I was planning to store the extras to prepare for when Mayor Tommins inevitably clears me out again." He really bought a ridiculous amount of them. It was a miracle that his heart hadn't given out by now, that much stimulant could *not* be good for anyone.

"If you say so. It just... feels weird."

I flapped my hand at her. "You worry too much. It feels perfectly normal here to me."

But that wasn't necessarily true. I always tuned out the magic around me, I would be overwhelmed if I didn't. I did notice that my spells were coming more naturally in recent weeks, though. My potions, too, took less strain. I assumed I was just becoming more talented. I was an excellent witch... But maybe they were coming a little *too* easily.

Magic was a tricky thing. It was everywhere, sure, but only in remnants. Magic wasn't nearly as abundant as it was when the Old Gods roamed the realm. Or so the texts said. These days, it was a limited resource. Crumbs of magic could be found in old relics, clinging to trees, gathering in quiet places. It condensed in areas of extreme emotion, it slithered through forgotten corners of the realm. Wisps of it followed around every living creature, some folk more than others, but most didn't realize it. Witches were the most attuned.

Most of the remaining magic in the realm could be found within the bodies of the magical folk—witches, wizards, and the few lucky others.

Fiella stood, breaking me from my thoughts. "No offense, but I need to get out of here. I'm afraid I'm going to touch something I'm not supposed to in this mess." She looked around distastefully. "And that thing is giving me the heebie jeebies."

She glared at my cauldron, flashing her fangs in a threatening snarl.

I laughed at her antics. "Fair enough! Have a good day! Sell lots of shit and smooch your man for me!" I blew her an exaggerated kiss, grimacing when I realized I'd touched my lips directly to my sludge-tainted hand.

"Sure, Kiz. I love you to the moons!"

"I love you to the suns! Even if you're a pansy about a harmless ruined cauldron brew."

She chuckled under her breath as she left, pulling the door shut behind her with a muffled thud. She opened it a moment later, sticking her head inside. "Oh! I almost forgot. What are you bringing to the annual Moonvale potluck? It's only a few days away."

I had completely forgotten about the potluck. With all the madness happening lately, it had slipped my mind. "Shit! Something easy, I guess. Maybe stew?"

Fiella snorted. "You think anyone will eat *your* stew when Ginger will be bringing hers? Not likely. You better think of something else. I'm bringing blood smoothies."

I gagged. "Nobody is going to drink those except for bloodsuckers. That's revolting."

Fiella flashed a fanged grin. "That's exactly the point. More for me. And Redd too, I guess. And the others. Whatever, there aren't any rules against it."

"I'll figure something out. Don't worry." My mind whirled through the possibilities.

"Meet at Ginger's Pub for dinner?"

"Of course." I would definitely not be cooking for myself.

Fiella gave me a thumbs-up and shut the door again, heading to her trinket shop. She was always a late riser, starting her days when the rest of us were already up and moving.

If I was being honest, I was a horrendous cook. I could brew potions and poultices and tonics like nobody's business, but the edible stuff was a completely different story. Flavor was the hardest part—no amount of magic could improve the taste of something foul.

Unfortunately, a new rule had been implemented for the annual Moonvale potluck this year and it was very clear; you could only indulge in the feast if you brought something to contribute.

I would certainly bring *something*. Would it be delicious? Definitely not. But would it be edible? Probably. Maybe.

Hopefully.

I returned to my largest cauldron, planting my hands on my hips in contemplation.

It would take a *lot* of work to clean the horrendous sludge out of the bowl, and I was *not* in the mood for that kind of manual labor at the moment. I shoved the cauldron into the corner, out of the way, so I could deal with it another day.

I was huffing and puffing and glistening with sweat by the time I got the massive bowl far enough out of the way to avoid impacting my workflow. I could have sworn it was much heavier than it should have been. Like it was filled with rocks instead of slimy potion.

I dusted my hands off, proud of myself for such an impressive physical feat, and returned to my lists of daily tasks. I would have to brew my potions in my smaller cauldrons now that my favorite cauldron was temporarily out of commission, but that wasn't a problem. Only a minor inconvenience.

I refastened my green wavy hair back into a tighter bun, pulled a fresh apron over my tunic, and got to work.

I paid extra attention to my ingredients, triple checking everything and watching the cauldrons like a hawk to ensure no surprises were added.

Damned sprites.

My biceps were aching and my back was straining from the effort by the time I finished the day's brews; a new batch of energizing tonics for Mayor Tommins, ten sachets of healing poultice for the healing clinic, a pain reducing potion for the coven leader and oldest witch in town, Ani, a pouch of sobering dust for Ginger's Pub, and a bucket of magical blue dye for the clothing shop.

I set off to make my delivery rounds.

Some folk in Moonvale chose to come by the shop to retrieve their orders, but if I had the chance, I preferred to deliver them. Especially these days, when every extra moment they lingered in my shop was an extra opportunity for those damned sprites to get their grubby mitts on them.

I strapped my heavily laden satchel onto my back, glared at the cauldron in the corner one more time for good measure, and slipped out the front door of my apothecary shop, locking it behind me.

I had named the shop after myself, of course; Kizzi's. It was entirely practical. It was short and simple and got the job done. Everyone in Moonvale knew exactly who I was, and they knew to come to me for all their witchy or pharmaceutical needs.

My first stop was to the healing clinic, Moonvale Medical. It was in town square, close to my own shop, only a short walk away.

"Velline!" I called as I pushed the door open with a rusty squeak of hinges. "Are you in?"

The gorgeous angel flitted over to me, ridding herself of a mask and gloves and tossing them into a waste bin. Her glimmering wings flared gracefully behind her. "Perfect timing! Thank you!"

Velline's shoulder-length white hair was smooth and straight, framing her face perfectly. Her skin glinted with a healthy silver glow. It was nice to see her looking so bright, especially after the hardships Moonvale endured during the freeze season.

I dropped my satchel onto the floor and knelt to retrieve her order. I pulled all ten sachets of healing poultice out one by one, inspecting them and subtly sniffing their contents before setting them in Velline's waiting hands.

I couldn't risk any more mishaps. They were bad for business.

Damned sprites.

The sachets smelled how they should, like licorice root and lavender, and they appeared to be tied exactly how I had left them. Thank the gods.

I stood, brushing the dust off my knees and pulling my bag back onto my shoulder. "Alright, there you go! You should be covered for a while. If you need any more, you know where to find me."

"Thanks, Kizzi. You really are a gem to this town; I hope you know that." Velline stated matter-of-factly. My cheeks warmed at the kind words.

"It's nothing, just a little mixing and brewing." I coughed awkwardly. "Anyways! How have things been here? Any crazy illnesses recently? Old Man Wilbur still driving you up the wall?"

Old Man Wilbur was an elf, somewhere around seven hundred years old, and he was an absolute piece of work. He was once the primary healer in Moonvale, but he was slowly passing that responsibility onto Velline so he could have more time to himself. What he did with that time, nobody knew for sure.

"You know what, it's been calm, actually. I shouldn't say that too loudly, lest the fates hear me, but things have settled into a pretty normal rhythm." She tossed one of the sachets idly back and forth. Her silver fingernails caught the light and sparkled prettily. "Old Man Wilbur is exactly how you'd expect him to be." She glanced at me conspiratorially. "But I shouldn't speak ill of him. He has been an excellent mentor."

I snorted. Velline was always so polite, so sickeningly *nice*. She didn't have a mean bone in her body.

It was baffling. I adored her for it.

A hacking cough from the back of the room interrupted the conversation.

"Duty calls—my patient is awake. I better go tend to him. I'll see you around!" Velline flitted away before I could respond, wings trailing in her wake.

I peeked around the corner, hoping to catch a glimpse of whoever was sick today, but Velline tugged the curtain closed before I could see anything identifying.

Bummer. I loved knowing what everyone was up to. Sticking my nose into other folks' business was my favorite pastime.

I headed off to Ginger's Pub next.

The smell of lingering ale and warm vegetable broth wafted over me as I opened the door to the pub. I inhaled deeply, loving the way the smell comforted me. It wasn't necessarily the best smell in the realm, but it was familiar, and it wrapped around me like a calming embrace.

Early in the day, Ginger's Pub was practically empty. There were a few patrons enjoying a lunch or a goblet of wine but most of Moonvale saved their pub visits for the evening. Today, only a handful of folk were sitting at tables, chatting quietly.

"Hello!" I called out. "Are you here, Ginny?"

I waited for a few seconds, wandering idly toward the bar. I didn't see the faun anywhere, nor did I hear the telltale clack of her hooves on the stone floor. I huffed out a sigh, plopping my satchel on the bar top to give my tired shoulder some relief.

"Ginger?" I shouted, louder this time. "Delivery!"

"Hang on!" a voice called from the kitchen, deep and booming. Certainly not Ginger. I leaned my hip against the stool, tapping my foot in a quick rhythm. I wasn't necessarily in a hurry, but I didn't like to be kept waiting. It made me snappy.

Tandor, the barkeep and Ginny's most loyal employee, bustled through the swinging kitchen door, two bowls in each hand. He used his shoulder to plow the door open. It was an impressive feat, if I was being honest. I certainly would have spilled something.

He glanced in my direction, cracking a quick smile when he met my eyes before hurrying to drop the bowls off to the two humans sitting in the far corner. I tapped my foot faster.

The orc was massive, with skin the color of springtime moss and hair so shiny it made me jealous. He was also wasting my time.

I pulled the large pouch of sober dust from my satchel and dropped it onto the counter. Ginger had arranged a regular delivery of the stuff, and she went through it quickly. One handful, blown in a folk's face, had the ability to stop a blubbering drunk from crying, or if Ginger was in a bad mood, snatch a pleasant buzz away from an annoying patron. It was one of my favorite recipes that I had created, with its mild stimulating effect and fun method of delivery.

I crossed my arms over my chest. "Tandor! Ginny owes

me five silvers for this one, did she leave that out somewhere?" I leaned over the counter, looking for anything that might resemble a payment. Unfortunately, nothing did. I glanced over at Tandor, but he was chatting with the humans, smiling and laughing at something the man with long blonde hair had said.

I sighed. Slow folk.

CHAPTER 2
Tandor

"Of course, yes, let me know if you need anything else," I said hastily to the group of humans enjoying their lunch. I took a step backwards, hoping to extract myself, smiling in a way I was pretty sure looked genuine.

I didn't want to offend the humans—and any other time I would be happy to linger and chat with them—but I had more important things to handle at the moment. I threw a glance over my shoulder at the witch standing by the bar, looking irritated. Her green hair was pulled up off her neck, highlighting her delicate throat and dainty pointed ears. Her tapping foot grew more incessant, practically vibrating through the floor.

I sighed. Starting off on the wrong foot, again.

"Hey, Tandor, can you bring us another round?" the blonde man asked. He was slurring slightly, a bright flush in his cheeks as he tossed his arm around the shoulders of the darker skinned man sitting next to him. "It's our anniversary. We're celebrating,"

I clenched my teeth. "Sure, sure. Just hang on a second—"

"You know what, it's fine. I'll just drop this off and get the payment sometime later!" Kizzi's voice called out.

"No!" I shouted a bit too loudly, my voice echoing in the mostly empty room. I hurriedly turned to face Kizzi again to find that she had slung her bag over her shoulder and was heading for the door. A seed of dread sprouted in my stomach. "Don't leave. I'm coming."

To my patrons, I uttered a hasty, "One moment, please, and I'll bring you those ales."

I abandoned the dining humans with a hasty wave, hustling over to the bar. Kizzi rolled her eyes but made her way back to the bar with a huff. The soles of her boots clacked against the floor with a slow, even rhythm as she moved.

I wasn't sure why she made me so nervous. I was usually the confident one, but it was hard to be myself when just looking at the witch made my palms sweat.

"In a hurry today, princess?" I asked, ducking below the counter to retrieve the silvers from the safe. If it took a few seconds longer than necessary, I hoped she didn't notice. I fumbled the coin pouch twice before I had a secure enough grip on it to stand up and place it on the counter.

Kizzi snatched it quickly.

"Always. I've got a million things to do, of course." She squinted her eyes at me, her ears twitching. "And don't call me princess. It makes me sound bitchy. Princesses are only in books."

I cracked a grin. "I can't help myself when you're flitting around like royalty. You stood there for less than thirty seconds before you started huffing and puffing."

"Maybe I've got more important places to be."

My smile faltered, but I fought to keep it on my face so she wouldn't notice. "Right. Of course. Well, thank you for this. We ran out a few days ago and things have been rowdy with the potluck coming up. And then Hallow's Eve. Ginger was hoping you'd have her order ready today. She's out, by the way. I'm sure you noticed." I laughed nervously. I was babbling—I knew it, but I couldn't stop myself.

"Right..." She held the pouch of coins up with a tight smile before she tucked them in her satchel. "I'll be going, then."

"Of course, of course. Thank you."

"You said that already."

I gulped, my smile now absolutely painful. It surely looked more like a grimace. "Right."

She gave me a finger-wagging wave before she drifted toward the door, leaving the light scent of magic and toasted apples in her wake. My smile (grimace) finally dropped from my face, and I let out a heavy sigh.

Maybe next time.

I wiped my sweaty hands off on a dish towel, tossed it over my shoulder, and set to pouring ales for my remaining patrons.

I cast a quick glance around the room to see if anyone had witnessed that absolute wreck of an interaction. I made brief eye contact with the mothman in the corner, who gave me a commiserating grimace before returning to his fruit salad. My shoulders rounded.

I had been looking forward to seeing Kizzi again. Her delivery schedule varied, but she always came by at least once a week, and I made it a point to interact with her every time. It was like a game, almost, trying to make the witch smile. She had such a lovely smile. I knew how much responsibility she carried on her shoulders, running the apothecary that took care of the entire town.

If I could lighten her mood for a moment, it gave me a strange sort of satisfaction.

Too bad I had absolutely blown it. Again. The witch hardly even noticed that I existed. Or maybe she could tell I was absolutely infatuated with her, and she simply didn't feel the same way. I sighed heavily.

Maybe I'll get it right next time.

CHAPTER 3

Kizzi

I finished my day's deliveries with plenty of time to spare—I was even able to crack open the new shifter romance novel Fiella loaned me before I had to meet her for dinner.

I had covered the nasty sludge-filled cauldron in my shop with a sheet on my way in. Fiella might've had a point... the stuff was a little unsettling.

If it was out of sight, it was out of mind. More or less. At least the weird, popping bubble splatter would be contained. How it managed to boil without a heat source was a mystery that I chose to ignore for the time being.

I curled up in my bed, tugged my fluffiest fur blanket over my head and lit my enchanted lamp with the smallest wisp of magic from my fingertip. The warm glow allowed me to see the pages in the darkness of my cozy cocoon. I couldn't even feel the magic leaving me, the amount was so miniscule. These were some of my favorite magics—the delicate, subtle ones.

I latched at every opportunity for leisure time I could grasp. Being idle was one of my favorite pastimes, that's why I rushed through my tasks so quickly. As soon as I finished my work, I could just *relax*. I could rot away in bed with a good novel for a few hours and nobody would bother me.

It was glorious.

Though most of the folk in Moonvale lived in cottages on the edges of town or dispersed throughout the Greenwood Forest, I chose to live in the back room of my apothecary shop. It was simply more convenient. I wasn't someone who craved separating my work from my home. I was often finishing up potion brews at odd hours, so it was easier to keep my entire life in one building.

And I was rather fond of this building. With its uniquely curved walls, its heavily laden shelves, and the comforting smell of cinnamon that permanently stained the air, I never wanted to leave.

My personal room was my favorite part. My bed, huge and fluffy and filled with as many pillows and blankets as it could carry, took up a large portion of the space. I had it shoved in the far corner under a net full of tiny, enchanted twinkling lights, so it almost looked like the firefly-filled sky.

The front wall of my room—by the door—held a cabinet with my most valuable finds. The rarest ingredients I had sourced from the farthest reaches of the realm. The lock was spelled, of course, so if a thief tried to lay their hands on it, they would be trapped in a thick layer of slug slime, with their feet frozen to the floor.

A witch liked to protect her valuables.

If preferring the dramatic is a crime, lock me up in the mayor's dungeon.

The cabinet held other marvelous finds, like shining pink diamond dust from Rockward's mountains, harvested by the near-mythical mining gnomes. And the dried wings from an extinct species of butterfly. And many other fabulous (and fucked up) things.

The cabinet also housed the most dangerous potions and tonics I had brewed—like the mixture that induced a long, deep sleep. The memory blurring tea blend. And the outlawed love potion.

A broad, arched window covered the side wall, letting in as much light as possible. The sill was crowded with potted plants that reached for the light with curling tendrils and vining leaves. I kept the curtains open as much as possible.

Sometimes, on my darker days, I hoped the bright light would sink under my skin and brighten my insides too.

Everything that I needed was here in my shop. Well, except for Fiella. I needed her too. It was always us against the realms, and since she had become mated, I didn't have unrestricted access to her friendship like I used to.

It ate away at my insides like a mild acid.

I was thrilled for her, truly. She deserved happiness more than anyone else I knew, and Redd treated her well. I just missed her. I missed our spontaneous trips, and our daily dinners together. I missed our random middle-of-the-night gossip sessions.

I sighed, trying to shake off the grasp of melancholy.

I wasn't necessarily lonely—I had only ever really had Fiella and the witches in my life and I never needed anyone else. I just felt... a bit gray on the inside. Sort of hollow.

I focused harder on my book, hoping to distract myself. I was so absorbed in the story I could almost pretend I didn't catch glimpses of sprites flitting in my peripheral vision. The tiny, fairy-like creatures were almost impossible to spot, but if you weren't looking directly at them, you could occasionally see the glimmer of their wings, the sparkle of their streaming hair, or the sheen of their glowing skin. Sprites were everywhere—in the forest, in the depths of the river, even distributed throughout towns, but there was an ungodly amount of them infesting my shop.

Fucking sprites.

The book distraction worked, because a few chapters later, after a particularly fascinating spicy scene and a battle between rival wolf shifter clans, Fiella pounded on my shop's front door.

"Let's go, Kiz! I'm starving!"

I dog-eared the corner of the page (certain Fiella would curse me out for that later), pulled myself out of bed, and smoothed my hair, hoping my tunic wouldn't be too noticeably wrinkly.

"I'm coming, I'm coming, hold your unicorns," I grumbled.

I tossed my satchel over my shoulder and tugged my boots onto my feet, all the while listening to Fiella complain outside my door about how hungry she was and how she would drop dead if she didn't get a cider in her stomach in the next five seconds. Dramatic vampire.

The walk to Ginger's Pub was especially lovely in the evening. The mild season air was the perfect temperature, chill enough to benefit from long sleeves but not frigid enough for a cloak. It smelled of crisp, green leaves, a hint of warm stew, and something that reminded me of nutmeg.

The scents of small-town living were everywhere—of folk working and creating and eating.

Our boots clacked along the stones in sync. Fiella's legs

were much longer than mine, but she was mindful to shorten her stride.

Critters scurried across the cobbled streets without a care in the world, not even bothering to shy away from any roaming folk. Two squirrels chased each other in a circle beside my feet, chirping happily. I stepped away from them.

"So," Fiella said, nudging me with her elbow. "How was your day? Same as usual, or did something juicy and exciting happen?"

"Pretty much the same, I'd say. I made some standard deliveries. Medical, the pub, Mayor Tommins, Ani, the clothing shop."

Fiella hummed in contemplation. "And did you dispose of that ghastly cauldron concoction? I don't even know how you're going to do that. You'll have to take it to the Barren Lands and hope the scorching suns dry it out or something."

I sighed. "No. I did not have the energy to deal with that today. That's a problem for tomorrow. Oh! There was someone sick at Moonvale Medical today. Any idea who it could be?"

"I can't believe a folk with a stomach bug is the most exciting thing happening in town today."

"It is pretty pathetic. Nothing wonderful happened over at Fiella's Finds? Any rich strangers with mysterious backstories wander in to buy your most expensive items with suspiciously obtained silvers?"

"Ugh, no. I wish. Just the usual travelers and locals. You know I'd immediately send any suspicious but rich strangers in your direction."

"We're boring today. Maybe we need more curses to spice things up."

Fiella jabbed me in the ribs with her finger. "Don't even say that out loud. The fates might be listening."

I snorted, shaking my head as we neared the pub.

Raucous laughter drifted out of the propped-open doors, the smell of bread and crisp fermented fruit, and a mild twinge of magic wafting out to meet us. Music thrummed quietly somewhere inside—a musician earning a few extra coins. Tables were set up outside for folk to enjoy the evening air with their dinner and ales, crowding into the street and even turning the corner around to the side of the building.

Ginger's Pub was packed tonight. It was as if the entire town of Moonvale decided to come enjoy some ale and stew.

At a glance, I could see fae, elves, shifters, humans, and even a few of the more reclusive minotaurs tucked in the corner.

Luckily, we caught a couple as they were leaving and were able to snag their table.

"Gods! This is unreal, word must have finally gotten out about how good Ginger's stew is." Fiella shouted over the noise.

I snorted. "Fi, everyone is well aware of just how much of a delicacy Ginny's stews are. That can't be it."

"You're right. What in the realms is bringing everyone out then?"

I shrugged. "Beats me. Maybe it's the weather."

"As long as they have some blood in stock, I'll be happy. And a cider, of course. I really hope it's lavender blueberry today."

"Girl, I know you do." I looked around, hoping to catch a glimpse of Ginger's auburn hair or Tandor's hulking form. I could see the top of Tandor's head behind the bar, his dark black hair gleaming in the light from the wall sconces. "I'll head to the bar and grab us some drinks—if you see any bowls of stew floating around you better snatch them."

Fiella saluted me sarcastically. "Yes ma'am."

I rolled my eyes as I shouldered my way to the bar, careful not to push anyone too hard and knock them over but forcefully enough to let them know to get out of my way. Everyone was so gods damned *tall*. I utilized my elbows when I needed to, subtly jamming them into the guts of the stubborn drunks who wouldn't budge.

I didn't do any real damage—I was simply a woman on a mission. If I sent a flicker of magic zapping here and there, that was nobody's business but my own.

After the grueling journey, I popped up beside the bar, leaning my elbows onto the sticky surface.

Tandor's eyes zeroed in on me immediately. He drifted in my direction. I pretended not to notice the annoyed grumbles of the other folk in line that I had so smoothly stepped in front of.

"Kizzi!" He slung a wet towel over his shoulder, splattering the fae man behind him in mystery liquid. "Twice in one day! You couldn't get enough of me, could you?"

I snorted out a laugh. "That's it, exactly. It has nothing to do with the fact that you're the one serving alcohol here. I've been counting down the seconds until I could see you again, actually," I joked.

Tandor grasped two goblets, knocking an empty bowl onto the floor which he promptly kicked aside. "I would hope for nothing less. The usual?" He stretched his neck, searching for Fiella's bright blue mane of hair in the crowd. "Two or three today? Redd here?"

"Just two, Redd was held up with one of his projects. You know how he gets when he's got a saw and a chunk of wood."

A woman cleared her throat pointedly somewhere behind me. My ears twitched in irritation.

"Two it is." He slid the goblets toward me with impressive smoothness—not a single drop slopped over the side.

"Thanks! Oh yeah, I forgot to ask, do you have any blood left today?" I glanced down at the cups, noticing the red hue in one of them. "Never mind! You're a genius. Thanks again! And good luck with... all this!"

"You act like I'm new at this, I wouldn't dare deprive Fiella of her bloody ciders. I like my throat intact."

I snorted. "Smart man. Thanks!"

"You said that already."

The sass. Throwing my own words back at me. I couldn't help but smile.

I shouldered my way back to the table, throwing my sharpest death glares at everyone in my way. By the smell wafting up from goblets, today's cider was strawberry basil flavored, which was one of the best. I would curse a bitch if they made me spill any onto the nasty, mud-covered floor.

Luckily for everyone else in the room, I made it back to the table without incident.

Fiella stared pointedly over my shoulder with her eyebrow lifted. I glanced behind me, but nothing stood out, except for a pretty human woman ordering an ale. "What?"

Fiella shook her head, the corner of her mouth curling upward. "Nothing, Kiz. I just... saw something interesting."

I shrugged. Weird. I must've missed it.

I carefully sat the goblets down on the table, mindful to keep every drop of precious liquid from spilling. Fiella snatched one with supernatural speed. I would never get used to her quick vampire reflexes, no matter how many years I spent by her side. She had taken a deep drink, set the goblet down, and leaned her head back with a contented sigh before I even got myself situated on my barstool.

"It's no lavender blueberry cider... but it will certainly do." Fiella mused, running her tongue over the edge of her goblet to catch an errant drop.

I hummed in agreement, taking a sip of my own. The crisp, icy cold liquid slid down my throat with a slight fizz— the fruity, herbal flavor dancing over my tongue sent a shiver of delight down my spine. Delicious.

If I had a knack for brewing beverages, I would beg Ginger and Tandor for the cider recipe, but as it stood, nothing I brewed ever tasted even remotely pleasant. My tonics and potions were choked down, not savored.

"So, have you given any more thought to what you might bring to the potluck?" Fiella asked.

I sighed. "Sort of. I wish they would let me help with setup or something, I feel bad that anyone in Moonvale will have to try my cooking."

"Oh, come on. It's not *that* bad," Fiella chided. "Remember that one time you made toasted-cheese sandwiches? Those were edible."

"I convinced Mitz to help me with those."

"Oh... right. Never mind on that then. What about that one time you made a mirthroot-spiked punch? It tasted fucking nasty but it sure was fun."

"Fiella, I can't drug the entire town."

"Well, you *could*—" I kicked her under the table before she could finish that sentence.

"I'm not drugging anyone."

Fiella laughed under her breath as she took another swig. "Fine, fine. Be boring. How about," she stared off into the distance as she thought, "fried tomatoes?"

"That sounds like a disaster waiting to happen," I grumbled.

"Well, figure something else out then. There's got to be *something* you can make that won't induce vomiting."

I caught sight of Ginger out of the corner of my eye—she was making her way toward our table with two bowls in hand. My spirit brightened immediately. "Oh, you're a goddess, thank you, Ginger!" I shouted to the faun woman when she stepped within earshot. Her auburn hair was tied up into a tidy bun that made her antlers stand out, and her brown freckled skin was flushed and glowing. Her long, lean frame was draped in an apron with a few mysterious stains on it. Her hoofed feet were bare, as usual. A bright smile pulled at her cheeks, lighting up her face in a way that was infectious.

"I thought I saw my two favorite cider drinkers. Hello, ladies!" She carefully placed the bowls in front of us, and though the place was packed, and she was clearly busy, she lingered for a few extra moments. "The place is packed, right? Isn't it wonderful?"

"Right... wonderful. That is exactly the word I would use," Fiella said, not very convincingly, as she glared at a shifter that brushed past her.

"Good business, that's for sure," I said.

"Oh, business has been excellent! Things usually begin to slow down as the mild season comes to an end, but if anything, there have been more customers than ever," Ginger said wistfully. "I wish it was always like this."

"You're nuts. I would simply drop dead if I had to handle this many customers every single day," Fiella said.

Ginger snorted. "You're just saying that. It's pretty fun, tending to so many customers. I make a game out of it. Like right now, I can feel twenty sets of eyes burning a hole into my back, but I bet I can help every single one of them in ten minutes flat. Time me."

She flitted away from the table without another word, bee-lining toward a large table full of folk.

"Absolutely crazy," I murmured.

After Fiella and I finished our ciders and our bowls of chicken and veggie stew, I glanced up at the bar to gauge the line. The pub was settling down as the minutes passed by, and the crowd wasn't quite as dense as it had been when we arrived.

My eyes locked with a dark, almost black gaze, so swiftly it was as though he had been looking at me first. Tandor lifted his hand with a slight wave. My eyes drifted to his forearm, huge and tightly muscled and exposed beneath scrunched up sleeves. I waved back, then held up two fingers, tilting my head in question. Tandor smiled, rolled his eyes, and pulled out two goblets.

I had expected the orc to ignore me, but surprisingly, he stepped out from behind the bar and brought the ciders over to the table.

"Wow, I didn't think that would work," I laughed as Tandor made his way over to the table, bumping into more than one customer in his path. The large orc wasn't very agile.

"Princesses don't retrieve their own drinks," he joked with a mocking smile.

I rolled my eyes at him. "Come on, not the princess thing

again. You didn't *have* to bring them over here; I would have gotten up eventually."

"Whatever you say, princess," he mumbled. His ear flickered lightly. "Good to see you, Fiella," he said a little louder, flashing a tusk-bearing grin at the vampire as he turned and weaved his way back to the bar.

Fiella just stared at me knowingly.

"What? Is there stew on my face?" I asked, self-consciously wiping at my chin.

"Nothing, nothing. Never mind." She stared at me for a few seconds longer before diving into her next goblet of cider. She was being very ominous today. It was annoying.

CHAPTER 4

Kizzi

Morning light filtered beautifully through my shop's arching windows, begging me to crack them open and let the fresh air in.

I resisted the urge, though. There was a heavy, charged quality to the air that made the hairs on the back of my neck stand up, and I was determined to figure out what it was.

It was probably the damned sprites messing around again... but I needed to be sure.

"You little fuckers can leave whenever you want, you know," I called out into the seemingly empty shop. I couldn't see the sprites, but I knew they were lurking. "You don't have to keep harassing me. I've been punished enough for whatever moral crime I must have committed. I'm cured of my wrong-doings. I'm not above bribes, either, if you're receptive to that." I waited for a few seconds, but nothing changed, so I let out a frustrated huff and got back to work.

Of course I had tried speaking to the sprites. I spoke to them so often that a fly on the wall would probably think I lost my mind. But they never spoke back. They never commu-

30

nicated with me in any way that I could understand, besides endlessly messing with me and my shop.

Little shits.

I worked methodically through the apothecary to determine the source of my unease, starting at the front door and making my way to the back—shelf by shelf, basket by basket. I trailed my fingers over everything, keeping my senses open and letting any lingering traces of magic register in my mind.

Everything was normal... until I got closer to the cauldron I had shoved into the corner and tried to forget about.

The giant cast iron bowl reached all the way to my hip. As I neared, my eyes began to water, and a vaguely sick sensation settled in my stomach. My ears flattened back to my head.

Gods, this feels weird. This feels wrong.

I could have sworn I left the cauldron covered with a sheet, but that sheet was now neatly folded on the floor a few paces away. Had I folded it up and just forgotten about it? I bent down to pick up the fabric. The remnants of magic that leached into my fingertips were stronger than I expected.

A shiver crawled down my spine—a seed of fear taking root in my chest and threatening to bloom.

"Come on, Kiz, don't be a baby. Just look in the cauldron," I murmured to myself in an attempt to steel my nerves.

I took a few deep breaths, feeling like an absolute idiot, while I mentally hyped myself up. Surely, there was nothing abnormal in the cauldron. Surely, the sludge would look the same as the last time I saw it.

Surely, I was overreacting.

With one last deep breath that pulled in as much air as my lungs could hold, I leaned over the rim of the cauldron and peered inside. My heart galloped in my chest.

What I saw was... exactly what I expected. Just thick, viscous liquid filling about two thirds of the pot, slowly gurgling. It had a purple sheen that I hadn't noticed before but nothing about it was remarkable in any way.

I had freaked myself out for nothing. "Old Gods spare me," I sighed as I gripped the edge of the cauldron and fought to still my racing heart.

Waves of magic traveled through my fingers and up my arm in shuddering, unsettling pulses. I snatched my hand back and clutched it to my chest. I examined my palm to make sure I hadn't been burned, but my skin was the same shade of olive green it always was.

A fleck of sludge clung to my thumb, which I hastily wiped onto the sheet I was still clutching.

Well, that answered that question. I knew I put a little extra oomph into my last brew, but I didn't think I'd put *that* much extra magic into it. The thing was practically radiating magical energy, setting the air abuzz.

I covered the cauldron with the sheet again, paying extra attention to weigh the corners down with selenite crystals so it wouldn't slip off. I didn't know how strong the sprites were, or if they were the ones who removed the sheet in the first place, but I hoped the crystals would be too heavy for them to dislodge.

Only the fates knew what would happen if anything else was added to the cauldron. I really needed to clean that out sooner rather than later.

I tossed the windows open as wide as they would go, hoping some of the trapped magical energy would dissipate and relieve the uneasy feeling lodged in my stomach. A mild breeze flowed in, fluttering a basket of dried butterfly wings and rustling hanging herbs.

I didn't remember until much later that the cauldron had only been half full when I initially pushed it aside.

With the annual Moonvale potluck rapidly approaching, I agonized over what I would prepare. My best bet would be something simple—something that required as little hands-on work as possible so I would have fewer opportunities to screw it up.

I tapped my chin with my fingernail.

Baked goods were out of the question. As were coffees, teas, any hot beverages, as those would certainly be covered. There wasn't a sign-up list or anything, but it was expected that every folk would bring something different.

I thought about foods I had eaten in other towns during my travels. Vegetable soup would be too difficult to get right, sandwiches were too complicated, dried meats were delicious but were a nightmare to make.

Then the perfect solution came to me.

Chili.

Fucking chili!

Of course! It was *perfect*. Chili was similar to stew or soup —one of those toss-the-ingredients-in-and-leave-it types of recipes. All I would have to do was throw the ingredients in a cauldron and let it sit. Almost like a potion.

Potions I could handle, so surely something potion-like would be easy as well.

It was exactly the solution I needed.

I had first tried chili in the breezy, hilly town of Oakhollow. I could remember the moment vividly. I was on a trip to collect some potion ingredients, and Fiella had come with me, of course, on one of her trinket shopping expeditions. She was off bartering for a better price on woven blankets while I sat down at a diner for something to eat. I was so famished that I could have eaten an entire cow. Instead, a tiny, smiley waitress had plopped a steaming bowl in front of me. The chili had been the perfect temperature—hot enough to waft steam over my face but not hot enough to blister my mouth. It was rich, tomato flavored, and full of wonderful textures.

Eating that chili had been a damn near religious experience.

I had been so enraptured by the delicacy that I begged the chef to give me the recipe. I had convinced myself that I would be able to make it at home. I ended up needing to use a truth spell on the chef. I only felt a little bit guilty about it.

He refused to offer up his secret ingredient, but I extracted most of the recipe from him, and I kept the scribbled note tucked away in my personal room's locked cabinet for safe keeping.

Reciting the unlocking spell and using my fae-iron key, I quickly retrieved the recipe from its hiding space and nudged the door shut with my elbow. I unfurled the crinkled note and laid it flat on my worktable.

Excitement thrummed through my veins.

The recipe read:

Ingredients: tomato (both fresh and jarred), green pepper, red pepper, onion, ground beef, beans, broth, herbs of choice, salt and pepper, garlic (omit if folk of the blood sucking variety will be ingesting). Secret ingredient still a mystery.

Combine ingredients and simmer for at least two hours. The longer the better. Serve hot, with bread on the side, or poured over a grilled cheese sandwich.

The potluck was in two days, so *surely* two days of simmering would make the chili *extra* delicious. Delighted with myself for my brilliant idea, I skittered to the grocery store to secure my ingredients.

The cellar underneath Ginger's Pub was a room I had become increasingly familiar with over the years. I couldn't begin to count the hours I had spent in the damp, dark space, adding herbs to brews and monitoring their developing flavors.

Though the pub belonged to Ginger, I had been working for her for so many years that I had slowly acquired more and more tasks and responsibilities. We were more like partners than we were employee and boss.

My favorite task was brewing. I enjoyed interacting with customers, but nothing beat the joy of creating the perfect beverage.

It took five years for Ginny to even allow me within two paces of the cellar that housed her precious brewing barrels. She even bought an expensive enchanted lock for the door to keep nosey folk out.

These days, I understood her protective tendencies. The brews were my pride and joy.

While Ginger still handled most of the ales and the

wines, ciders were my domain. Trying new flavors was one of my favorite pastimes. They weren't all successes, and some of them were raging failures, but it was the experimentation that kept me intrigued and kept my mind whirling. The possibilities for improving kept me on my toes.

I poured a few drops from the barrel that I had been working on for weeks—my concoction for the annual potluck. The liquid was an orange, golden brown, gorgeously smooth and artfully rich. I examined the brew, holding it up to the glow of the lamplight. Not an impurity or imperfection in sight. The aroma was fruity and hoppy, with a cinnamon finish that rounded off the profile. I inhaled deeply, feeling very satisfied with my spice choices.

With only a moment's hesitation, I poured the liquid into my mouth. The last time I sampled my concoction had been days ago, and the fermentation was nowhere near complete. Now, I was out of time, so I silently prayed to any of the Old Gods that were listening that the brew would be ready.

The cider caressed my tongue and slid down my throat. I groaned in delight.

Absolutely perfect.

My newest creation was my best one yet—spiced pumpkin cider. It had taken weeks to find a traveling salesman willing to find pumpkins and bring them to Moonvale. The massive orange fruits were rare, only growing naturally in the fields surrounding the mountains of Rockward.

The fruits then had to be chopped up, the skins and seeds removed, chilled, dried out, and then boiled down into a syrupy pulp. It had taken ages of painstaking labor.

The hassle was worth it.

I took the annual Moonvale potluck *very* seriously, and this cider would surely be a crowd pleaser.

I poured myself another sample, tossed it in my mouth, and savored the crisp, almost nutty flavor. I had used one of the largest barrels in the cellar, but now, I wished I had brewed multiple batches.

This stuff was going to disappear faster than a water sprite in a forest fire.

Kizzi and Fiella were going to love this one. The corner of my mouth curled as I thought about the two women and their deep, almost reverent love for ciders. Of all the folk in Moonvale, I could count on them to give me the most elaborately honest opinions.

I could also count on them to drink any cider I placed in front of them.

Those ladies could handle their alcohol with impressive gusto. Even more so than some of the older, larger folk that frequented the pub.

I poured another small dribble of cider into the goblet and tucked it under my arm, tidying up the space before making the climb back to the pub's kitchen.

I shouldered open the cellar door with a flourish while calling out, "Ginny! You've got to try this one."

When I last saw Ginger, she was in the dining room polishing tables to perfection. I assumed she would still be out there.

The unlucky faun was right behind the door.

My mindless entrance knocked the woman right off her hooves and she fell on her ass with a muffled *oomph*. The plate she had been drying clattered to the floor and cracked in half.

"Gods above, Tandor! Use your eyeballs for once and look around before you come storming in here!" she scolded.

"Sorry, boss. I got too excited." Still clutching the goblet with my precious pumpkin brew in one hand, I reached out with my other and hooked my fingers under the bewildered woman's arm and hoisted her to her feet. She landed gracefully. Everything she did looked graceful—even falling flat on her ass.

"I can stand, I can stand, you brute." She pried her arm from my grasp and ran her hands over her pants to brush off any clinging dirt. "Thanks for the hand, I guess. Though it is your fault that I needed it. What do you have there?" she asked when she finally noticed what I was holding.

Wordlessly, I presented the goblet to her. She took it, examining it with a practiced skepticism. She swirled it around, held it up to the light, and then took a tentative sniff, exactly as I had done in the cellar.

Sparing just a moment to meet my eyes and arch a full eyebrow, she raised the glass and poured it into her mouth.

A moment passed. Two. Anticipation boiled under my skin, buzzed in my stomach. I clenched my hands together to stop myself from wringing them.

Then Ginger burst out laughing.

"What... what is it? That's not exactly the reaction I expected," I asked nervously.

Ginger slapped a hand on my shoulder and squeezed. "You've finally outdone me. This is the best cider I've ever tasted."

"And that's... funny?"

"No, not funny. Hilarious. I never thought I'd see the day,

but I should have paid more attention to you. You'll steal this business out from under me if I'm not careful."

My breath whooshed out of me. I finally cracked a smile. "It's pretty good, huh?"

"Pretty good? This stuff is borderline magical." She paused for a second. "Or is it *actually* magical?" Her eyes narrowed slightly. "What did you do, Tandor? Am I poisoned?"

I snorted. "Nope. No magic here. Just talent."

"Just talent? Well, I'll be damned. Can I have some more of this?"

"Sure—at the potluck with the rest of Moonvale. You better be quick, or it'll run out before you get any," I said smugly.

She glared at me for a second before bolting for the cellar door. She almost made it.

I stepped smoothly in front of her, barricading the path and grinning broadly, my tusks on full display. I crossed my arms over my chest and planted my feet.

Giving up, she strode away with a huff, her hooves clanking rhythmically on the stone floor. "Ugh. You're the worst, you know!"

"Love you too, Ginny," I laughed.

She flapped her hand dismissively before flipping me her middle finger.

I smiled for the rest of the day, pride blossoming in my chest at what I had accomplished. The folk of Moonvale were going to *love* my pumpkin cider.

The air had cooled to a comfortable briskness by the time I decided to head back to my cottage for the night. Ginny and I took turns closing when we weren't swarmed with customers, and tonight had been on her.

I really needed to talk with her about hiring someone else to help us during busy days. We had briefly discussed and dismissed the notion in the past, but having an extra set of hands to wash dishes and run bowls back and forth certainly wouldn't be unwelcomed.

The two moons slowly climbed a path across the sky, rising timidly from the horizon as the two suns slipped from view. The first moon would reach its peak within the hour, and the second shortly after.

Unseen insects chirped from every direction—fireflies fluttered lazily on the cooling breeze. Darkness was creeping into the realm's edges, but the enchanted torch lights of town square kept things from feeling eerie. Instead, the town was cushioned in a gentle, warm glow.

My boots thumped heavily along the cobblestones.

I waved at the few folk I passed, but I didn't linger to start any conversations like I normally would. I was craving a good night's sleep more than a casual discussion.

A crisp breeze tossed my black hair over my eyes, and I absentmindedly batted it away. The ending of the mild season meant that Hallow's Eve was rapidly approaching. It was only a few weeks away, now. The green leaves in the Greenwood Forest were already beginning to deepen in pigment, settling into their emerald coloring that would soon fade into shades of orange and red.

Hallow's Eve was a holiday celebrated throughout the entire realm of Aldova—from the Dragonspeak Mountains, across the Barren Lands, all the way to the sea. Every town and every species celebrated in their own way, but we all celebrated. It was a chance to embrace our natural darkness. To cling to our baser instincts.

And for some of us, to act out our more beastly, wild tendencies.

For orcs, Hallow's Eve was an even bigger deal than Merry Day or Year's End. As a species, orcs prized strength above all else, both physical and mental. We liked to participate in competitions to prove our strength to each other. Moonvale's Hallow's Eve celebration would involve more prowling than proving strength.

The holiday season made me miss my family. There were other orcs in Moonvale, sure, but none that I was especially close to.

The resounding *thunk* of my boots on the solid wood of my newly repaired front porch was music to my ears. The wood had begun to rot, and Redd, the new vampire woodworker in town, had transformed it into something fresh and sturdy. I would call myself handy, but I was nowhere as talented as that man. My quick patchwork fixes had held, sure, but they had been hideous.

Now, I didn't have to worry about my heavy feet busting through the wood—I could stomp as hard as I pleased.

Two wooden rocking chairs wobbled in the breeze, as though ghosts were sitting upon them. They creaked quietly —a whisper in the night.

With a groan, I bent to unlace my boots. My back muscles protested as I righted myself again. I left the boots on the threshold before I stepped inside my cottage.

The familiar scent of clean linens and comfort greeted me like an old friend. I didn't bother to light a candle, instead feeling my way through the space by memory. My eyesight was sharp, but with my curtains drawn and the faint light of the moons blocked out, I could see almost nothing. That didn't matter, though. The space was clean, as always, and the high roof built for the tallest of folk guaranteed that I wouldn't hit my head on anything.

I preferred to spend my time in town among other folk rather than in my cottage by myself. My cottage was my place to relax, unwind, and rest, and not much else. It housed my belongings, though there weren't many of those. I wasn't the collecting sort.

I didn't have much in the way of furniture, either. A hook on the back of the door held my cloaks that I wore during the freeze season. The front of my cottage consisted of a sitting area with a couch, a low table, and an oversized chair. A small, spindly fern lived in a blue pot that sat in the corner beside the window. I didn't have a dining table—that would be a waste of space when I took all my meals at the pub anyway. Storage trunks remained tucked off to the side until I needed to use them, and my kitchen and washroom were small and unobtrusive.

My bed took up most of the back half of the cottage. It was the largest bed that silvers could buy, and I still wished it was bigger. It fit my frame with little room to spare.

I yanked my tunic over my head and tossed it into the

wash basket in the corner, mindful not to pull too hard and tear any threads.

I pulled my window open to let the night breeze in. I wouldn't get to enjoy the nighttime winds much longer, soon the air would be too cold and unpleasant.

My thoughts skittered to a certain green witch, as they too often did. No matter how many times I chastised myself for being foolish, I couldn't shake the seed of affection that the tiny, stubborn witch had planted within me.

Kizzi had actually smiled at me yesterday at the pub. My cheeks lifted on their own accord as I remembered it. I could picture exactly what she had looked like. She had been wearing a pretty brown tunic, pulled in at the waist with a corset, tucked into a green skirt that hid the shape of her curvy legs. Her usual leather boots laced over her ankles. Her throat was adorned with a thin chain.

She looked as beautiful as ever, and when she smiled, she knocked the breath out of my lungs.

Even if she never returned my affections, at least I had these small, precious moments.

I hope she'll like my spiced pumpkin cider at the potluck...

CHAPTER 6
Kizzi

My second-largest cauldron sat above my firepit, happily bubbling away.

The chili mixture had taken longer than expected to come to a boil, but after a night on the heat source, it was stewing wonderfully. The whole shop smelled of spices and smoked tomatoes. The home-cooked-meal scent was a welcome change from my shop's usual flowers-and-suspicious-liquids aroma.

I was quite proud of myself. I had only tried one small spoonful, but the chili was *edible*. I couldn't call it *good*, because I had scalded my tongue in the process of sampling it and could hardly taste anything, but it certainly hadn't made me gag.

And that was a great sign.

All in all, this whole thing was a massive success so far. It was going much better than I expected.

I stirred the cauldron wistfully, smiling down at my creation. It even *looked* nice. Well, nice enough. The veggies were chopped fairly evenly, and the chunks looked enticing rather than repulsive. The beans settled wonderfully next to the beef pieces, and the green onions added a nice splash of color.

I leaned in and inhaled deeply. The boiling hot steam almost burnt my eyebrows off, but the lungful of deliciously scented air was worth it. I let it out slowly. "Ah. That's good shit." I glanced around to see if any of the sprites felt like celebrating my victory. Perhaps a round of applause, or a song and dance.

Besides a few flickers in my peripheral vision, I didn't see an audience. Bummer.

There weren't even any cats around to turn into pretend audience members. I wasn't much of a cat person, but there were a few that meandered through Moonvale, and I didn't mind them. Fiella's cat Sookie was one of the better ones. The large gray tabby just minded her business, ate a lot of snacks, and followed Fiella around when she felt like it. She even had a large orange boyfriend cat named Pumpkin. It was like some sort of twisted happy family over there. They were disgustingly precious.

I would tolerate a critter following me around. I bet I would even like it. Probably. Maybe. As long as it wasn't a damned sprite.

"How about you, cauldron slime? Anything you'd like to say?"

A bubble popped noisily beneath the sheet that was still weighed down with selenite crystals.

"That's what I thought. Bitch. My chili is so much cooler than... whatever the fuck you are."

Sassing the sludge in the corner was becoming a weirdly entertaining pastime. I chose not to examine that impulse too closely—if I was losing my mind, that was none of my business.

The cauldron made me angrier and angrier every time I thought about cleaning it out. My resentment had built to impressive levels. I had almost decided to let the sludge rot in the corner for the rest of eternity so I would never have to deal with it, but it was inhabiting my favorite cauldron. My largest, most valuable cauldron. I couldn't let my own laziness impact my business.

I had inherited the cauldron from the coven ages ago, when my aptitude for potion brewing began to present itself. I had been a natural, they said. But really, I was just so interested in it. I loved the thought of mixing things together to create something *new*. Something new and *special*. Something that could help folk.

That childlike curiosity never really went away—I still loved mixing things together, saying a chant under my breath, and trying to predict the outcome. Most of the time, my predictions were right. But I still surprised myself occasionally. Almost thirty years on this realm, and a potion mishap still made me giggle like a little one. I snorted when I remembered Fiella's face the day she stormed into my shop after my thirst tonic accidentally transformed her normally golden-brown hair into a startlingly bright blue color.

Some of my best work, truly. The color was impressively vibrant. It wasn't really my fault—the sprites were responsible —but I eventually figured out how to concoct a bluebell potion to keep her strands from fading back to their natural color after she'd grown fond of the look.

I left the ladle perched on the edge of the chili cauldron as I packed up the day's orders and prepared to make my deliveries. The potluck was tomorrow, and I had a few stops to make: enchanted fertilizer for Lunette's plant shop, soaked candle wicks for the coven to make some new summoning candles, and fumigation sage for a cottage with a mouse problem.

As I walked out the door, I paused and turned around. I waved my finger threateningly around, trying to glimpse any flashes of movement. "You little fuckers better be good, or I'll banish you with another seance. I know you didn't like *that* very much." As usual there was no response, but a slight breeze pushed a tendril of hair behind my shoulder. I shivered and ran my fingers through my curls, pulling the strands back into place.

"And you!" I shouted to the cauldron in the far corner. "Fuck you!"

I glared menacingly into the interior of my shop for a few moments for good measure.

Feeling better, I tucked the strap of my satchel higher onto my shoulder and set about my deliveries.

Later that evening, I returned to my apothecary to find everything seemingly undisturbed and wonderfully aromatic. The fragrance was growing stronger and stronger— I could practically smell it from down the street. The stirring ladle I had been using had clattered to the floor, but that was my own fault for leaving it perched where I shouldn't have. It probably fell on its own.

Maybe my threats had worked and the sprites behaved for once.

I tossed the ladle into my washbasin and grabbed a clean one to give the chili a stir. Tomorrow, I would have to haul the heavy cauldron to the park in the center of town square, but it would be worth the effort when everyone saw that I had *actually* prepared something edible this year.

In previous years, I simply arrived at the potluck empty handed. The folk of Moonvale didn't mind sharing, especially since I helped everyone with their potion-related needs. This year, though, the rules were stricter. Everyone had to prepare their own dish to bring. No exceptions. No ifs, no ands, no buts. Ridiculous, if you asked me.

The chili was coming together beautifully, turning a rich, deep brown color. It was thickening up, too. After another night of stewing and a few finishing touches, it would be perfect.

I pulled off my dress and slipped into my nightgown as I prepared for bed.

A gentle creaking made my ears prick to attention. I froze, listening intently, but the sound didn't repeat.

Maybe my mind is playing tricks on me...

With a sigh, I picked up an enchanted lantern and made another round, ensuring that everything in the shop was secure so I could go to sleep with peace of mind.

I quickly discovered the source of the creaking sound; I hadn't shut my personal cabinet properly when I retrieved the chili recipe earlier, and the door was gently swinging on its hinges. Back and forth, back and forth. Rolling my eyes at my own carelessness, I locked the cabinet properly, ignoring the gentle bolt of magic that skittered up my palm, through my forearm, and across my collarbone.

I slipped into my washroom to rinse the day's grime from my skin. Quickly, I cleaned my hair with my favorite honey scented soap and braided it down my back so it would be smooth and wavy for tomorrow's festivities.

As I grabbed my book and curled up in my bed, I made plans for how I would dispose of the cauldron sludge. I would need my largest cauldron for Hallow's Eve and the coven's rituals. Hallow's Eve was the night when the veil between the realms was at its thinnest. When magic flowed more freely and could be manipulated with more ease.

It would be soon, I decided. I was tired of looking at it. But not tomorrow—tomorrow would be busy. Maybe the next day. I would drag the cauldron to the border of the Barren Lands and let it dry out, and then I would dump the dried remnants in the river and forget about the demonic sludge once and for all.

I drifted off to sleep with my book still open and my mind full of magical worlds, swashbuckling pirates, and annoying sprites.

CHAPTER 7
Tandor

Town square park was a cacophony of noise and movement. This early in the morning, the dual suns had yet to reach their peak, but the folk of Moonvale were awake and moving.

Tables had been set out—pulled from the diner and the pub and spread through the entire park. Some folk even brought their own tables and chairs from their cottages to guarantee they would have somewhere to sit and enjoy the festivities.

I lost count of how many tables I hauled. The wooden things were easy to hoist over my shoulder, but after at least twenty of them, my muscles were warm and loose, thick with blood flow. Every single one of the pub's tables was now sitting in the park. It felt strange, seeing the worn wood out in the broad sunlight of morning. The color was lighter, the brown pulling more toward orange than toward red as it did in the glow of the dim pub lanterns.

Amid the table arranging chaos, I had dragged myself to the pub's cellar to haul the barrels to the event before all the good tables were taken. I even brought Ginger's—there was no way the small faun woman would have been able to hoist it herself. She was strong, but she wasn't *that* strong. She had prepared both wine and stew for the potluck because she couldn't pick a favorite. Typical Ginny.

I preferred the space on the far end of the park, toward Fiella's Finds and Lu's Blooms. Most of the cottages were situated that way, which meant that most folk would pass by the table to enter the event and would visit me first.

It was all very strategic. I wanted to be the first smiling face they saw when they entered the park, and I wanted their mugs to be filled with my cider before they had the chance to be filled with anything else.

There wasn't much competition for the far table, so my ridiculously early rise had been pointless. My spiced pumpkin cider and Ginger's mulberry wine were set up, ready to be enjoyed, and the event didn't start until the suns reached their peak. Ginger situated herself in the center of the park, in the middle of the action, where she would be in the core of the crowd. The thought made me cringe a little.

I held back a yawn for what felt like the hundredth time.

I tried to force my groggy thoughts to wake up. Dumping a bucket of cold water over my head in my washroom had not been enough—my eyes ached to be closed. I decided I would close them for *just* a second. Five seconds, max. Taking a seat on a rickety stool, I leaned my elbows on my table and propped my head up, leaning against the barrel for balance.

Just... going to... rest... my eyes...

Thwack!

My head smacked onto the table with a resounding thud, snapping me awake. My eyes scanned the area for a threat.

Ginger stood above me, chuckling darkly. Her hair was slicked back in a style that made her antlers especially prominent. "You're an asshole," I grumbled.

"And you're going to miss all the good stuff if you don't get yourself *up*. Come on, it's about to start!"

I glanced around, surprised to find that so much time had passed. Most of the tables were full.

I scrubbed my eyes. "You're right. Thanks, I was just resting my eyes for a moment."

"Tandor, I can see you from my table. You've been asleep for over an hour."

I rolled my eyes, waving a hand at her dismissively. "Lies."

Above the noise of the crowd, a strained, grunting voice caught my attention. My ears perked. "Old Gods damn it, damn everything, damn it all. Fates!"

I clapped a palm over my mouth to smother my laughter.

The source of the cursing was Kizzi, straining beneath the weight of a cauldron that was half her size. It wobbled precariously with every step she took, threatening to upend and drench the witch. Her hands were covered with ridiculous fluffy mitts, which were clearly impacting her grip.

A large white cat brushed against her ankle, nearly tripping her, but she hardly seemed to notice.

I bolted in her direction without thinking.

"Hey there, Kizzi! Let me help you with that. Princesses shouldn't carry heavy things." I snatched the cauldron from her grasp despite her protests, lifting it with mild strain. It certainly was a burden—it was a wonder the woman had carried it this far.

And then the heat registered. I yelped, forcing my fingers

to maintain their grip on the cast iron though my flesh was screaming at me to *drop it*.

"Damn it, Tandor! If you would have waited one second, I would have warned you that it was as hot as Hell's Realm. It's been boiling for two whole days." Her mitted hands fluttered anxiously in my direction as I turned and carried the cauldron to the nearest table as fast as physically possible. It was only a few long strides away, thankfully. I could practically feel my skin broiling, burning, blistering. I set the cauldron down on its stumpy legs, released a deep, shuddering breath, and then tucked my hands behind my back in embarrassment.

I would examine the damage later, when Kizzi wasn't around to witness it. My ears flamed in humiliation, drooping slightly.

"There you go, all set." I chuckled tightly. I prayed to whichever Old Gods were listening that she couldn't hear the slight quiver in my voice.

I avoided Kizzi's sharp green gaze—my eyes settled instead on her cauldron.

The contents looked... interesting. Brown, thick, vaguely soupy. Slightly congealed.

I caught a glimpse of what looked like a goose feather drenched in the brown, muddy liquid before Kizzi yanked the fluffy mitts off her hands and plopped her ladle into the cauldron. She gave everything a great, hefting stir. The feather disappeared beneath the surface.

I plastered a strained smile to my face, fighting the urge to gag.

I coughed to clear my throat. "What... what is it? It looks

good!" I breathed through my mouth to avoid any errant fumes.

Kizzi glanced at me, then returned her attention to the cauldron, stirring with gusto. Her forearms strained. "It's called chili. It's a recipe from Oakhollow."

"Oh, how nice. I can't wait to try it. Later, though. Later. Not right now." I shifted my weight on my feet, trying to hold my palms perfectly flat behind my back so my blisters wouldn't chafe.

"Thank you for the help, but I had it under control. How are your hands? Not feeling great, are they?"

I gulped. "It's no problem, I'm here to help. They're fine."

"Really? Why are you hiding them, then? Let me see." She released the ladle, and it remained suspended in the thick, chunky substance. She turned to me, held her hands out, and arched an eyebrow.

"That's really not necessary. Like I said, they're fine." My forehead broke out in a clammy sweat.

She just lifted her eyebrow even higher, brokering no argument.

I sighed and slowly pulled my hands from behind my back, holding them awkwardly in front of me. Kizzi grasped my wrists. Her hands were warm and soft, but her grip was surprisingly sturdy.

My skin tingled at the contact and my ears perked up. My cheeks threatened to lift in a bashful smile. She was touching me. Actually touching me.

Then Kizzi released one of my wrists and ran her fingers gently over my palm. The pleasant tingles vanished, replaced with sharp, burning pain. "Ouch! Gods be damned!" I tugged at my hand, but she held firm.

"I knew it," she tsked. "You burnt yourself pretty good. This'll take a few days to heal. Next time, let's ask permission before we snatch a cauldron out of a perfectly capable lady's hands, shall we?" With a gentle, chastising pat to my damaged palm, she finally released me.

"Of course, I was just trying to help." My shoulders drooped in shame. "I'm sorry."

"Don't apologize to me when you're the one burnt to a crisp! I feel bad that you're hurt."

"It's nothing, really. I've had much worse." I was lying, of course. It stung ferociously. But I would rather choke on chili than admit that.

She stared at me knowingly. "Whatever you say, tough guy."

Kizzi pulled a few more ingredients out of her satchel and began tossing them into the cauldron, and I quietly took my leave. I heard Fiella's bright voice behind me, alongside Redd's deeper tone. They must've noticed Kizzi's arrival.

I huffed a deep breath out through clenched teeth, glancing down at my useless hands as I wandered back to my table on the far end of the park. Pouring drinks from the barrel all day was going to be a nightmare. If only someone could help me. Ginger had her own barrel to worry about, though, and I didn't trust anyone else to do it.

I would have to suffer through it.

Ginger flitted by my table only long enough to drop off a steaming mug filled with coffee. "I saw that, by the way. You're an idiot!" she called over her shoulder as she pranced away.

"You have no idea..." I mumbled under my breath. I lifted the mug, careful to make as little contact with the hot ceramic as possible. The coffee was dark and rich with flecks of ground cinnamon dotting the surface. A faint nutmeg scent slipped through the coffee's strong aroma. I inhaled gratefully before taking a sip. Hot, but not painful—the perfect temperature. I took another longer swallow, relishing the warmth that slipped down my throat, settled into my stomach, and spread all the way to my fingers and toes.

At least, now that I had some coffee in my system, I was more likely to survive the hectic day.

I glanced at my blistered palms skeptically. *Let the potluck begin.*

CHAPTER 8
Kizzi

My chili was truly a masterpiece. It was a miracle that I didn't have a crowd of admiring onlookers surrounding my table to watch me add the finishing touches to the delicacy.

"Do you have to get yourselves set up?" I asked Redd and Fiella. The two mated vampires had teamed up and brought blood smoothies in two different flavors. More than half the folk of Moonvale would avoid their table, for obvious reasons, but the blood guzzlers would have plenty to enjoy themselves.

"Nope, we got here before you did, we're all set," Fiella said.

"Overachievers," I mumbled.

The potluck was only lightly structured. Folk milled around as they pleased. It was common courtesy to ignore any unoccupied tables and come back later when the table was manned again. We looked out for each other, and we all feasted at our leisure. The event didn't officially start until Mayor Tommins declared it, though.

I pulled out my final chili ingredient, along with a small knife.

It's garlic time, bitches.

I began slicing the garlic in quick, even strokes.

Redd let out a garbled shout, somewhere between a shriek and a gasp. "Kizzi!"

"What?!" I glanced up to see that all the color had drained from his face. He was clutching his chest dramatically. "Oh, Old Gods spare me. Are you kidding me right now?"

"What is it—AHH!" Fiella screamed, quickly ducking behind Redd's taller frame and clutching his shoulders.

"You guys are ridiculous! It's just a little garlic—it won't hurt you!"

"You don't know that," Redd said with a shaking voice.

I picked up a clove and held it out threateningly. "Boo!"

Both vampires startled and scrambled back a few steps. "That's not funny!" Fiella wailed.

Laughter burst out of my mouth, shaking my entire frame in massive, belly-quaking cackles. "It's hilarious!" I dropped the garlic clove so I could clutch my stomach. "You should see your faces right now!"

Fiella flipped me off. "You're a bitch." Her voice was still hollow and shaky, but color was slowly returning to her complexion.

"Yep, and you love me anyway." I fought to reign in my laughter. "I couldn't help myself! I had to."

"Yeah, yeah. Whatever. I hope you know we're not eating that, not with *that stuff* in it."

"That stuff? You mean garlic?" I asked.

Fiella flinched. "Quit it!"

"I'm sorry, I'll stop, I swear." I finally choked down the

rest of my giggles. "You weren't going to eat it, anyway, let's not kid ourselves."

Fiella snorted. "Can't blame me."

Truly, I couldn't.

"We better get back to our table, it looks like the potluck is about to start. To the suns, Kiz."

"To the moons!" I called back.

As Redd tossed his arm over Fiella's shoulder and guided her gently back to their table, I tossed the chopped garlic into the cauldron and gave it a quick stir.

There. Now it's perfect.

The garlic brightened the scent to perfection. I lovingly examined the chili, stirring it slowly and letting the steam caress my face. I was so ridiculously proud of myself. Maybe this was a sign from the fates that I needed to start cooking more often.

A loud, booming clap in the center of the park captured my attention and everyone turned to face it. Mayor Tommins stood on a chair, his golden hair tied back into a neat ponytail. The gryphon was tall—not as tall as Tandor but taller than most of the other men in town. His voice projected impressively. "Folk of Moonvale! Thank you for coming out to celebrate with us as the mild season slips away—it's time for the annual potluck! This year, *everyone* has brought a dish to share. Take this opportunity to socialize, to catch up with other folk, to enjoy a variety of treats. Love your neighbor, treat your neighbor, treat yourself, and have a good time! Let's feast!"

Applause broke out, followed by hoots and cheers.

"Yeah! Let's feast!" I shouted with the crowd.

Folk began milling around like frenzied ants. I retrieved

my mug from my satchel and beelined to the nearest table serving tea to grab a steaming drink. I hadn't had time to caffeinate myself before the event—I spent entirely too long carefully stirring and admiring my chili.

I swiped a chocolate croissant from Mitz's bakery table on my way back to find that a few curious folk had gathered beside my table, hesitantly peering over the edge of my cauldron to catch a glimpse of the contents.

"Hello! Give me a second and I'll serve you up." I shoved the entire croissant into my mouth and chewed ferociously as I set my tea down, climbed onto my stool, and grabbed the ladle.

"Hey there, Kizzi! What do you have there?" a voice asked. The question came from Daine, the mothman who ran the grocery store. His elegant fingers were tucked together in front of him, resting on the edge of the table. His wings fluttered in the mild breeze.

"It's called chili!" I announced loudly so all the nearby folk would hear. "It's a recipe from Oakhollow. Folk in the hilly regions eat it all the time."

"Oh, that's cool! And did you... make it?" Daine asked hesitantly.

"Of course I made it!"

I reached for the man's plate and snatched it out of his hands, ladling a generous serving onto it. I pushed the plate back into his grip before grabbing the next folk's plate and repeating the process. They looked a bit bewildered.

"Well, it certainly smells nice," Daine said.

"Tastes even nicer! Try it!" I insisted.

He took a tentative bite, chewing slowly. His eyes widened—his pupils dilating to saucers before constricting to pinpricks. He swallowed hastily. "Wow, that actually isn't bad. I might even say that it's *good*." He shoved another bite into his mouth. And then another.

"Kizzi brought something *good*? I've got to try this!" a voice announced.

"Me, too!"

Before I knew it, I had served chili to dozens of folk, my cauldron was half empty, and I hadn't enjoyed any of the potluck aside from my initial tea and croissant.

"Hey, Linc!" I hopped off my stool, reached out and grasped the human's arm. He was tall, but lanky, and his brown hair was cropped close to his scalp. His eyes widened in surprise when I caught his attention. "Can you make sure nothing happens to my chili while I step away?"

"Uh... Sure. Do you want me to serve any?" He asked, flummoxed.

I shrugged. "If you want to. Just make sure no critters get into it. And protect my cauldron, too."

"How am I supposed to do that?"

"I'm sure you'll figure something out. Oh, and Linc?"

"Yep?"

"If something happens to my cauldron, I'll skin you alive and wear you like a coat."

"Oh... Okay. Fair enough." He only looked mildly frightened. I was losing my touch.

"Thanks!" I grabbed my plate and mug and bolted away from my table. My cheeks ached from the ferocity of my smile. My chili was a hit! Everyone loved it!

Nothing could bring me down—I was riding a high.

I skipped to the far end of the park where Tandor's table always was, craving a crisp, refreshing beverage. A crowd surrounded his table, everyone chatting and laughing loudly. My curiosity piqued. I gently (with my elbows pointed outward) shoved my way through the crowd to the table.

"Hi, boo boo hands!" I greeted Tandor when I finally made my way to the front. The orc had removed his shirt and ripped it into strips, using those to wrap his wounded palms. He was sweating slightly, and his muscles glistened in the sunlight. He poured his brew into mugs with impressive efficiency.

He was truly a sight to behold.

My eyes traveled over his arms, past his bulging shoulders, down his chest, to his stomach... lower...

I yanked my gaze back to his face to find him already watching me. He cracked a crooked smile. "I was wondering when you were going to make it over here. I was afraid it was going to run out before you got to try it."

"I've been a little busy. Try what?" I lifted onto my toes to get a better look into the mugs surrounding me, but I couldn't see much.

"You'll see." He winked and snatched my mug from where it dangled by my side.

He filled it with liquid, his bandaged hands turning the knob on the barrel with practiced precision. His eyes danced with anticipation. He carefully handed the mug back to me— it was filled to the brim.

"You won't tell me what it is?"

"Nope." His smug smile grew.

"Is it going to kill me?"

"Try it and find out."

I shrugged, lifting the mug to my mouth for a hearty swallow. My eyes rolled to the back of my head, and I let out an ungodly groan before swallowing again. And again. The rich, smooth flavor rolled over my tongue and down my throat like it belonged there. By the time I finally came up for air, Tandor was laughing heartily with a massive smile on his face. His small lower tusks gleamed in the sunlight.

"That bad, huh?" he asked. His cheeks were flushed a warm healthy green color.

"Terrible." I held my mug out to him. "More, please?" I smiled sweetly at him and batted my eyelashes.

"For you, I guess." He poured me another mug full, and then filled another mug for himself. I held mine out for a toast.

"What are we toasting to?" he asked.

"To your Gods-blessed hands, for creating the most astoundingly delicious thing I have ever tasted. Even if they are burnt right now."

He chuckled. "I suppose I'll take that." He clinked his mug to mine and we both swallowed.

"Has Fiella been by yet?" I asked.

"She has. She said the lavender blueberry was better."

"Hmm. That's a load of shit."

"That's exactly what I said." He turned to fill another mug for someone else.

"Can I just stay over here with you for the rest of the day?" I joked.

"Who will hand out your... chili?" His voice was strangely tight.

I shrugged. "Someone will, I'm sure. Linc is watching it right now. Speaking of my chili. Do you want some?"

"Oh!" He fumbled nervously for another mug. "Maybe later. I'm full right now."

"Suit yourself. It's been quite a hit."

"It has?"

I tilted my head. "Is that surprising?"

He choked. "Of course not! Of course not," he stammered hurriedly.

An amused chuckle escaped my mouth. "I'm surprised, honestly. It turned out so much better than I expected it to."

"Kizzi!" Fiella called from a few paces away. "You've got to come try this cake!"

Oh, fuck yeah. I love the Moonvale potluck.

"That's my cue. Thanks! Come by my shop tonight and I'll treat those hands with some healing salve, I can tell they're really bothering you." I reached forward and patted Tandor on the back of the hand before whirling and weaving through the crowd to find my best friend.

Hours later, the suns began their journey to the horizon and daylight began to fade. My stomach threatened to burst. It was actually painful. I had tried as many foods as possible until I physically couldn't swallow anymore.

There were pastries, cakes, sandwiches, stews, rice dishes, smoked meats, sour drinks. Lunette had made an incredible leafy salad. Velline brought spicy ginger juice.

My favorite treats were the new cider from Tandor, and the gooey chocolate cake from Mitz.

The rare steak from a wolf shifter was my least favorite. I shivered when I thought about that one—it had been a struggle to swallow.

And my chili was gone. Every single spoonful of it. I was pretty sure Linc had licked the cauldron clean.

Empty, the cauldron wasn't nearly as difficult to carry. I hoisted it up, braced it against my hip, and hauled it back to my apothecary.

My shop was strangely still when I entered. I didn't sense a single flicker of movement, I didn't catch any flutters from the corner of my eye, and I didn't hear any of the telltale sounds of tiny creatures finding hiding spaces.

My ears pricked to attention, straining to hear *something*. Anything.

There was nothing to be heard—not even a popping bubble in a cauldron. The sprites must've really taken my last threat to heart.

I dumped the cauldron onto the floor and picked up a cloth, a bucket, and a container of soapy solvent. I couldn't afford to let this cauldron stay dirty like the large one had. I glanced to the corner and stuck my tongue out at it, just for fun.

Then I got to scrubbing.

The shop felt weird without the irritating presence of the sprites. It was almost... lonely.

How pathetic that my biggest pests had become a twisted sort of comfort.

I didn't particularly enjoy the solitude. I kept turning my head sharply, hoping to catch a sneaky sprite unawares, but there were no sneaky movements to be caught. I huffed out a sigh. "Where did you go, you little assholes? Decided to go bother the other witches instead?"

Silence.

The cauldron was easy to clean, all things considered. I set it out to dry and packed away my cleaning instruments in no time. If only all messes were this easily disposed of.

I made a final sweep of my apothecary, tucking baskets into their nooks, tightening jar lids, tossing dirty cloths into the wash bin. Satisfied with the contained, organized chaos of the shop, I got myself ready for bed.

I brushed my hair, still smooth and wavy from last night's braids, and twisted it back into a loose knot to keep it out of my face. I was standing over my wash bin in my undergarments, washing my trousers, when a knock sounded at the front door. Harsh and loud.

BANG. BANG. BANG.

I froze. My muscles locked and my ears flicked to attention.

The racket was jarring in the unnatural quiet of my shop, kickstarting my heart to a dangerous rhythm.

Then I remembered the instructions I had given Tandor earlier—to swing by my shop for some salve for his burns. My muscles slowly relaxed from their tense position.

"Gods almighty! You're going to break the door down, hang on!" I grabbed a dressing gown and tossed it over my shoulders, hastily pulling it shut while I scurried to the front door.

"Why is the door locked?" Tandor's deep voice boomed, slightly muffled through the wood.

I unlocked the latch and pulled the door open quickly. "Because it's nighttime? I forgot you were coming by!" I looked behind Tandor to the folk milling about. The streets were more lively than usual—the potluck attendees must have not wanted the festivities to come to an end.

"Oh, is it nighttime? Huh. I guess it is." He glanced

around awkwardly. "Do you want me to come back in the morning?" His gaze landed on my face and then slid down slowly. To my throat. To the vee of the dressing gown. To my bare feet. His eyes jumped away immediately, back to the empty shop behind me. "Or I could go see Velline..."

I shuffled my feet, feeling strangely exposed even though I was fully covered. "No, no, come on in, I'm still up. It's my fault that you're hurt. I can help."

I stepped back, pulled the door open wide, and held my hand out in a gesture to let him pass. He had to duck his head just slightly to step through the door, and his body took up most of the door frame. I always forgot how *huge* he was, but suddenly I felt crowded. Like there wasn't enough air in the room. He stepped past me quickly.

I pulled the door shut with a resounding clang.

Something about nighttime, the darkness creeping in, made the shop feel entirely too small—like I needed to throw the arched windows open and stick my head out to get a deep breath.

I cleared my throat. "So, how did the hands hold up? Were you miserable all day?"

His ears twitched. "It was... alright."

I cracked a smile at his embarrassment. "You don't have to lie to me—I know burns are unbelievably painful. You forget that I deal with hot cauldrons every single day, I've been burnt more times than I can count."

"Well, it definitely wasn't pleasant. But if I drank enough cider, I could almost dull the edge of it."

I nodded sagely. "That is a good tip. Maybe you should start picking up shifts with Velline over at Moonvale Medical."

"Very funny. I didn't really have a choice, now did I?"

"I suppose you didn't. Now let's see if we can do something about your little situation." I pulled my rickety work stool out for him to sit on but thought better of it. He might crush the thing. Instead, I retrieved a sturdier stool for him from the back. "Sit."

"Yes, ma'am." He sat obediently and rested his hands on his knees, palms up. They were still wrapped in the strips of his shirt, but he must have grabbed another before he came over here because he was now fully clothed.

Bummer. I chuckled to myself at the thought, imagining a man showing up at my door, half naked, at night, and how scandalous that would be.

He lifted an eyebrow. "What's so funny?"

"Oh nothing, I just noticed you have a shirt on again. May I?" I asked, gesturing to his wrappings.

"You're in charge here."

I rolled my eyes. His blisters had burst throughout the day, and the cloth was soaked through with sticky blood. I tsked in dismay. "Gods, Tandor. This is worse than I thought. We should've taken care of this earlier."

He just shrugged, but I could see the way his back was ramrod straight, and the way the muscle in his jaw twitched when I started to remove the bandages. I worked slowly, carefully, barely touching him. My grip was as light as the brush of a butterfly's wing. Still, I could practically smell the discomfort radiating from him.

"So, about that cider..." I said as a distraction. "That sure was something."

"Oh, that. One of my best, I'd say." His voice was strained.

"You're not wrong there. What's in it? I could taste the cinnamon, but I didn't recognize the rest of it. What else?"

One hand was now free of its wrap, and I moved on to the other, using the same feather light touch.

"Pumpkin, mostly."

"Pumpkin? I've never had that in a drink before, no wonder I didn't recognize it. Pumpkin doesn't grow around here, how in the realms did you get it?"

"It wasn't easy. But I found a trader who would source some for me. For a hefty price, of course."

"Can they get you any more?"

He tilted his head. "Why? Do you need a pumpkin for something?"

I shrugged. "Maybe. I've heard it can be used to enhance potion recipes. But really, I was hoping you would get yourself some more."

I flicked my gaze up to his face to find him already watching me. It was strange seeing him at this level—I was so used to craning my neck and looking up at him. I returned my attention to his hands, pulling off the final bandage and discarding it in a waste basket.

He let out a quiet sigh of relief and lightly curled his fingers before straightening them out again. "I had the same idea. I think I might add spiced pumpkin to the normal cider rotation, if I can. If only we could grow pumpkins in Moonvale."

I hummed in contemplation. "Has anyone ever tried?"

"You know what, I'm not sure. I had assumed so, but I've never witnessed it. We could talk Lunette about it, see if she has any ideas."

I nodded. Surely, there had to be a way. Maybe the coven could do something about that.

I wandered over to one of my shelves, flipping through containers until I found what I was looking for. "Don't touch anything, let your hands breathe for a few moments."

"Whatever you say, princess."

That damned nickname again. I flipped him off over my shoulder. He huffed out a quiet laugh.

I collected the ingredients I needed: two mushroom stalks, a dried dragonfly wing, a spoonful of rainwater, three hairs from a baby squirrel, and a dash of cinnamon. I brought them over to my mortar and pestle and got to work, grinding the ingredients into a smooth pulp while humming an enchantment.

Mentally, I sang a song. *Oh, mother of the Old Gods, grant me the healing touch. Grace me with your magic, your strength, so that I may sooth what has been burned.*

I didn't have to sing or chant to get my magic flowing, but it always helped. I used less energy that way. The words came almost instinctively—I didn't recall ever learning them or memorizing them, but they always came to mind in times of need.

The salve came together quickly, forming a thick paste. I gave it a quick sniff to make sure it smelled right.

Luckily, it did.

Screw you, sprites, wherever you are. A quick glance around the shop showed that they still hadn't returned.

When I turned to Tandor, I found him staring intently at the corner, his eyes burning a hole into the side of the giant cauldron. It was still covered, but the sheet looked different. I would have to examine it later.

"Uh, Kizzi." He tilted his head. "What are you making over there?"

"Nothing. Why do you ask?"

"Nothing? Really? I don't know, there's something about it..."

I shook my head. "It's nothing. I need to clean it out, is all. I don't want to talk about it."

He stared at the cauldron for a few moments more before finally tearing his gaze away. "If you say so. Let me know if you need help—that thing must be heavy."

"You want to help with another cauldron?"

He glanced down at his hands. "You're right, maybe that's not a great idea."

I smiled. "Maybe not. Thanks for offering, though." I set the healing salve down and snatched a clean cloth out of a bucket, wetting it with cold water. I approached timidly, stepping into his personal space. "Ready?"

"As I'll ever be."

"I'll go easy on you." I cleaned his hands quickly, removing all traces of dried blood, dirt, and cider. He held dutifully still, his muscles strung tight as a bowstring. He hardly even breathed.

This close, I could smell the gentle musk drifting from his skin. It was surprisingly pleasant. Like rain, but warmer. A soothing rain. The rain during the mild season. And a hint of something spicy that I couldn't put my finger on.

"How are you doing over there?" I asked, peeking up at his face. His expression was strained, his cheeks a paler green than usual.

"Great," he gritted out between clenched teeth. "Thank you."

"It'll be over soon," I promised.

He nodded hastily.

"Just the salve, then I'll wrap them up again, and then we're done. Think you can handle that?"

He kept nodding, his head continuously bobbing. *I think he's broken. Poor guy.*

"You're tough. You got this," I insisted. The nodding continued.

I tossed the blood-spotted cloth into the wash basin and grabbed the salve mixture, holding the pestle out for him to examine. "Okay?"

"Do I want to know what's in it?" he asked.

"Probably not. But I swear, it'll help."

"Go ahead, then." He refused to watch while I gently slathered the mixture onto his palms, instead examining my face. When the salve touched his skin, he let out a deep, relieved breath. I worked carefully, one finger at a time, taking care to coat every bit of damaged skin. I layered extra onto the bleeding bits.

"Better?" I asked.

"So much better," he sighed. His strained posture finally relaxed, and he slumped on his stool. His knees drifted open slightly, one of them bumped into my hip. I pretended I didn't notice. It was probably an accident.

Tandor was completely relaxed by the time I finished applying the salve, looking as comfortable and at ease as he usually did. It was a relief to see—tense Tandor was unnerving.

"Let me grab some clean bandages. I have a stack around here somewhere. I hate to break it to you, but I'm going to burn those shirt strips."

"I think I'll live. Are you going to perform a witchy ritual with them?"

I snorted. "Maybe I will. Mind your business."

I found the bandages tucked in a basket next to my collection of plucked flower petals.

"Almost done. Ready?" I held up the bandages. Obediently, he raised his paste-smeared hands, his elbows propped against his knees. To see such a huge, intimidating orc curled over on a stool with his wounded hands propped up was certainly... something. I fought the smile that threatened to lift my cheeks.

I stepped into his space again, grabbed a bandage, and got to work. I grasped his wrist for stability with one hand while I gently wound the fabric with the other. I started the wrap around his thumb, on the meaty flesh there, where the burns were the deepest. I wrapped it twice. Then around the palm, again, and the fingers. One at a time. Tandor's warm breath tickled my face as it drifted past me. I tied the bandage into a neat knot. Not beautiful, but it would do.

Next hand.

I picked up another bandage. I started with his thumb, again. This hand was burnt a little worse. I added an extra layer to his palm before moving onto his fingers. Pinky first. Then the third finger. Middle finger. Pointer.

"Kizzi."

"Hmm?" I glanced up, and my gaze collided with liquid onyx. I was trapped like a fly in honey. His face was much, much closer than I expected it to be.

I was frozen. Our faces were mere inches apart.

His gaze flicked down to my mouth briefly before

returning to my eyes. Heat traveled up my neck, over my cheeks, settled in the tips of my ears.

My hands were still hovering over his palm, gripping the tail of the bandage, and he slowly curled his fingers into the fabric.

I couldn't help it—I leaned toward him and let my eyelids fall shut.

BANG.

BANG. BANG. BANG. BANG.

I gasped, breaking through the weird trance I had fallen in.

What the fuck *was that? Was I about to kiss him? Where the fuck did that come from?* Hot embarrassment flamed in my cheeks.

Bewildered, I scurried backward, unable to meet Tandor's gaze.

"Is that the door?" he asked.

"Sure sounds like it."

He cleared his throat. "Expecting someone else?" His voice was full of gravel.

"No."

"Oh. Who would just show up to a business at night?"

"Besides you?"

He glanced at me sideways. "Besides me."

"I don't know!"

"Are you going to answer it?"

BANG. BANG. BANG.

Thankfully, the distraction lightened the strange tension that had settled over the room. I hoped Tandor wasn't feeling it as thoroughly as I was—maybe he didn't notice how close I had come to planting a big fat unsolicited smooch on him.

"I guess I have to. Will you protect me if it's a monster?" I joked. There were no monsters in Moonvale.

"Of course, princess."

That damn nickname. My cheeks warmed for some reason. I yanked the waist tie on my dressing gown impossibly tighter before I stomped over to the front door.

"This better be good!" I shouted to the nighttime intruder as I yanked the door open. What I saw perplexed me. "What the fuck. Linc? What are you doing here?"

He smiled broadly. "I came to see you, of course!" He spread his arms wide, beckoning me into a hug.

What. The. Fuck.

CHAPTER 9

Tandor

My bandaged hands hung uselessly by my sides as I stared at the situation in front of me with absolute bewilderment.

Linc, the human man that was always fluttering around town, was standing outside Kizzi's door, in the dim light of the gleaming dual moons, grinning at the witch with his arms thrown out wide and a manic gleam in his eye. His cheeks were flushed to an alarming degree, and I could hear his heart thudding from where I was standing. *Thump. Thump. Thump.*

Kizzi and... Linc? I hadn't seen that coming. Sure, the man was handsome, but he was sort of... odd. And not necessarily in a good way.

Lead settled deep in my gut. I swallowed, trying to ease the tension that was growing inside me.

Part of me wanted to punch the human. My knuckles wouldn't even split with how neatly they were wrapped with bandages.

I stepped forward, just once. The floor creaked beneath

my feet. The sound seemed to break Kizzi from whatever stupor she had fallen into, and she looked around frantically.

"Linc, what in the realms do you mean? You came to see me? It's nighttime!"

"I couldn't wait any longer," he said, still holding his arms out.

"Do you need a potion or something? I'm not going to make anything else tonight—"

"No, not a potion. I just need you." He stepped forward, reaching his hands toward Kizzi's shoulders. She hastily stepped back.

"Hey there, Linc. What's going on?" I asked.

His glossy eyes fixed on me. "Oh, hey, Tandor. Were you just leaving?"

I crossed my arms. "Not anymore."

Kizzi glanced at me strangely. "I can't do this right now, Linc. You're probably drunk. If you still need something tomorrow, you can ask me about it then, when you've sobered up."

His eyes widened. "No! But—"

The witch slammed the door in his face. She locked it, tested the knob, and then tested it again. It held.

Linc knocked on the door again, more gently this time. "Please, honey, let's just talk."

"Go home, Linc," she gritted through clenched teeth.

"Not before we talk."

"We can talk tomorrow."

He paused for a long moment. "You promise?" he finally asked, quieter this time. He sounded forlorn. Sad.

Kizzi let out a heavy sigh. "I promise."

It took a while, but eventually, the sound of light footfalls heading into the distance could be heard, breaking the weighted silence of the night.

I just stared at Kizzi. She stared back. I thought again about earlier, how close she had been to me, how every muscle in my body ached to lean in, to kiss her, to capture her lips with mine. I could have sworn she leaned in, too. That must have been my hopeful imagination.

Eventually, she broke the tense silence. "So, that was weird."

Which part? The almost kiss or the interruption? I almost asked, but I stopped myself. Instead, I said, "It was. Does he do that often?"

She scoffed. "No! Never. Linc and I aren't even really friends. He helped me hand out chili today, maybe I gave him the wrong idea? I hardly spoke two words to the guy!"

The knot in my stomach loosened slightly. Kizzi didn't belong to Linc, after all. I still had a chance.

Deep down, I pitied the human. He was ensnared in Kizzi's web just as I was.

"I think he was just drunk, and he'll probably forget all about it come the rise of the suns," I offered.

"One can only dream."

I held my right hand out to her, where the final ties dangled loosely. "Would you mind fastening this last knot? Then I'll get out of your hair and let you get to bed. You must be tired."

"Oh! Right, of course," she said hastily. She fumbled with the strips of fabric for a moment before she found a secure grip, and then she tied the knot with impressive speed. She retreated to the other side of the room. "You must be more tired than me, after slinging drinks all day. I saw how crowded your table was."

I shrugged, admiring the neat, secure bandages on my hands. They really felt *so* much better. It was miraculous how much of a difference a little magical salve could make. "I have more energy at night, usually. The mornings are when I really struggle with being tired."

"That's backwards."

"I guess I'm a night owl."

"Right. Well, sorry again about the hands. If you need another round of healing salve, just let me know."

I nodded. "Thank you, Kizzi, for this." I held my hands out as an explanation. "This really is incredible."

She brushed me off. "It's just a quick enchantment and a few herbs. Nothing special."

"Still, thank you."

Her cheeks darkened slightly, but she said nothing else. With a nod in her direction, I unlocked the door and stepped out into the night. I resisted the urge to peek over my shoulder to catch another glimpse of the woman in her dressing gown. I heard the glide of metal on metal as the lock clicked into place behind me.

The cool night air was pleasant against my warm ears. I let out a deep breath, allowing the tension to drain from my shoulders, my forearms, my wrists.

The walk to my cabin would be a much-needed distraction.

Surprisingly, a few folk were still out and about, even though the moons were high in the sky, and it was far past the time when most of Moonvale settled down for sleep. I even saw a fluffy white cat scurrying around the corner, chasing something I couldn't see. I thought it might've been the same cat from earlier, the one that rubbed against Kizzi's ankles.

I took a slight detour to pass through the park in town square, checking for any heavy items that still needed to be returned to their proper homes. The park benches were all that remained.

On the closest bench sat Linc, hunched in on himself, staring at his shoes. His gaze was fixed but not focused, and his eyes still held a strange, glossy sheen. His eyebrows were pinched as though he was upset, but his mouth was lax.

Was he... waiting for something?

A glance around the park showed nobody else looking at him or heading in his direction. He was on his own, it seemed.

My jaw clenched. Was he waiting for Kizzi?

Absolutely not.

"Hey, Linc!" I called out as I approached the man. "What are you up to?"

He didn't look at me when I stepped closer. "Oh, nothing, really."

"Are you okay?"

"Yes," he answered simply.

"You don't look okay, man. Are you going to sit here all night?"

He shrugged. "Maybe." His gaze remained unfixed, pointed at the ground.

"You should really get home," I said hesitantly. "Can you walk?"

He nodded. "I can. But no, thank you."

"I'll help you," I insisted. I placed a hand tentatively on

his shoulder. He didn't even flinch. His muscles were loose and relaxed. "Would that be alright?"

He simply shrugged again. Nervously, slowly, I grabbed Linc's arm and pulled it over my head, around my shoulders. He let me. "I'm going to help you stand, okay?"

I secured my arm around his middle, grasped his wrist, and gently hoisted him to his feet. He was not very heavy, but I had to crouch to keep his feet from hovering above the ground.

"Do you still live over by the river?" I asked.

"Yes."

"Okay, then. I'll take you there." I began walking in that direction. He walked with me—clumsily but willingly. His feet moved as though commanded by an external force.

The human was silent the entire way, gazing off into the distance with glossy eyes and pinprick pupils. He didn't seem drunk.

Mirthroot, maybe? Linc really didn't seem like the recreational drug type, but folk could be surprising.

Luckily, the door to his small, tidy cabin was unlocked. I pushed it open and led the human inside. He allowed me to place him onto his bed, where he clumsily crawled under the covers. He was still fully dressed with his boots on, but there was no way in Hell's Realm I was going to undress him while he was acting so strange.

"Are you good here, Linc?"

He didn't answer—he just stared at the ceiling above him.

"Okay then... I'm going to leave. Just go to sleep. Don't go anywhere else. You'll feel better tomorrow." *Hopefully.*

Silence.

Feeling confused and vaguely concerned, I left Linc in his

bed, marched out of his cottage, and pulled the door closed behind me.

The walk to my own cottage was less eventful. Chirping insects, scurrying critters, and my own thoughts were all that kept me company.

My cottage was uncomfortably quiet. Stiflingly so. I tossed my windows open wide, welcoming the sounds of the lively forest a few paces away.

It helped. A little.

My mind couldn't decide where to settle, flitting back and forth between Kizzi, her soft hands and kind treatment of my wounds, and Linc, and his baffling behavior. Both were enough to scramble my brains.

Was Linc really interested in Kizzi, or was it just a drug making him act that way? It didn't seem like she returned his affections but... she didn't return mine either. I wasn't in a position to care, but I couldn't help myself.

Maybe tomorrow will be more normal...

CHAPTER 10
Kizzi

The knocking on my front door started before the suns had even risen in the sky. Incessant. Constant. Neverending. I ignored it for as long as I could, but eventually, I forced myself out of bed. If I was going to be awake against my will, I could at least be productive.

I glanced at the giant cauldron in the corner as I sleepily made my morning shop rounds, checking for any damage the sprites might have inflicted overnight. It was full, uncovered, and perfectly still.

Everything else was exactly as I had left it the night before. The sprites still hadn't returned. Assholes. Whether they were assholes for bothering me or assholes for making me worry, I couldn't decide. I plopped down on my stool and rested my head in my hands.

I was exhausted—tired all the way down to my bones. Between the late night, the racing thoughts, and the ridiculously early morning, I hardly caught a wink of sleep, and I was feeling the consequences.

Knock. Knock. Knock.

"Go. Away!" I shouted for what felt like the hundredth time that morning. "I'm not open yet. Don't you have something better to do?"

"Gods, who crapped in your cauldron this morning?" a bright, familiar voice called out. Fiella.

I sighed. *I guess I prefer her over the others.*

Hoisting myself from my stool, I dragged my feet to the front door and pulled it open. "Quick. Don't let anyone else in."

"You look like shit," Fiella declared, looking me up and down. I would have slammed the door in her face, but she was carrying a pouch from the bakery and two steaming mugs of tea. And I was not above delicious bribes, even on my grumpiest of days.

"Come on! Hurry!" I tucked my arm around her back and yanked her inside before I ducked back in and threw the door shut.

I let out a heavy sigh of relief.

"What the fuck was that?" Fiella asked, heading to a table and making herself at home as she always did.

"I honestly don't know," I responded. I massaged my throbbing temples, trying to ease the ache that was slowly settling beneath my skull.

"Are you running a crazy sale that you didn't tell me about? Why are so many folk waiting outside?"

I snatched a mug of tea and a peach biscuit from her. I took a slow sip of the hot beverage, letting it soothe me. Earl grey and spearmint. "Nope, no sale. Do you think they're playing a prank on me?"

She considered this. "No, it didn't seem like it. They were just waiting out there. They wouldn't tell me why."

"Ugh," I groaned. "How many of them?"

"Do you really want to know?"

"Gods, is it that bad?"

She nodded sagely. "It's pretty bad."

I took a huge bite of the peach biscuit, chewed it slowly, and swallowed, not even caring about the crumbs I was dropping everywhere. I washed the bite down with a sip of tea. "I'm ready. Lay it on me."

"At least half of the town is out there, Kiz."

My jaw dropped open. "You're joking."

"I hate to tell you this, but I'm not. Look for yourself."

"No way! How do I make them leave?"

She shrugged. "Have you tried just... telling them to leave? Asking what they want?"

"Of course not! I refused to open the door."

"Well, I'd say that's a good place to start."

I sighed. The vampire was right. I had been so grouchy from the early morning and all the pestering that I hadn't felt like entertaining any of it. I simply left my curtains pulled shut and ignored the problem, hoping it would go away. I occasionally shouted curse words at them, but that hadn't done much either. Clearly my plan wasn't working.

Speaking of ignoring problems and hoping they'll go away...

Bracing myself, I turned slowly to the cauldron in the corner. I hadn't questioned what it looked like this morning, but now that I was more awake, the discovery was... alarming.

The cauldron was full to the brim, the sheet that had been covering it, weighed down with selenite crystals, was crumpled against the wall, and it was oozing magic. I could almost *see* the waves of magic drifting down the cast iron, over the floor, cascading across the shop. It was a wonder I hadn't noticed it before—I had gotten so used to tuning it out.

"Hey, why did you stop breathing? I can't hear your breaths anymore—" Fiella started before she noticed what I was looking at. Her spine straightened in a jerk. "Oh, fuck. Did you add something to it? Wasn't that thing like half full the first time I saw it?"

I shivered and ran my hands over my arms. Goosebumps rose on my skin. "I didn't add anything."

"Okay. Let's not panic. So, the mysterious and extremely unsettling cauldron creation is... growing?"

I nodded. "It sure seems like it."

"And we're not panicking."

"Nope. Not at all." My teeth began to chatter.

We stared at the cauldron for what felt like ages. I could almost feel it staring back—my paranoid imagination was out of control.

"Why hasn't it dried out? Shouldn't it be shrinking?" she asked.

"It should be. I've been keeping it covered, maybe that's why it hasn't dried?"

"You should really get it out of here."

"I could hardly move it to the corner, there is no way I'm going to be able to pick it up and carry it outside!"

"What was your plan?"

"I didn't have one, clearly! I've been ignoring it!"

She snorted. "Yeah, that sounds about right."

Knock. Knock. Knock. A gentle hand rattled the front door. "Kizzi? Are you in there?"

Shit! "Depends who's asking," I responded.

"It's Mayor Tommins."

"Oh... Yes, I'm here. Hang on." I pulled the door open and let the man in, hastily shutting it behind him. "What can I do for you, Mayor?" I hoped he couldn't tell how tense I was.

The tall gryphon waltzed into the room, his fluffy, golden hair smoothed back into its usual ponytail at the nape of his neck. His tunic was a bright blue color that reminded me of Fiella's hair.

Mayor Tommins looked at me strangely for a second. His pupils dilated and his nose scrunched. He shook his head, as though trying to clear his thoughts. Then he stepped backwards, putting as much space between himself and me as possible.

Tentatively, I sniffed my underarm. *Do I smell that bad? Rude.*

Mayor Tommins cleared his throat. "It seems there is some sort of... situation going on here. Care to explain why so many folk are camped outside?"

I shrugged. "Truly, I have no clue. Can you ask them?"

"I tried that. They didn't seem to have an answer for me." His gaze traveled from my face, down to my feet, and then back up again. He hastily looked away, his expression strained.

"Can you demand that they leave, as mayor? I don't want to deal with them."

"I suppose I could." He glanced around the shop suspiciously. "What have you been up to in here?"

I gulped. "Why do you ask?"

"Something feels strange..." He slowly walked around the room, examining jars and shelves at random. He glanced at me from the corner of his eye. "When I look at you, I feel this —this unpleasant sensation."

Fiella snorted from where she sat across the room before drowning her laughter with a swig of tea.

"I'm... sorry? There isn't much I can do about that. I didn't realize I was so unpleasant to look at."

His cheeks flushed. "That's not what I meant. You're a lovely lady, Kizzi. It's just... he glanced at me again and shuddered. "It doesn't usually feel like this."

I shrugged helplessly. "Well, I didn't do anything, I swear! Just business as usual!"

"You haven't been making potions with *those* plants again, have you?"

"No! By the Old Gods, I swear I haven't!" At least not the plants I was pretty sure he was referring to—the poisonous ones that caused extreme anxiety and solidified skin if ingested. You don't make that kind of mistake twice.

He squinted at me for a moment before finally relaxing into a more normal posture. "Alright, then. I have no reason not to believe you. Let's just all go back to normal, okay? I don't like how the folk of Moonvale are acting out there."

I nodded quickly. "Yes, of course. Normal sounds great."

"Alright then. I'll see what I can do about the crowd outside. Good day."

"Good day!"

"See you, Tommins!" Fiella called out.

Mayor Tommins waved absentmindedly as he exited. He pulled the door shut with a bang that echoed through the room. My ears shrank back to my head.

"Am I losing my mind, or was that whole interaction extremely weird? What is going on with everyone?" I asked.

"That was definitely weird. Was he trying to tell you that you're smelly and ugly?"

"You caught that too? It sure seemed like it!" I shivered. "I thought he was more polite than that!"

"He usually is. Maybe it's the aftermath of the potluck stress, or he ate too much yesterday and his stomach hurts."

"Maybe," I agreed halfheartedly.

"Well, I promise that you are beautiful, and you smell like sunshine and daisies." She stood from her stool. "I better go start my day. If any folk are still lingering out there, I'll threaten to bite their throats to make them go away."

"You're the best."

She flashed me a fanged grin. "That's what best friends are for! Moons, Kiz!"

I laughed. "To the suns, Fi."

She waved as she left, and I heard the muffled sounds of her ferociously snarling through the door. I snorted out a laugh, wishing I could witness that spectacle for myself.

My mirth died quickly. Why was everyone losing their minds? First me, when I almost kissed Tandor against his will. Then Linc, Mayor Tommins, and half of Moonvale?

It was almost like *the Josten incident* all over again. But this felt different. This didn't feel sinister—it just felt strange.

Well, hopefully everything goes back to normal soon.

I worked for what felt like hours in tense, charged silence. My skin felt too tight. It itched, and I couldn't get comfortable.

I refused to leave the shop to make deliveries—I was

pretty sure everyone outside had gone but I didn't feel like risking it.

But I couldn't handle the silence anymore.

"Do any of you little shits feel like bothering me today?" I shouted into the empty shop, hoping to startle a sprite into revealing itself.

Silence was the only response. My ears drooped slightly. I stood, spreading my arms wide and turning in a circle.

"Good! I'm happy that you're all gone!" I shouted louder. Silence again.

"I've been trying to get rid of you for ages and I'm so glad it finally worked!" I screamed. My voice cracked at the end.

Nothing.

"I'm so glad you left me here all alone!" My voice crumpled. A wave of sadness and fury washed over me. I felt abandoned. I felt betrayed, even though I had no logical reason to.

I stormed over to the cauldron in the corner. "And you! Fuck you! Fuck you most of all!" I grabbed the edges of the cauldron, not caring if any of the strangely smooth and thick substance got on my hands. I needed to scream, and this was my best outlet.

"Fuck you for ruining my potion. Fuck you for causing a mess. Fuck you for making my shop feel weird. Fuck. You!" I screamed until my voice fragmented like shards of broken glass, and then I started to cry. Tears welled up in my eyes and dripped down my cheeks. They traveled the curve of my jaw and collected at the point of my chin.

Slowly, so slowly, a tear dripped from my chin and landed in the giant cauldron.

The tiny drop settled on top of the sludge for a moment before it began to spread, becoming a thin layer that I could hardly see. Then it began to sink into the sludge. I watched curiously.

Heavy waves of magic shot through my hands, up my arms, into my shoulders. A massive boom resounded, throwing me across the room and shattering my eardrums. Darkness stole my vision. Darkness took over the entire shop.

Faintly, I could hear ringing, metal cracking, and what almost sounded like... laughter?

And then there was nothing.

CHAPTER 11

Tandor

G inger's Pub hummed with a strange energy. I refilled goblets, delivered plates, and wiped down tables, trying to figure out where it was coming from.

My hands, still wrapped securely in the bandages and salve, didn't ache nearly as fiercely as they had before Kizzi's treatment. They barely even stung. I was able to use them as I normally would, with only minor hindrances.

I was hesitant to remove the bandages and look at my wounds beneath. I was occasionally a squeamish orc, especially when it came to my own injuries.

There were more folk in the pub than usual this early in the day. Folk that would normally be going about their daily tasks, running their businesses, or staying at home.

It was like they were... waiting for something. My mind flitted to Linc, and his strange behavior last night. He had appeared to be waiting, too. Like he was frozen—ready to move only when he received orders.

A small white cat was perched in the corner of the room, watching with alarmingly bright green eyes. It gazed at the crowd with an almost folk-like intelligence. I didn't bother trying to shoo it away—I let the cats come and go as they pleased as long as they didn't irritate anyone. They kept the more invasive critters away, like mice, squirrels, and spiders.

And they were cute to look at, too, if I was being honest. I often tried to pet them, but they usually didn't let me. They were intimidating for some reason.

I recognized the critter—it was the same cat that had nearly tripped Kizzi before the potluck. Weird. I was seeing it everywhere.

"What's up with everyone?" Ginger asked as she swept in front of me to drop a bowl off at a table of fae and witches.

"I'm not sure..." I answered. "I was wondering the same thing."

I looked around, examining the pub's patrons. Daine, the mothman from the grocery store, sat in the corner with Velline, both of them stiff and awkward. A few shifters hovered by the door looking like they might bolt at any moment. A pair of humans dined at the bar, but they spent more time staring into nothingness than they did eating. Everyone looked *almost* normal... but not quite.

"Well, if they're paying customers, I suppose we'll keep serving them how we usually do." Ginger shrugged.

"This weird thing happened with Linc last night, do you think it has anything to do with it?" I asked. As the faun and I wandered back to the kitchen, I explained the situation that had occurred the night before in Kizzi's apothecary. How Linc had shown up, insisting on coming in to speak with Kizzi, and was forced to leave. How I found him on a bench in the park with none of his wits about him. The crazed, faraway look in his eye. The way I dragged him home, mindless and compliant.

"Gods. That is strange," she mused. "Late night at Kizzi's, huh?" She raised an eyebrow knowingly.

I rolled my eyes. "She was helping me with my burns." I held my hands out as proof. The neat bindings were beginning to loosen from how much I was using them.

"Sure. Whatever you say, Tandor." She smirked at me. "I've seen the way you watch that little witch. Kizzi's a treat—only a blind folk wouldn't be interested."

"Exactly!" I agreed.

"I knew it!"

"Wait, you tricked me!" I huffed out a sigh. "Okay, fine. I might be interested. I just find her lovely, is all. And interesting. And she's so hardworking, always fixing up potions for everyone in town. And—"

Ginger cut me off with a laugh. "Enough, enough, I get it. She's amazing. Why haven't you done anything about it?"

"I've tried! Well, I've sort of tried. Every time I feel like we're having a moment, she clearly doesn't feel the same way. I don't think she even sees me."

"You're gigantic, it's impossible not to see you," she teased. "Have you tried telling her how you feel?"

I sighed. "No. I should, I know, but I'm not prepared to face that rejection yet. And she makes me so *nervous*. If things must stay exactly how they are, I'll be content with that. I'll take a few friendly words here and there rather than scaring her away forever."

"I don't think you'd scare her away. She likes your ciders too much."

I elbowed her in the shoulder. "That's all I have going for me, huh?"

"Yes. But it's better than nothing," she agreed solemnly.

"Do you think I should go over there and check on her? She seemed pretty rattled after the Linc situation last night, and I'm afraid he'll go back and bother her some more."

"Go, go, check on your woman. Just come back before the evening dinner rush."

I bent and plopped a kiss onto the top of her head, pulling my apron off and tossing it aside. "You're the best, Ginny!"

She shoved me toward the door. "I know it. Good luck!"

I saluted her as I hustled out of the pub and practically ran to Kizzi's apothecary.

The shop was dark when I approached. Unnaturally dark. I couldn't even see through the windows. I pressed my face to the glass to get a better look, trying to peek through the gaps in the curtains, but all I could see was thick, shadowy darkness.

Was she still sleeping? It was past midday. I knocked tentatively.

No answer.

I knocked again, louder this time.

Still nothing. A kernel of worry bloomed in my gut. Something about this didn't feel right.

I knocked a third time, banging so hard that my healing hands ached. "Kizzi!" I shouted. "Are you in there?"

I heard a small rustling sound from inside. My ears flicked out, trying to gather as much of the sound as possible.

"Kizzi? Is that you?" I held my breath. I heard the strange rustling again, followed by a small, pained whimper.

"Kizzi!" I shouted. "I'm coming in!"

I yanked on the door with all my might, but the lock was solid. Probably enchanted to be un-pickable. The wood, though, didn't seem to be enchanted.

I backed up, braced myself, and delivered a mighty kick to the center of the door. It buckled slightly. Yes!

I kicked the door again. And again. And again. Finally, wood splintered, and the door flew open.

I stormed inside. The first thing I noticed was that the darkness was indeed smoke—and it was suffocating. It billowed out the open door, seeking fresh air to taint. I yanked my tunic over my mouth and nose and dropped to the floor, where the air was less densely smokey. I felt around with my bandaged hands as I traveled the perimeter of the room on my hands and knees. "Kizzi! Where are you?!" I shouted, slightly muffled through the fabric covering my face.

The quiet whimper sounded again, closer to a groan this time. I crawled faster.

Slowly, the smoke began to clear.

What I saw made me pause. It wasn't a fire that had caused the smoke, because nothing was damaged. There was no flame, no ash, and nothing was burnt. I tentatively got to my feet.

A flurry of movement in the far corner caught my attention. It was a fluttering, bustling mass of movement that I couldn't quite distinguish.

Until I noticed a flash of green curly hair peeking out. I bolted for the corner. "Gods almighty, Kizzi!"

The mass broke apart into shimmering flashes of movement and dispersed, spreading throughout the shop. I hardly noticed—my attention was fixed on the small witch curled up on the floor.

Kizzi appeared to be asleep, but her position was unnatural. She was slumped sideways, partially propped against the shelf on the wall, and one of her arms was squashed beneath her.

"Can you hear me? I'm going to sit you up, alright?" I wasn't sure if she could hear anything in this state, but speaking to her made me feel better. My heart was thundering in my chest.

Gently, carefully, I tucked a hand behind the nape of her neck, and the other grasped her shoulder. I slowly sat her upright, being cautious to keep her head still in case she was injured. A small rivulet of blood trickled from her ear. Her eyes fluttered, and she groaned again.

She began to slump, so I grasped her head with both hands, bracketing her gently but firmly. Her eyes fluttered again. "Wake up, Kizzi. You're okay," I insisted. My blood thundered through my veins with an almost painful ferocity, but I fought to keep my panic at bay.

A moment passed. Ten. Endless moments. Eventually, her eyes slowly opened. Her gaze was groggy, unfocused, but the green of her irises was the prettiest sight I had ever seen. I decided right then and there that green was my favorite color. I huffed out a sigh of relief.

"Tandor?" she asked, confused. "What are you doing here?"

"Did you fall? What happened?"

"I don't know…" she mumbled. She tried to look around, but I held her still. Her eyes jumped to mine, startled.

"You were slumped on the ground. Are you hurt?"

She closed her eyes for a moment. "I ache, but I think I'm alright." She lifted a hand to the back of her head, her fingers lightly brushing mine where they grasped her. She prodded her scalp for a bit and then brought her hand into her line of sight. "I'm not bleeding. I think I just bruised myself."

"Are you sure? Your ear is bleeding. Do you need to go see Velline?"

"No, no. I can hear you—I'm fine." She slowly looked around, and her eyes widened into saucers. "They're back."

"Who's back? Nobody else is in here, Kizzi. Are you sure you didn't hit your head too hard?" Worry flooded my thoughts. I leaned over to get a better look at where she hit the shelf.

"No, I'm okay. I promise."

I didn't want to release her, but she pulled my hands from her head and used them as a support to stand herself up. I let her.

She winced and gritted her teeth, but she was steady on her feet, and I took that as a good sign. I stood as well, hovering close in case she fell again.

"What happened? Do you remember why you were on the floor?" I asked gently.

She didn't answer, instead her gaze danced around the shop. Her mouth held a small, serene smile, and her eyes glistened.

It was a punch to the gut, how beautiful she was. She nearly brought me to my knees.

I committed her expression to memory—I wasn't sure what was causing the strange, wondrous reaction, but she was worthy of a painting.

I let her enjoy her moment. She slowly drifted over to a worktable and stretched her hand out, reaching for something. Her smile grew. "You came back," she said quietly. I couldn't quite see what she was reaching for—my eyes were having a hard time focusing. Something small shimmered, distorting the light.

Then it dawned on me. It was a sprite. I glanced around the shop, furrowing my brows, trying to focus my struggling vision, but the effort was futile. The sprites were everywhere —in every corner of the shop. I couldn't quite see them straight on, but I could catch flurries of their movement out of the corner of my eye, and I could see them in my peripheral vision.

The sensation was disorienting. The way I couldn't *quite* see them, even though I knew they were there.

Kizzi let the sprites dance over her fingers, climb onto her arms, settle into her hair. She seemed at peace with them. Happy, even. I had never noticed the small creatures in the shop before, but it was clear that she was familiar with them.

I stayed quiet, content to just observe the moment.

She laughed quietly and then her gaze flicked to the corner of the room, where her giant cauldron sat. The smile dropped off her face.

"Oh, fuck."

<h1 style="text-align:center">CHAPTER 12
Kizzi</h1>

My stomach churned with dread. My minor aches were forgotten, the strange joy of having the sprites return evaporated in an instant.

What I had been doing before I blacked out slowly came back to me. I had been hunched over the cauldron, shouting, and I had started to cry. And then the boom—I was tossed across the room. And then I woke up staring into Tandor's concerned face.

It was the cauldron.

The cauldron sat in the corner, but something was different—it was cracked down the middle.

My treasured cauldron was broken. Ruined. A cracked cauldron was a witch's worst nightmare. I gulped, feeling the blood drain from my face. My ears drooped. The coven was going to be *pissed* that I ruined our biggest cauldron just weeks before Hallow's Eve.

A small wisp of smoke curled up and drifted away, dispersing into nothing.

Slowly, carefully, I approached the corner. The air

surrounding the cauldron vibrated with so much magic that it was almost painful. My teeth chattered and my hair fluttered on a phantom breeze.

I reached the cauldron. Leaned forward. And hesitantly looked inside.

It was empty. Completely empty. Not even a crumb of residue, or a drop of liquid remained. "What in the realms?" I asked aloud.

"What is it?" Tandor asked. I jumped, his voice startling me.

"It's... nothing. Absolutely nothing."

"Then why do you look like you're going to throw up?" He approached with timid steps.

"Because that's a problem. It wasn't nothing before..."

I leaned further into the cauldron to be sure, ignoring the overwhelming waves of magic, but there was nothing remaining. No ashes, no evidence of any kind.

"Before?" he asked gently.

"Before the explosion."

"Okay... can you explain that more?"

I nodded, trying to gather myself. I walked over to my stool and sat down, and Tandor followed, sitting as well. I massaged my temples.

One of the tiny sprites settled onto my head and massaged my scalp with nimble fingers. Strangely enough, it helped ease the ache.

I explained the situation to the orc, and he listened intently. I told him about how the cauldron had started out as a failed potion brew with too much magical oomph behind it. How the sprites had probably added things to it. How I had let it sit for days, not wanting to clean it. How it started off as half-full, and eventually (damned sprites) expanded.

"You could have asked me for help, I would have hauled it to the Barren Lands for you," Tandor interrupted.

I smiled slightly. "In hindsight, I probably should have. I thought I could handle it."

I continued my story. About the cauldron sludge growing. About how I had been shouting at it, and then how I cried, and the boom that followed, throwing me across the room.

"And then you arrived," I finished. "And now you're all caught up."

He nodded slowly, absorbing. "Okay... so the cauldron sludge exploded and just... vanished?"

"Yep."

"And this is a bad thing?"

"It's definitely not great. There's no residue, no ash, no remains. It didn't burn. It didn't dry out. So where did it go?"

He pondered this. "Did you cast some sort of disappearing spell?"

I shook my head. "No, no I didn't cast anything. Not intentionally, anyway."

"Do things happen accidentally sometimes?"

"They shouldn't, but things have been so weird lately..."

A new voice called out from across the room. "Hey, Kizzi!"

I damn near jumped out of my skin. I glanced at the door to find it splintered and broken, floating open on its hinges. Standing in the entryway was Linc, looking much more himself than he had last night, aside from a strange sheen in his eyes. "Linc. You're back. Fantastic."

I shot an accusatory glance at Tandor to find him gnawing on his lower lip nervously. His small tusks poked out between his full lips. "It was an emergency. Sorry about that. Don't worry, I'll fix it."

I flapped my hand at him dismissively. "That's a problem for later."

Linc stepped into the shop and glanced around. "Your door is broken, by the way." He picked up a mushroom and sniffed it.

"I had no idea, thanks!" I said dryly. "That's toxic, by the way." It wasn't, but I was annoyed that he was touching my things without asking.

He dropped the fungus immediately and dusted his hands off on his trousers. He spun and faced me with a cheesy grin on his face. "It's good to see you, Kizzi!"

"What do you need? Are you here to place an order?"

"I'm here to see you, of course," he stated matter-of-factly.

Tandor shifted on his stool, clearing his throat. I ignored him.

"And why is that?"

He stared at me blankly, as though the answer were obvious. It certainly wasn't obvious to me.

Tandor crossed his arms over his chest and tapped his foot against the floor. Tap tap tap tap tap tap. I just stood there, unsure what to do. Linc and I weren't necessarily friends—we had only spoken in passing when seeing each other around town. The interaction at the potluck was the longest conversation we'd ever had, as far as I could remember.

"Are you going to buy anything?" I asked.

He gazed longingly into a jar filled with berry powders.

"No, I don't think so." He continued to wander, just looking upon the items filling my shop.

After long, awkward moments, I said, "Well, you've seen me. You can go now."

Linc smiled brightly. "Okay, then! This was nice, I would love to do it again some time!" And with that, he abruptly strode out through the broken door.

Tandor chuckled quietly under his breath, a deep rumble that vibrated the air around him. "Well, that was fun!" he joked.

"Shut up," I grumbled. "That was painful."

"I'm just glad to see him up and moving, after last night."

I whirled to face him. "Last night? What happened last night, do you mean after he tried to get in here?"

His lips flattened into a line. "I saw him after I left. I was taking a stroll through the park and, what do you know, our human friend was sitting on a bench, looking... lost. Dazed, almost. I didn't want to leave him out there, so I had to practically carry him back to his cottage. It was bizarre."

"And you're just telling me this now? That he was waiting for me?"

"It slipped my mind—I was a little busy finding you unconscious on the floor..."

My cheeks warmed. "I suppose that's fair enough. I must have really given him the wrong idea at the potluck—"

The broken door swung open again.

I groaned, dropping my head into my hands. "Who is it?" I asked.

Lunette, the lovely druid who ran the plant shop, tentatively strolled in. She looked vaguely confused. Her long orange hair was twisted back into an intricate braid with leaves strung throughout and a pretty gray cloak adorned her tall frame. She was followed by a werewolf man with an intimidating muscular build and shaggy white hair who looked just as confused, if not more so. Both of their eyes held a strange glossy sheen.

Lunette's twinkling voice was quiet in the now-crowded space. "Hi, Kiz."

My annoyance dropped. "Oh, hello Lu. What can I do for you? Do you need more of those fertilizing powders for your plants?"

She drifted toward me, her cheeks flushed. "No, no, I still have plenty from my last order."

"Oh...kay," I said. "Something else then?"

She swallowed tightly. "I just had the strangest urge to come see you. I don't really know why, it's just this—this *pull* in my chest. This weird nagging to visit." She drifted even closer but stopped herself before she touched me, hovering right inside my personal space. Her unique cherry scent drifted over me in a pleasant wave. I inhaled deeper than I necessarily needed to.

Lunette had always been friendly, and I enjoyed talking with her. We bonded over our shared love of poisonous plants and pretty flowers, and she always had the best gossip. And she was beautiful—nobody could deny that. But through the years of knowing each other, there had never been a romantic spark.

But the way she was staring at me now made me wonder...

I gazed into her eyes, examining the strange sheen there. The same sheen that was in Linc's eyes. And Mayor Tommins'. I didn't remember Tandor's eyes being glossy, but I glanced at him to check, only to find him scrubbing his eyes with his fists and quietly sniffling. An opened jar of snap-dragon pollen sat beside him that he had clearly been tinkering with. I stifled a laugh. *Idiot.*

The white-haired werewolf hovered near the door, watching Lunette with a keen eye but not looking like he wanted to come in any further.

"Lu?" I asked cautiously.

"Yeah?"

"Are you... are you feeling okay?"

"I do feel a bit strange..." she admitted. She pressed the backs of her spindly fingers to her cheeks. "A little warm, I guess. My skin is a little flushed. My heart is beating too fast."

"Why don't you go sleep it off, and we'll grab coffee and pastries sometime soon?" I suggested.

She considered this. "Sure, that sounds lovely. I have all kinds of fun gossip I gathered during the potluck, and I've been dying to share it. See you!" She lifted her arm like she was going to wrap it around my shoulders before she stopped herself and let it drop to her side.

"Bye." I smiled tightly and fluttered my fingers at her.

She gave me one last wistful but confused look before she exited with the white-haired wolf following closely behind her.

Tandor stood up from his stool. "Gods almighty are you popular today!" he declared, stretching his shoulders and rolling out his neck. His muscles bulged beneath his tunic at the motion. "I better get going, in case you need to entertain more visitors." He dropped his arms and looked at me intently. "Are you sure you're alright? Do you need to visit Velline? I can carry you there."

I blushed at the suggestion, but I flexed my arms, legs, and neck to be sure. My aches were minor—nothing that a simple healing potion wouldn't fix. The ringing in my ears was more annoying than painful. "I'm okay. Really. Thank you, though, for checking on me."

He stared at me for a moment longer before nodding reluctantly. "I'm glad you're alright. You gave me a fright there—don't do that again."

"Yes, sir. I promise you won't find me unconscious on the floor again. Well, I can't actually *promise*, but I will try very hard to make sure it doesn't happen."

He hesitated for a moment, looking like he might argue. Conflict clouded his gaze. "As long as you promise. See you later, Kizzi." He strode out of the shop and pulled the broken door shut behind him. It immediately swung back open. "Uh," he stammered. "I'll fix this."

I brushed him off. "I'll have Redd fix i, that vampire will have it done in a blink. Don't worry about it."

Looking bashful, he nodded again before departing, pulling the splintered door as closed as it would go.

The sound of hammering echoed through the shop as Redd repaired my door with fresh wood. The tall, brown-haired vampire looked disheveled and slightly dirty, as if I'd pulled him from another project. "Why did Tandor kick your door in?" he shouted over the noise. "You should have just unlocked it. This oak wood isn't going to match."

"I obviously didn't want this to happen. It's a long story," I answered drily. "But he thought he was saving my life."

"Saving your life, huh? Do I want to know?"

"Probably not," I answered honestly. "But I'll tell you anyway. So, I was making a potion, but the sprites fucked it up, so it turned into this awful sludge. I didn't want to clean the cauldron, so I just shoved it into the corner. Long story short, the cauldron exploded and tossed me across the shop and knocked me out. And that's when Tandor showed up."

The hammering stopped and Redd turned to stare at me, his expression slack jawed. His fangs caught the light. "Kizzi, you can't just tell that story like it's something nonchalant."

I shrugged. "Just another day as Moonvale's favorite apothecary witch."

He sighed in exasperation. "Fiella's going to have a field day with this one."

"She already knew about the cauldron, so she probably won't be very surprised when she finds out that it blew up in my face. Literally."

"Oh, I meant the part about Tandor kicking your door in and finding you on the ground." He turned back to the door.

"That part? That's the less interesting half of that story. He was just checking on me after a weird situation we had last night."

He simply hummed in response, but I swore I saw his eyebrow quirk and a knowing smile tug at his cheek. He finished the rest of his work in comfortable silence as I flitted about the shop gathering ingredients. The sprites watched me, perched around the shelves as though they were happy to just watch me conduct my mundane activities. It was nice.

I appreciated how Redd never tried to fill silence with unnecessary words. If he didn't have anything to say, he simply said nothing at all. It was refreshing.

When Redd eventually slipped away after a brief farewell and only accepting more of Fiella's blue-hair tonic as payment, I made my rounds, checking the shop before going to bed.

Just because I was glad that the sprites were back didn't mean that I trusted them... I knew they were still menaces.

The chili recipe was still sitting out on the counter, so I grabbed my fae-iron key, mumbled the unlocking spell, and pulled the cabinet open. I tucked the recipe inside, but I couldn't fight off the nagging feeling that told me something just wasn't right. I stared at the open cabinet for what felt like hours, trying to figure out what was out of place.

And then it hit me. My stomach dropped to the floor beneath my feet and my palms broke out in a clammy sweat.

Something was missing. And not just anything... The love potion was missing.

Fates.

I frantically searched through the cabinet, pawing aside delicate bottles, reading every single label to be sure, but my initial observation was correct.

Someone stole my love potion.

With a huff, I slammed the cabinet shut and sat on the corner of my bed. I dropped my head into my hands and fought back tears.

I wasn't supposed to have a love potion in the first place —I just wanted to see if I could pull it off. I never intended to use it, hence why I kept it locked up. I was just proud of myself for being able to accomplish such an impressive potion brew.

And now it was gone.

Nausea roiled in my stomach. Love potions were

outlawed for a reason. In the wrong hands, they could cause catastrophic consequences. Messing with a folk's free will was never acceptable. At a high enough dose, they could warp a folk's mind, never to return to normal.

I wallowed in misery for what felt like hours. Who could have possibly broken into my shop? I kept enchanted locks around for a reason—they were virtually infallible. Nothing else had been disturbed...

A sprite landed on my knee, fluttering into my field of vision. I swatted at it. "Get off me, you heathen. You could have stopped the thieves, and you chose not to," I accused.

Another sprite took its place. And another. I could hardly see them, but a handful of them perched on my knees, tilting their faces up at me pleadingly.

The knot of dread in my stomach tightened. "You... No." I stood, swiping the sprites off me and pacing across the shop. "No. No no no no no. No!"

The sprites.

The missing love potion.

The townsfolk acting so strangely...

It was all connected.

It was all my fault.

I halted my pacing and whirled to face the nearest sprite I could see, settling on one resting on the corner of my worktable. "What did you do?" I shouted at it. "How could you?!"

The glow around the sprite shrank to almost nothing. I wasn't deterred. "You stole my love potion, didn't you? You dropped it into the chili! Why?" I whirled to face the opposite direction. "You fucking sprites just can't leave me alone, can you? I was glad you were back, but now I wish you never found me at all!" My anger exploded out of me in hateful waves, but I couldn't contain it. I was ready to burst.

And then the tears started. At first, they silently streaked down my cheeks as I bolted around the room, swatting at any blurs of motion I could see and firmly closing jars and lids. And then the silent tears turned into quiet blubbering sobs.

Eventually, the sobs became deep, gut-wrenching, folding my body in half until all I could do was sink to the floor and cradle my face in my hands as I let my sadness and frustration tear through me.

I ignored the barely-there brushes against my back, along my hair, next to me on the floor.

I cried until I had nothing left. I was a shell of a witch, empty and dry.

Even my magic felt drained, though I hadn't used any of it.

I scraped myself off the floor with all the energy I had left and flopped onto my bed.

I didn't even notice the warm mass curled up in the bed next to me.

CHAPTER 13
Kizzi

As the first streams of rising sunlight peeked through the cracks in my windows, I groaned and yanked my pillow over my head.

I was not ready to face the day yet. My throat was sore, my eyes were puffy, and my head pounded with the beginnings of a day-ruining headache. I begged sleep to pull me back under, even if just for a moment. Anything to delay my day for a little longer.

Just as darkness began to close over me, I felt something brush the back of my calf. A whisper of a touch, barely anything at all. A pulse of magic zinged into my skin.

I froze, holding my breath.

A long moment passed. Two. I exhaled.

"You sprites better leave me alone. Fates. I'm still mad at you." My voice was muffled through the pillow.

Nothing. The movement didn't feel like a sprite, with their bright, delicate, barely-there magic...

Maybe I was imagining things again. It was probably just the blanket settling over me.

But... my feet felt cold in the open air. I wasn't under the blanket...

I'm going to throw up. Right here, under this pillow.

I didn't move a single muscle. My ears perked, straining to hear any sounds in the still, quiet morning. The only sound was my strangled breathing, scraping in and out of my chest.

I remained frozen for what felt like minutes. Hours. Eons. And then eventually, I heard a quiet rustling... coming from the sheets right beside me on the bed.

Fucking *fuck*.

My heart hammered in my chest, pounding so hard I was surprised it didn't burst free. I mentally tallied my options.

One, I could keep laying here like a little bitch, pretending not to notice the other presence in the room even though I was clearly awake and had already blown my cover by speaking.

Two, I could whirl around and attack whatever beast was in bed with me with whatever spell I could muster and hope I was stronger than it was.

Three, I could cry and pray to the Old Gods that I might drop dead or something before having to face this problem.

Unfortunately, two was my best option.

Old Gods, if you can hear me, please burn my stash of smutty books if I die. Or at least don't let Mayor Tommins find them.

I took a deep, quivering inhale.

And then I *attacked*.

I screamed as I flipped my body over, gripping my pillow like my life depended on it and absolutely walloping the bed beside me.

Smack! Smack! Smack!

I was prepared to inflict a death blow with my beloved pillow.

Feathers plumed in the air, billowing around me and settling onto the sheets.

I kept swinging.

Smack! Smack! Smack!

I couldn't even think of any spells to save me, I simply swung the pillow like a weapon.

My voice crumbled beneath the screams I was forcing out, and eventually I quieted.

And then I stopped swinging.

My forehead glistened with sweat, and I could hardly hear over my pulse pounding in my ears. All I could see in the bed beside me was... nothing. Nothing except for a slight bulge under the covers.

Gathering any crumbs of courage I had left in me, I gripped the blanket and yanked it off the bed, immediately brandishing a pillow again to defend myself.

The blanket settled onto the floor with a quiet whoosh.

And then my heart stopped beating altogether.

I couldn't believe my eyes.

Settled in the bed next to me, pummeled into an unrecognizable (and slightly lumpy) pulp... was the cauldron sludge, bright purple and *alive*.

I screamed bloody murder.

Ani's cottage was much messier than my shop, full to the brim with magical items and ingredients. The curtains were pulled shut, letting in no natural light—the only illumination in the space came from enchanted lanterns. A brown striped cat napped peacefully on the fluffy rug.

Tiny dust motes floated in the air. They danced and fluttered idly, disturbed by my movements. The scent of lavender and warm magic permeated the space. It almost smelled like home.

I clutched a mug of rose and sage tea with trembling fingers, fighting to still my quaking as I slowly brought the drink to my lips. I managed a small sip without spilling any.

A jar sat on the table between me and the coven leader.

I tried not to look at it, but I couldn't help myself. My eyes were drawn with a mind of their own.

The jar contained a small, roiling bit of the iridescent purple cauldron sludge, and I could tell that it was *pissed*. It hissed and snapped, splattering against the sides of the jar over and over again.

I was the one who deserved to be angry. After discovering the twitching, slimy mass curled up in bed beside me, I had done what any respectable lady would do.

I panicked.

I screamed, I cried, I screamed some more, then I threw up in the washroom. And then after shedding a few more tears, I grabbed a jar, blindly scooped up some of the sludge, and scrambled my way here: to my coven leader's cottage—so she could tell me what to do.

The tea, though expertly brewed, hardly brought me any comfort. I couldn't even appreciate the warm, floral flavor as it slid down my throat because I couldn't stop staring at the damned jar.

Ani peered me with a calm but questioning gaze. She wasn't nearly as panicked as she should have been while sitting in front of a magical monstrosity.

Her waist-length silver hair glimmered in the enchanted lighting of the cottage. She was swathed in a thick dressing gown, but her knobby feet were bare. She had clearly not been expecting visitors.

I exhaled a shaky breath. "Ani, I need help. What am I supposed to do?" I asked.

She glanced at the jar with only mild interest. "What do you mean, dear?"

"I mean—how do I get rid of it?"

She gently picked up the jar, rolling it between her gnarled hands and examining the contents with a knowing gaze. The sludge sloshed and crackled. "I'm afraid you can't get rid of it, Kizziah."

My eyes snapped to Ani's lined face. "What? You're joking. Yes, I can."

Her expression held no humor, just a calm steadiness. "I'm afraid this isn't a joke. It seems you've created yourself a familiar."

My jaw dropped open.

No fucking way. It was *impossible.*

I knew what a familiar was, of course. Familiars were things of old witch legends. A critter or a creation, bound to a witch's soul. A guardian, an assistant, a companion. A friend. It took immense magical power to create one, often requiring the assistance of an entire coven. Familiars assisted with spells and rituals, granting stability and control to their witches.

They were extremely powerful—all the strongest witches had one.

Or so the legends said.

Witches hadn't had familiars for ages—there wasn't enough magic left to create them. Not since the Old Gods abandoned the realm.

Nope. Not possible.

I slowly shook my head back and forth. This was some elaborate prank, surely. The coven was messing with me.

I waited for the punchline to drop.

I took another sip of my tea, but it roiled like the tides in my stomach, so I set it aside.

Ani's expression remained as steady as ever. There was no joke to be told.

I cleared my throat, fighting through the tension there. "A familiar?" I asked.

She nodded. "Yes. I can feel it. I haven't felt this much raw magical power in ages." Her gaze flicked to my face. "You didn't do this on purpose?"

"No!" I exclaimed. And then I told her the story of the sludge's creation.

She nodded knowingly the entire time, as though this entire situation made complete sense. It was infuriating, how calm she was.

"Heightened emotions can make our magic volatile," she mused. "And those sprites have been following you since you were a wee little thing. I can't say I'm surprised."

"And you're saying I can't get rid of it?"

The old witch shook her head, placing the jar back on the table. "No."

"Can I... destroy it?"

The sludge popped in the jar, lurching in my direction. I flinched.

Ani shook her head vehemently. "She didn't mean that, Old Gods forgive her," she murmured as she glanced upwards. She paled slightly. "This is your *familiar*. It is of your very *soul*. To destroy it would be to destroy a part of yourself."

I sighed, dropping my head into my hands. So I was stuck with this nasty, sticky, gooey, ugly cauldron sludge. Forever.

Things couldn't possibly get any worse.

"What am I supposed to do with it?" I mumbled toward the floor.

"Whatever you'd like, I imagine. Use it, ignore it, put it to work." I heard her dressing gown rustle as she shrugged. "A witch's familiar is a very powerful tool."

"If you say so." I reluctantly lifted my head, dreading the news I was about to deliver to Ani next. I took a deep, bolstering breath. "I haven't told you the worst part, yet."

She lifted an eyebrow. "And what would that be?"

I gulped. "The cauldron I accidentally brewed the sludge in... it was the giant cauldron you gave me."

Ani waited expectantly.

"And... it cracked when Sludgey over there came to life." I braced myself for her response, preparing to be scolded, slapped, or shouted at. The sludge gurgled noisily in the jar.

Ani inhaled deeply through her nose, held the air in, and then let it rush out of her mouth. Her breath rustled my hair, and I felt a delicate wisp of magic kiss my skin. She folded her hands in front of her with a white-knuckled grip.

She stayed like that for a few long moments before she spoke.

"You're saying the cauldron is... broken?"

I nodded mutely.

"Moonvale's largest cauldron. It's unusable. Right before Hallow's Eve?"

I nodded again, anxiously tucking my hands under my thighs.

Ani pinched the bridge of her nose in exasperation. "This is not ideal, Kizziah."

"I know."

"We need that cauldron so the coven can perform all the necessary rituals. Smaller cauldrons just won't do."

"I know," I repeated, quieter this time. Something about Ani's regal presence always made me feel young and naive. Especially when she was unhappy.

She exhaled harshly before brushing her hands off and meeting my gaze. A glimmer of disappointment shone in her light brown eyes, but not anger. Never anger.

"It was an accident," she murmured.

"It was," I agreed. "I didn't mean to."

She nodded before she stood up and moved to sit beside me on the couch. She tossed a skinny arm around me and rubbed my shoulders soothingly. I slumped. "You didn't mean to. And something amazing came out of it," she said quietly.

I exhaled heavily. "I'll fix it. Somehow."

Ani shook her head slightly. "It's not possible, dear. The creation of a familiar would have stripped the cauldron of its magical abilities."

"Then I'll find a new one," I insisted. The plan solidified in my mind. I would travel, as far as it took, to find a new cauldron. I refused to ruin Hallow's Eve for the coven.

"I don't know where you will be able to find one," she warned. "It's been ages since I acquired that one, and it was a family heirloom. There is no telling where in Aldova will have a big enough cauldron."

"Wherever it is, I'll find it." I declared. "I'll find it."

I allowed Ani to comfort me for a few moments longer before I extracted myself from her grasp and stood up. I tentatively grabbed the jar with Sludgey in it. The boiling mass stilled immediately.

"I'll get out of your hair, then. Thank you, Ani." I grasped the witch's hand and squeezed briefly before stepping toward the door. "You've never steered me wrong."

She nodded sagely, but a small smile tugged at the corner of her mouth. "You have never needed much steering."

I snorted out a laugh but accepted the compliment. That was a load of shit.

Before I could leave Ani's cottage, another thought struck me.

The love potion.

My shoulders slumped and my ears drooped.

"Oh my, you just had a heavy thought. What is it?" Ani asked as she stood up from the couch.

"Something else happened," I confessed.

"Something else, besides you breaking the largest cauldron in Moonvale?"

I nodded, biting my lip. "Something worse."

"Worse?" Ani asked.

"I may have... drugged the entire town with a love potion."

Ani stared at me blankly for a long time. "Is that a joke?"

I shook my head.

"Oh... dear. We're going to have to call a coven meeting for this one."

"You're kidding," Hyacinth blurted out with an astonished look on her face. The witch's coal black eyebrows nearly reached her hairline. The whole coven portrayed varying levels of shock—from mild surprise to mouth-clutching awe.

I stood in front of them all, awkwardly clutching Sludgey's jar in a sweaty grip. Luckily, everyone was too shocked to pay the jar much attention.

The coven sat in silence while I explained the tale of how the love potion came to be. And how it ended up inside the folk of Moonvale.

"Unfortunately, I am not," I admitted.

"You drugged *everyone?*" Another witch asked.

I coughed. "Well, everyone that tried my chili."

"I was wondering why you looked so pretty today. Fates! I ate some of that!" Hyacinth groaned in exasperation.

I winced. "I'm sorry about that."

"I did too!"

"Most of the town did. Everyone was so shocked that Kizzi brought something *edible* to the potluck this year that they just had to try it for themselves." Hyacinth glanced at me abruptly. "No offense."

I brushed that off. "None taken. I thought the same thing, honestly."

"What do we do?" someone else asked.

I shrugged helplessly. "That's what I came here to ask. Does anyone have any ideas?"

"Is there an antidote? A cure?"

"If there is, I don't have any." I glanced at Ani. She simply shrugged.

The coven leader drifted to a shelf on the wall, pulling out a massive, haggard grimoire, and began flipping through it.

"Maybe it will wear off on its own? Has anyone ever taken a love potion before?" I asked.

"Love potions are outlawed..." Hyacinth murmured.

I quirked a brow.

"Okay fine, I might have tried one before, but I screwed it up. I could never get it to work. Did yours work? Or do I just think you're hot?"

"I think so..." I recounted the story of Linc, of Mayor Tommins, of the weird behavior I had been seeing.

"It sounds like it definitely works. Old Gods be damned!"

"Shh!" someone hissed. "Blasphemous!"

"Oh, whatever—"

"I think I found something." Ani's voice broke through the discussion. She flipped the grimoire around, showing us the pages. "It says here, spells cast from strong potions can be broken by ingesting the powdered shell of a dragon egg. They're extremely rare, and only ever spoken about in whispers. As I'm sure you know, dragons haven't hatched since before the Old Gods left the realm." She flipped the page. "In old times, dragon eggs only hatched in certain regions."

"Where?" I asked.

"The belly of the mountain. Rockward, I would assume —that's the farthest mountain town. Though, this many years later, they could be anywhere."

I sighed. "Well, I guess I'm going to Rockward, too."

"Too?" Hyacinth prodded.

I glanced at Ani for help.

"She's buying a new cauldron," the coven leader explained.

"A new cauldron! A big one? How are you going to carry that?"

I shrugged. "Does anyone want to come with me? I'm sure two witches can carry a large cauldron. Probably."

"No way, those things weigh as much as five folk. Why don't you ask Tandor? That orc has arms the size of tree trunks," Hyacinth joked.

I tilted my head, considering. That actually wasn't a bad idea. "Maybe I will."

CHAPTER 14
Tandor

Dry tendrils of a broom wisped across the floor with a scratchy, comforting rhythm. My hands were now completely healed, no longer needing any bandages. I could clutch the broomstick without any trouble. I swept the day's dirt through the propped-open door, wishing it a silent farewell as it went.

It wouldn't stay outside the pub for long—it would quickly come back in tracked under clogs and boots—but it was satisfying to see it go, even briefly.

The crisp outside air drifted in, cooling the room to a temperature that tempted me to tug down my scrunched sleeves. I didn't catch a chill easily, but I wasn't impervious to the cold.

I continued to sweep.

Kizzi fluttered in the door, tracking spots of dirt onto the clean floor. A breeze followed her in. It carried the smell of falling leaves and toasted apples. I inhaled greedily. The witch was wearing a black tunic tucked into a long, flowing skirt that kissed the ground as she walked. Her boot-clad toes barely peeked out from below the billowing fabric. Her hair was down and wild, settled around her shoulders and curling at the ends, hiding her ears from view.

Every folk in the room turned their head when she walked in, some openly gaping. I couldn't blame them. I felt the same way.

That didn't stop the twinge of jealousy from twisting my stomach, though. Of course they would stare—she was magnificent—but irrationally, I wanted to be the only one to lay eyes on her.

I set the broom aside. "Hey there, Kizzi. Here for lunch?" I asked hopefully.

She shook her head. "I'm actually here to ask a favor."

I nodded quickly. "Sure. Anything."

Her eyes darted to my face. She tilted her head. "Hmm..." She stepped closer to me, examining my expression with a strange intensity. I gulped, nervous under her scrutiny. A bead of sweat trickled down the side of my forehead and I hastily swiped it away. I scrubbed an irritating speck of dust out of my eye. Still, she watched me.

"Is... everything okay?" I asked.

"That depends. Did you eat any of my chili at the potluck?"

I met her gaze abruptly, confused by the random question. "Did I eat any of your chili?"

She nodded, stepping closer and inspecting my face even more intensely. My skin tingled at her proximity.

"Uh... I sure did. It was delicious!" I grinned tightly, hoping she couldn't read the lie on my lips. I would die before I admitted to her that I had refused to try her chili because it had a dirty feather in it, and I was positive it would have made me vomit.

I would never admit to having such a weak stomach. Orcs were supposed to be tough, not squeamish.

I would never risk offending her, either.

She dropped her head back and groaned. "Old Gods be damned!"

Huh. That's not the reaction I expected.

"Was I... not supposed to?" I asked, dumbfounded.

She scrubbed her hands over her face. "No, no, it's not that." She dropped her hands and looked at me again. "Are you feeling okay?"

My stomach roiled. Were folk sick from her chili? I couldn't say that was surprising.

I shrugged, unsure of what the correct answer was. "I feel fine, more or less. Maybe a bit warm?"

"And are you itching to jump my bones right now? Confess your undying love for me?" she asked matter-of-factly, watching for my reaction.

My blood thundered in my ears. All of a sudden, I was achingly aware of how tight my trousers were. "Um... No?" I gulped. "I mean, not no. I didn't mean no. But I don't mean yes, either." This had to be some sort of trap.

She squinted her eyes and nodded hesitantly. "Okay. That's... fine. We can make that work."

I nodded too, unsure of what I was agreeing with but agreeing, nonetheless. "You said you had a favor to ask?" I reminded her. I subtly adjusted my apron, making sure it covered my nether regions properly.

"Oh, right. The favor." She looked nervous. "You're allowed to say no."

"Just spit it out—it can't be that bad."

She exhaled heavily. "Will you go on a trip with me?"

I waited to hear the rest, but she didn't continue. She just stared at me beseechingly. A little pleadingly. This was too good to be true. There had to be some sort of catch. "Sure. Yes. Where to, princess?"

"The problem is... I'm not really sure. Again, you're allowed to say no."

"Now I'm intrigued." I turned and faced Kizzi fully, crossing my arms over my chest so they wouldn't hang awkwardly by my sides. "You want to gallivant through the realm with me? That sounds rather romantic."

She snorted out an awkward laugh. "I need you and your big muscles."

My eyebrows reached for my hairline. "Kizzi, wow. I didn't realize you were so interested in my physique."

She groaned and ran a hand over her face. "This is not coming out right. Tandor, will you just come with me to a few towns so I can buy a new cauldron? And something secret that I can't tell you about. I need you to help me carry the cauldron—I won't be able to move it. I can ask someone else, but—"

"Yes. I'll do it!" I interrupted.

"You will? That easy?" she asked. She squinted at me again. "How much of my chili did you eat?"

I shrugged, waving a hand to brush away her chili comment. I wiped my sweaty palms on my trousers. "I've been meaning to pick up some fruits and herbs anyway. I've got more cider ideas to try, and the traveling salesman won't be back for a while. Besides, like you said—you need me." I winked at her, cracking a grin. My heart pounded in my chest.

The corner of her mouth lifted. "When can you leave? I have a few orders to prepare, but that shouldn't take too long."

"How about a few days? I have to start a few new batches of cider and make sure Ginger will be alright here without me for a little while." I hesitated, thinking. "How long will we be gone for?"

She chewed on her bottom lip. "It could be a few days... It could be a few weeks. I'm not sure how far we'll have to go."

I considered that. A few weeks on the road with Kizzi— I honestly couldn't think of anything I'd rather do more. Only one problem held me back. "Will we return in time for Hallow's Eve?" I would be disappointed if I had to miss out on celebrating Hallow's Eve here in Moonvale, but if I had to spend it on the road, it wouldn't be the worst thing...

"Oh, absolutely. I wouldn't miss Hallow's Eve. If I have to set out on another trip, I will, but I'll be damned if I miss out on celebrating with the coven."

I sighed in relief. "It sounds like we're on the same page, then."

"It sure does." She stared at me for a few moments before she subtly shook her head, resting a hand over her satchel at her side. "I better start preparing, then. Leave in five days' time?"

"I'll be ready," I promised.

She hesitated. "Do you have any of those spiced pumpkin ciders left?"

I snorted out a laugh. "I've been waiting for you to ask. Yes, actually, I have another small batch I set aside. Let me pour you one." I retreated to the cellar. I couldn't help the smile that pulled at my cheeks. I returned with two full goblets—one for her and one for myself.

"For you, pumpkin princess." I handed her a goblet and lifted the other out in front of me.

Kizzi smiled and tapped her goblet to mine. "I'll let the princess thing slide, just because I love this cider so much." She took a long gulp and hummed quietly. A drop of the liquid dripped from her bottom lip, trickled down her chin.

Hand trembling, pulse racing, I reached out and collected the drop on a fingertip, popping it in my mouth. I grinned when her jaw dropped open in surprise.

"Too good to waste even a drop," I murmured before lifting my own goblet to my lips and swallowing deeply.

Gods, I really outdid myself with this one. This is fucking delicious.

It tasted even better coming straight from Kizzi's skin.

We finished our ciders in companionable quiet, only speaking briefly about where our travels might take us and items we should bring. She requested that I bring a barrel of cider, but I had to turn that idea down, much to her dismay.

When she finally left, my stomach was feeling bubbly and warm, and not just from the cider.

Again, she snagged attention as she crossed the room. One man even started to follow her out before changing his mind and sitting back down.

It really was understandable. Of course everyone admired her. Kizzi was not only distractingly gorgeous, but she was also hard-working, and smart, and extremely loyal to the folk she cared about. She was the best this town had to offer. The whole realm, surely.

Many times, I had nearly gathered the courage to tell her

how I felt. To take a leap. But I always lost my nerve, or she simply laughed off my attempted flirty comments.

She would never see me the way I saw her. To her, I would always just be the orc at the pub serving her drinks. The orc willing to lend a helping hand.

The warmth in my stomach soured as I got back to work.

CHAPTER 15
Kizzi

M y feet dangled, swinging freely as I sat perched on the counter at Fiella's Finds—my best friend's cluttered and chaotic (but admittedly charming) trinket shop. I had shoved aside her messy ledgers to make room for myself— I refused to sit in the cozy nook and shout at her across the room as she worked. I preferred a closer seat.

She dealt with it.

Sookie, Fiella's fluffy gray cat companion, brushed against my ankle, taking the opportunity to use my boot to scratch her head. I held my feet still and let her. *Cats are so weird.* Eventually, she let out a quiet meow and moved along.

I chewed slowly on a toasted oat cookie, appreciating the gentle sweetness that was enough to satisfy but not overpowering. The perfect cookie. I ignored the crumbs that fell onto my lap.

I had brought Fiella two cookies, because I was the best friend in all the realms and nobody could say otherwise.

"So," Fiella said around a mouthful. "You're going on a

mysterious trip? And you're bringing Tandor?" She wagged her eyebrows suggestively. "That sounds fun."

I laughed, rolling my eyes at her. "I already told you, he's the only folk I know that's strong enough to carry the largest cauldrons."

"There are other orcs in town," she argued. "Or strong shifters."

"I don't really know them. They might be freaks. And you're forgetting the part about how I accidentally drugged everyone in town with a love potion."

Fiella snorted. "Oh yeah. Thank the Gods you put that —" she shivered dramatically "—*garlic* in there, or Redd and I would be chasing after you too."

I reached out and shoved her shoulder. "It's not funny!"

"I believe that's exactly what I said about the *garlic*," she retorted. "And you used it anyway."

"That was different! That was just a harmless joke, this is serious!" I whined.

"So, you're telling me that the entire town wants to get in your pants?"

"Ugh, no! At least I hope not." I stopped and considered. "A lot of them probably do. But they can't help it! The love potion affects all folk differently. Some of them will want to get in my pants. Some of them will just want to be around me. And some of them will obey my every wish and command."

"Shit. That's—that sounds kind of nice, honestly."

I groaned in frustration. "It's not nice! It's shaving away at their free will!"

"Okay, when you put it that way it does sound bad. Does

everyone know that you've drugged them and turned them into your own personal mindless drones?"

"No! Only the coven knows. And you."

"Tandor doesn't know?"

"Gods, no. And I'm going to keep it that way until I can figure out how to cure it."

"It won't wear off on its own?"

I shook my head slowly. "Nobody really knows. I can't risk it."

"And you figured out the cure?"

"Ani thinks that ground dragon eggshells might do the trick..."

Fiella gasped, clutching my wrist. "Dragon eggshells! Dragons haven't been seen since the Old Gods abandoned the realm. I've read about them in books. Are any eggs even left? How are you going to find one?"

I shrugged. "I'm going to have to look. There's no other option."

"Well... I won't judge you if you and Tandor..." She winked. "Get to know each other on this trip. I've seen the way he watches you."

I brushed her off. "That's just the love potion talking. Tandor hardly looks at me. Not any more than he looks at anyone else. And even if I wanted to take things further, have a little *fun* on the trip, that would be wrong considering he's quite literally drugged. Not happening."

Fiella just lifted her brows at me.

The days preceding the trip passed quickly—I kept myself busy enough that I hardly had time to breathe, let alone think.

I completed every order I had lined up, and even a few that weren't needed until after Hallow's Eve, just to be safe. I distributed what I could, and anything that couldn't be delivered now, I left with Fiella so they could be picked up while I was gone. I only had to bribe her two silvers for the trouble and swear that I would bring her back a baby dragon if I happened to find an actual dragon egg.

I didn't have the heart to remind her that dragons were extinct.

I sat on my favorite stool, tense, feeling uneasy now that I had my list of tasks completed. I was leaving in the morning and had gotten everything done. Absolutely everything. I had even cleaned my shop, wiping down every surface instead of utilizing a cleaning enchantment like I usually did.

I was still irritated with the sprites, but my anger had dulled, losing its sharp edges. I allowed them to follow me around, only threatening and cursing at them every once in a while.

They still tormented me, of course. They never stopped messing with my shop, moving things, opening jars, dipping their tiny fingers in ingredients. I just learned to expect it and deal with the consequences as they came.

I didn't let their presence rile me anymore.

The more time I spent around the sprites, tolerating them instead of trying to force them to flee, the more I was able to see them. Make out their actual forms instead of just vague blurs.

I could see that they were shaped like normal folk, for the most part. They were just tiny and winged. I could almost discern their elemental affinities, as well. The fire sprites had a brighter appearance, while the water sprites were murkier.

One water sprite in particular was bolder than the rest. She stayed out in the open longer. Approached me with boldness. Refused to flee when I fluttered my hand at her in a threat. She was currently perched on the lip of the cracked cauldron, sitting abnormally still. Watching me, always watching me. Like I was a performer there for her entertainment.

My new familiar was a huge pain in the ass.

The purple sludge was furious that I had unceremoniously shoved a portion of it in a jar (understandable, I guess) and it held a grudge impressively. Even when I opened the jar and reunited the sludge chunk with its larger counterpart, it hissed and spat at me. For three entire days, it sulked in the corner, hunkered in its cracked cauldron and covered with the sheet like it was literally hiding from me.

It was fucking ridiculous. Kind of hilarious, seeing an all-powerful magical concoction throwing a tantrum, but ridiculous all the same.

I ignored it as much as I could. When it couldn't be ignored, like when I needed to pass by or use that corner of my shop, I tried my best not to roll my eyes or flip my middle finger at it. It was sensitive, apparently. I learned that lesson very quickly after receiving a wayward drop of sludge to the eyeball.

I hadn't told anyone else about the situation. I still couldn't wrap my mind around how I'd accidentally created myself a familiar. A *familiar*. A thing of legends, of storybooks, of the witches from the time of the Old Gods. Familiars were a sign of power, of strength. Of immense magical control. I knew I was great, but I didn't know I was *that* great. If I'd thought defying the realm of possibility was an option, I would have attempted it a long time ago. I would've much preferred a cooler familiar, though. Like a cat. Or a squirrel.

The sludge gurgled in the corner, a big bubble bursting with an echoing *pop*.

My magical witchy companion, everyone. Behold.

I sighed inwardly. If I created it, I could at least attempt to form peace with it. Could familiars speak? I had no idea.

I cleared my throat. "Hey, cauldron sludge. How are you doing over there?"

The gurgling ceased, and the sludge stilled. Not a great sign. I walked over and removed the sheet covering the cauldron, clutching it awkwardly in front of me.

"I'm sorry for shoving you in a jar without asking first. In my defense, I didn't know what was happening and I was having a crisis."

The sludge shrank down, shriveling until it formed a tight mass that was about the size of my torso. It looked... petulant, almost.

"Come on, don't pout. It was just a misunderstanding."

The sludge didn't move, it just sat there looking mopey. I mentally cursed my life and what it had become. I was reduced to bickering with purple, gooey slime.

"What if we find you a real name? Would you forgive me then? I'll stop calling you Sludgey. Or any of the other terrible names I call you behind your back."

The sludge softened slightly, losing some of its rigid intensity.

Encouraged, I continued. "I'm great at names. Let's see." I cleared my throat. "Do you have a preference on typically male or female names? Something more in the middle?"

Nothing.

"... Okay then. I'll just start spit balling, you let me know if something sounds right. Sludgey."

The slime spat at me, showering me with tiny flecks of goo. I laughed, scrubbing the goo from my face. "I'm sorry, I'm sorry, I couldn't help myself. I'm serious this time. How about Bob? Suzan? Ivy?" I looked around the shop for inspiration. "Oh! Rose? Basil? Dragonfly?"

The sludge sat still, waiting. I hadn't nailed it yet, apparently.

"Okay let's try a new direction. Maybe something more magical?"

The sludge stretched slightly, standing at attention.

"Magical. Okay, I can do magical. How about Spell? Caster? Enchanta?" I thought harder. "Hmm... Curse? Hex?"

The sludge stretched and grew, filling the cauldron once more and hugging its edges. It jiggled slightly, the surface quaking like a puddle. "Hex? You like that one?" I shrugged. Not what I personally would have chosen, but it would do the trick. "Okay then, Hex. I'm glad we've got that settled. Now, are you just going to hang out here in the corner for the rest of time? I'm just curious. Not pushing, or anything." I grinned nervously, hoping I wasn't offending the magical slime.

The surface bobbed in and out. I nodded in understanding. "Fair enough, Hex. Fair enough. I would do the same if I had the chance. Now... am I supposed to take care of you somehow? I've never had a pet, but I assume I have to feed you?"

The slime bobbed again, more enthusiastically this time. I grimaced. "I was hoping the answer would be no. Okay, okay. What to feed a magical familiar cauldron sludge..."

I paced around the shop, peeking into baskets and glancing at jars. I stopped at a bowl of dried berries. "How about this?" I picked up one of the berries and tossed it at Hex. The berry hit the surface, and then slowly sank, engulfed by the slime.

I shivered. *Going to have to get used to that.*

Hex settled, curling up in the cauldron and somehow appearing content.

"Is that... enough?"

Nothing.

"Alright, then. Wow, motherhood is easy."

I smiled to myself as I packed up my traveling bag and prepared for the journey ahead.

CHAPTER 16
Tandor

I parked myself at a bench in the town square, my bag tucked beside my feet as I waited for Kizzi's arrival. I had a soft, light cloak tucked around my shoulders. It wasn't quite chilly enough for the cloak to be a necessity, but the air smelled like frosted leaves, so I knew the weather would be cooling down very soon.

Excitement thrummed through my veins. I loved to travel. Moonvale was my favorite place in the realm, but every opportunity to visit a new town was an opportunity I latched onto. Something about meeting new folk, trying new things, eating new foods, made me feel *alive*.

A squirrel scurried near my feet, chirping happily with an acorn in its mouth. It was headed toward the forest. I bent over, placing my upturned hand on the ground, wiggling my fingers in what I hoped was an encouraging manner. I wanted the squirrel to approach so I could pet its fluffy back. To my dismay, it didn't—but it didn't look terrified, either. It just continued on its path.

The park was quiet this morning. Only the delicate

sounds of scurrying critters, wind whistling through leaves, and my own calm breathing broke the silence.

Until the crunching stomp of boots plowing through leaves approached. I smiled. For such a tiny witch, she sure was noisy.

Kizzi strode to the bench and plopped down beside me, wordlessly dropping her bag and thrusting a mug of tea into my hand. I startled, not expecting the gesture. I held the mug out awkwardly for a moment. *Maybe she just wants me to carry it for her?*

She lifted her own mug to her mouth and took a sip. She gestured at me with her raised elbow. "Lemongrass and mint, today. It's good."

I nodded slowly, watching her. Her green hair was weaved back into a tight braid, keeping it off her face and making her pointed ears more prominent. She also had a light cloak tossed over her shoulders, but where mine was brown, hers was a soft lilac color. Underneath, I could see the crisp white fabric of a tunic peeking out, as well as a long flowy skirt. Her eyelids were dusted with something shimmery. Crystal powder, maybe?

"Try it."

I nodded again, but I slowly lifted the mug to my mouth, slow enough that she could stop me if she was joking. She didn't.

I sipped the tea gently to avoid being burned. It was delicious. It tasted green, light and refreshing. The heat was a nice contrast to the cool morning air.

We sat in companionable silence for a while, watching the critters scurry by as we drank our teas. I pondered how she was going to ride a horse with a skirt and corset on, but I didn't dare voice the question out loud. Surely, she had her ways.

The fluffy white cat I had seen around town sat across the park, perched on a bench. Watching. Its tail swished idly back and forth.

Kizzi pulled out a pouch from the bakery and reached inside, silently handing me a muffin with berry jam on top. I accepted it hesitantly. She scarfed her own muffin down with gusto, getting crumbs everywhere, which she idly brushed to the ground. A squirrel ran between her feet to collect the crumbs. She sat perfectly still so as not to disturb the small critter.

I resisted the urge to bend down and attempt another pet. I enjoyed my muffin at a more leisurely pace, purposely dropping crumbs so the squirrels would come near *my* feet instead.

Kizzi's eyes flitted to my hands. "Your burns healed pretty nicely, didn't they?"

I nodded, setting my breakfast aside and spreading my fingers so she could see my palms in their entirety. "They did. Not a single scar."

"Wow," Kizzi said appraisingly. "Not too bad for an apothecary witch."

I cracked a smile. "Not too bad indeed. I didn't even have to bother Velline at the healing clinic."

She smiled back. "She wouldn't have minded, but I'm glad we were able to take care of it."

I nodded in agreement. "What do you say? Are we ready to start this journey?"

She stood, gathering our mugs and hoisting her bag onto her back. "I'm ready, let me just drop these mugs off and then we can head on our way. Hopefully they have two good horses at the stables right now."

They did not have two good horses at the stables right now.

There was only one, and it was... scraggly. Tiny and brown and barely larger than a donkey. It looked like it would struggle to carry Kizzi—my weight would probably be enough to snap its poor back.

"Are you serious?" I asked the stablemaster—a fae man that looked to be around my age, just past his thirtieth year. "This is it?"

The man nodded. "This is it. Quite a few folk are traveling right now. The other horses are out on their journeys."

"Moonvale really needs more horses," I mumbled under my breath. Louder, I said, "Can it even make it through the Barren Lands? It looks fragile."

The Barren Lands were the harsh, uninhabitable stretch of desert that separated Moonvale from the other towns in the realm of Aldova. The Barren Lands were dry, leeched of every ounce of magic. Legends described the Barren Lands (once known as The Wild Lands) as a thriving oasis, full of unique critters and the most beautiful foliage in the whole realm. When the Old Gods abandoned the realm so many lifetimes ago, they destroyed the magical soul of the oasis, leaving us with a desolate and deadly landscape.

"Um... maybe?" the boy said hesitantly.

"Maybe! I don't feel great about that answer." I sighed in exasperation.

"You are quite big... this horse usually carries smaller folk."

"I can tell! It's practically a mouse!"

I glanced at Kizzi to find her a few paces away, covering her mouth with her hands and trying to stifle her laughter. She was shaking with the effort. I glared at her.

"Oh, wait," the man said. "I have an idea!" He bolted from the stables and around the back, disappearing from view.

Kizzi's laughter slipped free with a wild, choked snort.

"You shut up!" I griped. "It's not my fault that the only horse here is the size of a squirrel!"

Tears of mirth slid down her cheeks. "I just can't stop picturing you on that horse's back," she blurted out between giggles. "You're bigger than she is! You ought to carry her through the Barren Lands!"

"Find another travel companion, then." I crossed my arms across my chest and tilted my head in mock outrage.

She just flapped her hand at me. "You have to admit, it's funny."

"It's not that funny," I grumbled.

The man returned from behind the barn, dragging a wooden monstrosity behind him. He huffed and heaved with the effort, but the thing slowly rolled in our direction.

It was... I supposed it could be considered a carriage. It looked more like a giant covered wheelbarrow.

It was large—large enough to fit three smaller folk if they squeezed in tightly—and it sat on four sturdy iron wheels. It was vaguely square in shape. Old holes had clearly been patched with whatever scrap wood was lying around. Four wooden stakes held up a makeshift roof. The man hastily pulled a sheet off it—it was certainly in storage for a *long* time.

It was hideous. An absolute monstrosity.

"What is that?" Kizzi asked, her laughter reigniting. "A cottage on wheels? Don't let Redd see it, he'll drop dead."

"It's a carriage," the man said defensively. "It's perfect! You two can sit inside with your gear, and the horse can pull it. And the horse's back won't snap in two. Everybody wins!" His grin was tight and pleading.

"Well..." I said. "It's not gorgeous but I guess it does solve our problems."

Kizzi nodded in agreement. "They're not going to let us into the other towns, it's so ugly. I love it. It's perfect, we'll take it."

The man sighed in relief. "Five silvers, please."

I choked. "Five? For that hunk of junk?"

"It's a rare carriage..."

Kizzi tossed me an admonishing glare and presented the man with a handful of coins. "Thank you very much for your help. We will return it before Hallow's Eve."

The fae man collected the silvers and then scurried away without another word—scrambling to harness the scrawny horse and get it hooked up to the carriage.

This was going to be a long, slow trip...

The thought didn't bother me as much as it should have.

I held an arm out in a grand gesture. "After you, my lady."

Kizzi snorted and rolled her eyes, but she stepped up to the carriage door without complaint, yanking it open and tossing her bag inside. She immediately grabbed the bag and frantically peeked inside, sighed quietly, and then tucked it gently into the corner.

Then she hiked up her skirts and climbed deftly into the carriage. I yanked my gaze away when I caught a glimpse of a smooth, exposed thigh.

I allowed myself two deep breaths. And then I followed her, tossing my bag beside hers on the floor of the carriage. She stuck out a booted foot to prevent our bags from smashing together. The stablemaster beckoned me forward and briefly instructed me on how to control the horse from the carriage. The mechanics were roughly the same as riding horseback, but if the horse decided to go rogue, we were screwed. There would be no stopping it.

"It should be fine," the man assured halfheartedly. "Have a safe journey!"

I gritted my teeth and patted the man on the shoulder. "Thanks! Wait! Does the horse have a name?"

"It's Daisy." He saluted me and hurried away without another word.

"Let's go, captain!" Kizzi called from the carriage. "Let's see how fast this baby goes!"

I laughed, shaking my head. "Let's just try to focus on crossing the Barren Lands in one piece."

She crossed her arms. "You're no fun."

CHAPTER 17

Kizzi

Tandor wasn't the worst travel companion in the realm.

He was chatty, but he always had his wits about him. He was watchful, cautious, and controlled the horse with an impressive efficiency.

The worst part about him was how much space he took up. He easily occupied more than half of the carriage, and his thigh was firmly pressed to mine at all times. His elbow grazed my side every time he moved. I couldn't even scoot away—I was already squished against the carriage door.

I shoved against his shoulder. "Don't you have any more room over there?"

He shrugged lightly. "If I scoot over any further, I'll tumble right onto the ground."

"Maybe you should try it," I grumbled. His proximity was making me antsy, warming my blood to levels I wasn't happy about.

My body was far too aware of him.

His cheek twitched. "Does the princess need more personal space? We should have asked for a royal carriage."

"I didn't realize you were so massive. Somehow, you're even bigger when you're sitting down. It's absurd."

He flexed his bicep and it strained against his sleeve. "I can't help it. That's four hundred pounds of orcish muscle, baby." He patted his softer stomach. "With some pastries and ales on top."

I rolled my eyes. "I should have invited someone else."

He barked out a laugh. "Hush, you need my strong orc muscles, you said so yourself. Would you be more comfortable sitting on my lap?"

Warmth flushed my cheeks, seeping all the way to the tips of my ears. "Of course not!" But I couldn't help but imagine it. It probably *would* be more comfortable. His thighs were muscled, but not rock hard, and his cloak looked awfully soft. And I bet his arms would cradle me in such a nice way... My cheeks flushed even hotter.

"Suit yourself, princess. The offer stands if you change your mind." He peeked at me from the corner of his eye. His cheek lifted into a smirk when he noticed my flush. "We should stop for a break soon. Daisy is starting to slow."

I cleared my throat. "That's an excellent idea."

The Barren Lands weren't too miserable this time of year—only moderately so.

Tandor and I sat on a tattered blanket spread over the dry, dusty stone ground as we enjoyed a small meal of bread and cheese. Most of his ass was on the stone, but that was his own fault for being so large.

I ripped my chunk of bread into smaller pieces as I ate, making sure to pop an equal amount of bread and cheese into my mouth at the same time so I had the best flavor experience possible. Tandor watched me but didn't comment.

The horse slurped away at a small bucket of water that had been stashed below the bench in the carriage, as well as a few handfuls of oats. Her brown body shone with sweat. She would be able to eat a heartier meal when we reached the next town—Sunhaven.

If we had decided to take a roundabout route and travel through the Greenwood Forest, we could have gone straight to Tidegrove, but the carriage definitely wouldn't have survived that journey. The forest paths were hardly maintained, and the critters of the woods gave me the heebie jeebies. I shivered just thinking about it.

Sunhaven was a lovely town. It was hot. Dry. Crowded. But lovely all the same.

Redd was from Sunhaven, and his family still lived there. Redd's family was much more talkative than he was, though the sullen vampire was slowly opening up as time passed. That was certainly Fiella's influence.

We would reach the town by sundown if we kept a good pace. The horse was surprisingly tough—she kept going even when I expected her to tire. She might have looked fragile, but she was tough as rocks. Still, we didn't want to push her too hard. I should have crafted her some energizing potions to keep her endurance up...

"So, I take it your cauldron and secret ingredient aren't available in Sunhaven?" Tandor asked conversationally.

I shook my head. "No. I don't think so. I might as well pick up a few things while we're here, though."

"Of course not—that would be too easy." He laid back on the dusty ground, shutting his eyes. The light of the dual suns danced over his moss green skin, brightening the hue to a color that resembled fresh grass. He had removed his cloak only a few hours into the journey, when the air turned from crisp and mild to heavy and warm as we got deeper into the Barren Lands. I was still wearing my cloak—the warmth wasn't enough to bother me yet.

I kicked a small pebble aside and watched it dance over the flat, cracked land. "Are there any fruits you'd like to pick up while we're here? Or any spices?"

He hummed in thought. "I am running low on saffron, and my lemongrass stash is shrinking too. I'll see what I can find."

"For a new cider flavor?"

A smile stretched across his face. "Of course you would ask that. Yes, actually."

"See, it won't be a total waste of time."

He rolled over to examine my face. "No, not a waste of time at all."

I wasn't sure why that comment made my cheeks warm.

CHAPTER 18
Tandor

Sunhaven had surprisingly few accommodations available for such a bustling, crowded town.

There were three inns.

The first inn, near the entrance of town, was completely full. Though there were dozens of rooms, each one was occupied. The elf working the front desk was not friendly either—she was offended by my attempt of flattery.

The second inn was under renovation. By Redd's woodworking family, coincidentally. They were laying down new wood flooring and expanding the kitchen and common areas. The entire building was out of commission.

The third inn was our last hope.

The front of the building was lined with potted plants—spiky, succulent varieties that would never survive in Moonvale's milder weather. I glanced at Kizzi to find her admiring them longingly.

We strode into the front door. There were folk everywhere. In the streets, it was almost impossible to walk ten paces without crossing paths or bumping shoulders with someone. Inside the inn was just as crowded. There were comfy looking chairs spread throughout the large room, and every window was thrown open wide to let a breeze pass through. Every chair was occupied. There were even some folk standing in corners, chatting idly.

I didn't have much hope. *Maybe we can somehow curl up and sleep in the carriage...*

We had left the carriage with Sunhaven's stable attendants, as well as Daisy the horse, so she could be tended to until we left again. She was the smallest horse in the stable, of course. But I had to admit, her glossy brown coat made her look more beautiful than all the dusty, tan horses that were local.

A grinning, tall human man stood at the check in counter. "Hello, travelers!"

I smiled politely. "Hello. Do you have any rooms available?" I glanced at Kizzi over my shoulder. She was hardly paying attention, too distracted looking around the room. "Two rooms?"

The human hemmed and hawed. He idly flipped through a book, shaking his head occasionally.

A nervous sweat broke out over my skin. "Please, we'll pay extra. The other inns had nothing for us."

Kizzi elbowed me in the side. "Shh! Don't tell him that, he's going to charge us more," she hissed quietly, stretching on her toes to try to speak directly into my ear.

I glanced at her, bringing my face close to hers. "I've got this under control. Just watch."

She held my gaze for a moment before she shrugged, dropping back down to a flat stance and taking a step back. She returned to her folk watching.

The human tapped his finger onto a page. "Aha! I've got one." He smiled broadly. "Such happy news! Looks like this is the last room available today. More should open in a few days, but you never know how long folk will stay, I'm sure you understand."

"Oh, that's great! Wait—" I gulped, and my blood warmed. "We need two rooms."

The human's smile drooped. He turned back to his book, flipping quickly from cover to cover. He looked back up apologetically. "I only have the one."

I clenched my jaw, grinding my teeth. "How many beds are in that room?"

The human hesitated. "One bed, sir."

I sighed. "One bed. Excellent." I turned to Kizzi, expecting her to offer up an argument of some sort, but she just looked at me expectantly.

"One room. One bed," I repeated to her.

"Well?" she asked, quirking an eyebrow. "Are you going to pay the man? We better get the room before someone else does. Besides, you can sleep on the floor." I examined her face for long moments, searching for something I couldn't find.

"Okay, we'll take it."

"That'll be seven silvers, sir."

I recoiled. "Seven? Gods almighty. That should pay for an entire week."

The human shrugged. "It's the last room available in the entire town—the price is the price."

I grumbled under my breath, pulling out my pouch of silvers and paying the man. "Thank you," I forced myself to say.

He snatched the coins and placed a large brass key in my

hand. "You'll be in room twenty-three, just head up the stairs and follow the hallway to the very end. You'll see it." He retreated without another word.

An unexpected knot tightened in my stomach. I rolled the key between my fingers. "So, Kizzi. How about we drop off our bags and grab some dinner? I could eat an entire horse."

"Lead the way."

The room was small.

Much smaller than I had expected. It was near criminal that we were being charged seven silvers for this place —it was more of a closet than an actual room.

My head nearly skimmed the ceiling as I walked; I had to duck to avoid cracking my skull on the light sconces. A small washroom was tucked in the corner, barely wide enough to stand inside. A tiny table was perched by the entryway, and a chest sat by the wall. There was hardly any floor space, just enough to walk from place to place and none extra. Our bags would surely occupy every remaining inch.

There was definitely not enough room for me to sleep on the floor.

The rest of the room was occupied by the large bed. I breathed a sigh of relief when I saw it—at least we would both fit comfortably. I sent a silent thank you to the fates, in case they were listening. Two fluffy pillows sat at the head of the bed, and a smooth, muted orange blanket was draped haphazardly.

I knelt and lifted the blanket, peeking under the bed just to see... nope—it was a platform style with no space beneath.

Was I really considering sleeping *under* the bed? Possibly. But the idea was useless.

Kizzi squeezed into the room and settled her bag gently onto the floor. She pulled it open and peered inside, sticking her hands in and fiddling with something before closing it again. She glanced at me, glanced around the tiny room, and then looked at me again. She seemed to be debating something.

I held my breath, words refusing to form on my tongue. I shifted awkwardly from foot to foot. My heart raced in my chest.

Long moments passed.

Eventually, her gaze settled onto the large bed dominating the room. She let out a deep sigh, her shoulders rising and falling with the movement. "Well, at least it's a big bed. You better be a calm sleeper, and if you steal the covers, I'll curse you to make all your hair fall out."

I nodded sagely. "I would expect nothing less."

"I mean it—your head will be bald and shiny."

"Shiny?"

"Shiny."

I held my hands up placatingly. "I will be on my best behavior. If you'd prefer me to sleep on the floor in the hallway—"

"Oh, shut up. I was thinking the same thing, but the innkeeper would never allow that."

I shrugged. "I could try it anyway."

"If they kick us out because you're clogging up the hallway, I'll curse you twice. I'm starving, let's go find something to eat."

My stomach growled loudly, echoing through the quiet room. "I'm not going to argue with that."

Kizzi stooped, reaching into her bag one last time and murmuring under her breath. I tried to ignore the strangeness of the situation... I was not in the habit of judging magical women for their eccentricities. She sighed and stood up, heading for the door.

She hastily tucked her hands into her pockets for a moment before pulling them out and rubbing her palms against her trousers. *Nervous sweat, maybe? Weird.*

I followed her out of the room and into the narrow hallway. Her shoulder brushed against my elbow. She didn't immediately pull herself away.

We wandered out into Sunhaven as the dual suns dipped below the horizon, determined to fill our stomachs with something besides bread and cheese.

"You know, for how often we see each other around town, we hardly know each other," Kizzi said before shoving a spoonful of vegetable soup into her mouth.

I hummed thoughtfully. "You don't think so?"

She shook her head.

"I know you're the best apothecary witch in the entire realm," I said. "I know that Fiella is your best friend and has been for ages. Your only true friend, if we're being honest." Kizzi looked like she wanted to argue but I interrupted her.

"We both know it's the truth. You don't let anyone else get close enough to form a real friendship. You don't mind Redd, though."

She looked mildly startled. "You caught all that, did you?"

I nodded, munching idly on a chunk of bread. "You're not very friendly, but you're not unkind. You just speak your mind. You don't tolerate bullshit, or niceties. You're also the most impatient folk I've ever met, which is surprising, considering your line of work. One would think waiting for potions to brew would force you to tolerate waiting."

Her cheeks flushed, deepening her complexion to a lovely, warm shade of green.

"Wow. That's... okay fine, you know some things about me."

I pointed my spoon at her. "See, I told you."

She hummed in consideration. "And you..."

I brushed her off. "You don't have to—"

She interrupted me. "You love to chat. To an annoying degree. You'll speak to any folk who's open to conversation, even if other folk are waiting for you."

I snorted out a laugh. "I guess you could say that."

She continued. "You're loyal—you could have left Ginger's Pub and opened your own place years ago, but you stay. You don't get close to folk either. Well, except for Ginger, but she's technically your boss. Why is that?"

I ignored the question. "See, we know each other more than we think we do."

"I guess we do."

I picked up my pint of ale and took a long swallow. A shiver or revulsion worked its way down my spine. I ignored it and swallowed again. Kizzi watched me with a slight smile tugging at her mouth.

"Not up to your standards?"

I set the pint down with a thunk. "It's dreadful."

"Wow! I think that might be the first unkind thing I've heard you say," she laughed.

"I might be a nice folk, but I am not a liar—and I refuse to give this horrendous ale any more credit than it deserves. I brewed better my first year at Ginger's."

Kizzi picked up her own pint and gave it a sniff. Her nose wrinkled. "You're right, this smells like piss." She took a tentative sip and immediately gagged.

"Oh, come on, it's not *that* bad!"

She forced down another swallow, holding back the gag this time. "No, you were absolutely right the first time—it's dreadful."

I chuckled, holding out my pint to clink against hers. "Well, here's to shitty ales in new towns, then. It'll make returning to Moonvale so much sweeter, knowing we have the good stuff to look forward to."

She lifted her pint and gently tapped it against mine. "I'll drink to that."

We finished our ales quickly and then ordered another round. The second tasted much better than the first.

"So, what else should I know about you?" I asked, leaning back in my chair and kicking my feet out in front of me.

Kizzi shrugged. She leaned her elbows onto the table and rested her chin on her hands. "There's not much to know, really."

"Nonsense. There's more to you than just an amazing apothecary witch. Do you have any family?"

"No."

I nodded, giving her time to continue.

She sighed. "I've been alone for as long as I can remember. Well—not alone," she interrupted herself. "The coven has always been there for me. Ani took me in when I was young and practically raised me as her own. And Fiella, of course. And her Ma and Pa."

"It sounds like you have a wonderful family, then. Family isn't always your blood and bones."

She nodded thoughtfully. "I agree with that. How about you, are your parents running around the realm somewhere?"

I took a large swallow of ale. "Not anymore. My Ma and Pa both left the land of the living some years ago."

Her face scrunched. She reached over and patted the back of my hand where it rested on the handle of my pint. "Oh, Gods. I'm sorry, Tandor."

I tried to smile, but it was weighed down by the painful twinge in my chest. "I miss them every day, but they lived a long, full life. They wouldn't want to see me moping about them, wherever they are." I glanced up to the ceiling, imagining the sky and the two moons beyond. I pictured my Ma's face smiling down at me, her perfectly straight teeth and dimpled cheeks. And my Pa's, wrinkled around the mouth and at the corners of the eyes from a life full of grins.

We sat in silence for long moments, lost in thought and surrounded by the idle chatter of the diner around us.

Eventually, she broke the silence. "No siblings, then? Any other Sablesmiths out there?"

I glanced at her face to find her watching me intently. Her hands were tucked into her tunic pocket.

"One—a sister. Rune. She's a few years older. Settled

down with a family in Tidegrove. She always loved the waters." I smiled fondly. "I don't see her much, but every time I do, it's like we never parted. She's just... easy."

Kizzi's eyes brightened. "She sounds lovely. Does she have the same incredibly silky hair?"

I choked out a surprised laugh. "You think my hair is silky?"

"I regret asking."

I laughed louder. "Yes, she does. And her little ones do too."

Her face softened. "I can just imagine it—tiny, green-skinned orcs running around with pigtails. Do you want to visit them?"

"I would love to, but I know how out of the way Tide-grove is. If the fates take us there—absolutely."

"Up to the fates, then."

I nodded, and then a question tickled at my mind. "What happened to your parents? Any siblings that you know of?" I asked gently, afraid that I was prying too hard.

She let out a huff of air, pulling her hands out of her pocket to grip her pint glass. "I don't know. Isn't that strange?" She stared into the liquid in the glass, but her focus was faraway. "I suppose they could be out there somewhere, but they left me behind. They didn't want me. So why should I want them?"

"That's a terrible thing to do to a little one."

She nodded glumly. "They just dumped me in the park in town square. Left me on a bench all alone. I was three or four years old, I think." She lifted her gaze to mine, and my chest squeezed with tenderness. "I try not to think about it too much. It makes me sad for little me. She went through a lot." Her eyes bored into me with a painful heaviness.

I couldn't help myself—I ached to comfort her. I reached out and placed a gentle hand on her shoulder. My fingers curled over her shoulder blade and my thumb rested softly over her collarbone. I tried not to notice how soft her skin was there. "They are fucking idiots for leaving you. Whoever they were, wherever they went, whether they be alive or dead—I don't care what their story is. They're the dumbest folk in the realm for leaving you behind. I would slap them if I could."

She cracked a watery smile. "Wow, you'd inflict violence on strangers for me? How chivalrous."

I released her shoulder with a careful squeeze and snorted out a laugh. "Only when it's deserved. In this instance—yes, absolutely."

Kizzi looked at me strangely for a moment, tilting her head and squinting her eyes.

"What?" I asked.

She sighed, and her fragile smile drooped a bit. She just shook her head instead of answering.

She turned to a passing server. "Two more ales, please?"

I laid in the inn's surprisingly comfortable bed, staring up at the dark ceiling.

My body was exhausted, but my mind was painfully awake. My thoughts couldn't decide where to settle.

Speaking of my younger years had resurfaced memories that I preferred to keep buried. I didn't like to think of my Ma and Pa, whoever they were. They were witches of some sort, that much was evident in my magical abilities. But their identities were a mystery. They had left me behind in Moonvale with nothing but the clothes on my back—not even a letter. They hadn't spoken to anyone, either. Nobody knew where I came from.

Ani found me there, sitting on that park bench. She didn't ask a single question, she just saw me, offered her hand, and guided me to her cottage.

I also thought about Tandor, his body sprawled out on the bed next to mine, breathing rhythmically. Spending time with him was much more enjoyable than I expected it to be. I always knew he was friendly, and he was easy to look at, of course, but I was surprised by how easy it was to talk to him. How natural. I thought about the way he placed his hand on my shoulder—how he somehow knew I needed the comforting touch at that moment.

I couldn't help but wonder how much of his kindness was due to the love potion, and that thought made my heart sink in my chest with a strange wave of disappointment.

I wanted him to be kind to me because he *chose* to, not just because he was magically forced.

And that thought was... worrisome.

I also thought about the jar tucked away in my bag. I had brought Hex with me to the diner, too afraid to leave them alone at the inn. I didn't want them to throw any magical tantrums. They had insisted on coming with me on this journey—tucking themself into the jar before I left my shop. They snapped and spat at me until I relented. Hex was now idly sitting in my bag, alarmingly still and well behaved.

I was new to the whole familiar thing, but mine felt a little too clingy.

I was waiting for the other boot to drop.

The tiny room was pitch dark. There was one small window, and it was covered with wooden slats, blocking out the moonlight that might have crept in.

I stared at the ceiling, praying for sleep to pull me under. Tandor's deep even breaths should have been soothing, but they just made me antsy. Fidgety. Like my skin was too tight for my bones.

I should have brought some sleep tonics with me...

Even the noises from outside were unfamiliar. The chirping insects were not the same as those who inhabited

Moonvale, and the comforting scurrying of critters was missing.

I could hear hints of other folk, too. Boots on the cobblestones outside. A laugh from a room down the hall. The creak of wooden stairs.

It was all overwhelming.

I wanted to crawl out of bed, crawl outside, and soak up some fresh air, but I knew that wouldn't sooth me. The air was too different. Too dry and warm. Too heavily laden with the smells of a bustling town.

I was used to traveling. I traveled far and wide to find ingredients for my potions. But that was usually alone, or with Fiella. And Fiella was a comfortable presence—I was more familiar with her breathing than I was with my own.

I resorted to assembling potions in my head. I closed my eyes and let the familiar pattern tug my thoughts away from their swirling maelstrom.

I wonder what mixture would be helpful for calming a troubled mind. A potion, probably. With a liquid base. Honey. Honey is calming, rejuvenating. With chamomile flowers. And maybe some bark of an ever-tree from the mountains. If I boil it long enough, it will lose most of its pain-relieving properties but will relieve tension instead...

Darkness closed around me, slowly sweeping me away to blissful nothingness.

A large, strong hand slid down my back in a comforting caress. The touch heated my blood, and a pleasant shiver traveled down my spine. I hummed happily.

A dreamy, blissful warmth surrounded me. I was more comfortable than I had been in ages. The smell of warm rain curled around me. I snuggled in deeper, craving more of that warmth, and more of that lovely smell. My cheek pressed into firm, bulky muscle.

The hand slid up my back, slowly, inching over every divot of my spine. My nightgown was smooth and light and did nothing to diminish the warmth of that touch—it practically burned me. The hand reached the base of my neck and paused before sliding into the roots of my hair. Strong fingers massaged my scalp in slow circular motions. A quiet groan slipped out of my mouth before I could stop it.

I kept my eyes closed, soaking up the bliss of the moment.

I reached out a curious hand and my fingers brushed against smooth, hot skin. I let my fingers trail up, up, up, over the soft ridges of a ribcage, over strong, firm pectoral muscles, to a juncture where neck met shoulder. I lightly dug my fingers into the taut muscle there, experimenting. The muscle softened slightly in response.

The fingers in my scalp continued their magical movements, while another hand tentatively brushed over my hip. The fingers slid up, ghosting over my waist before curling around to the small of my back.

My pulse quickened in my veins.

I tossed my knee over strong hips, soaking up as much of that warming touch as possible.

My fingers slid up a strong neck, over a defined jaw, slipping onto a pointed ear. I tugged lightly—curious.

A groan sounded in the darkness beside me. I smiled wryly.

The fingers massaging my scalp clenched gently and tugged, lifting my head. Warm breath caressed my face. I relished it—the proximity. Knowing another was so close that I could almost breathe them in.

The hand on my back slid lower, ghosting over the curve of my ass and settling on my calf. Strong fingers curled, encircling my leg.

I leaned in, closer, slipping my hand behind a strong neck.

Lips whispered against mine, almost touching but not quite. I shivered.

The hands on me tightened, grasping urgently.

The lips surged forward, capturing my mouth in a searing kiss. I moaned against the onslaught. The kiss deepened—a tongue teased at the entrance of my mouth. I shifted my weight, pulling myself onto the deliciously warm, deliciously *comfortable* body.

I settled on top, my hips aligning perfectly with a massive, burning hardness. Heat flooded my core. I suddenly felt terribly, urgently *empty*.

"Kizzi."

I deepened the kiss further, my tongue dancing with another, hands gripping flesh. More. *More.*

"Kizzi." Louder, this time.

I sat upright and sighed, my head lolling back blissfully as I ground my hips against the delicious hardness beneath me.

"Tandor," I breathed.

"Kizzi!"

My eyes snapped open.

Blood thundered in my veins, blurring my thoughts. Remnants of sunlight tried to force their way in the window, but they couldn't make it through the wooden slats. The room was dark.

The body beneath me was perfectly still—practically vibrating with tension.

I froze. The arousal flooding my veins just a moment ago drifted away like a cloud of smoke.

I took stock of the situation, suddenly snapping back to reality.

I was in Sunhaven.

I was in an inn, a room, a *bed* with Tandor.

And I was shamelessly straddling the poor orc.

I could hardly see him in the shadowy darkness of the room. Tandor laid perfectly still beneath me, his breaths sawing in and out of his mouth. His arms were splayed wide, his hands curled into tight fists.

And he was impossibly, desperately hard.

"Oh, fates." I whispered.

He gulped audibly, and then forced out a strangled laugh. "Well, good morning to you too."

"Fuck!"

"I'm not complaining or anything, but..." he tapped my bare knee with the tip of his finger. "I'm trapped."

Mortified, I scrambled off his lap and onto my side of the bed. I hastily straightened my gown and yanked the hem down as far as it would go.

He rose to a sitting position then awkwardly adjusted himself in his thin sleep pants. I tried not to look. I really did. But I couldn't help myself.

My eyes widened at the impressive bulge in his pants. I knew he felt large when I was on top of him but... *wow.*

I was grateful for the low lighting. I silently prayed that his vision wasn't keen enough to see the flush surely staining my skin.

He chuckled quietly, and my gaze flicked to his. I found him already watching me. "Dreaming about me, princess? I'm flattered."

I tried to laugh, but it came out choked. "I wasn't..."

"Oh, was this you making a move on me, then? I'm certainly not saying no, why don't you come back—"

I threw a pillow at his head, smacking him right in the face. He laughed louder.

"Dreaming." I gritted out. "Just dreaming."

Curse that love potion... if he wasn't drugged I would... I would...

What would I have done? Would I have crawled back onto his lap to finish what my dream had started? Would I have shoved my undergarments aside and seated myself on his hard, massive cock? The thought reignited the heat in my blood.

I absolutely would have.

I shook my head, struggling to clear my thoughts.

It was no use imagining. I couldn't throw myself at a man enchanted with a love potion. That just—that just wasn't right. No matter how warm and comfortable and delicious smelling he was.

Or how much he clearly wanted me to. His body, at least.

Just the love potion working its way through his system, I reminded myself.

I ran my hands through my hair, smoothing back the snarled curls.

"Must've been a nice dream," he mumbled as he set a pillow over his lap.

"Shut up. We will never speak of this again. Deal?" I begged.

"Oh, but it's such a good story!"

"Never. Again."

He held his hands up in mock surrender. "Fine, fine, this never happened. Now, would you like to use the washroom first, or shall I?"

CHAPTER 20
Tandor

My cock throbbed with an incessant ache that was almost painful. I hunched over the sink in the tiny washroom, debating if I could spend any more time in the room without drawing suspicion.

I had already rubbed myself to release once, but that wasn't enough.

I kept thinking about Kizzi and her soft, malleable thighs, the way they cradled my hips so perfectly... The way she rubbed herself against my—

I groaned and scrubbed my hands over my face. The heated thoughts were *not* helping.

I had heard the door open and shut a few minutes ago—hopefully that meant Kizzi left the room to go find herself some breakfast. Maybe with the distraction, she wouldn't notice how much time had passed... I could go for one more...

No. I slapped my cheeks to focus myself.

It was just a dream. She wasn't thinking about *me*. She must have been thinking of some other man.

The thought settled like a stone in my stomach, heavy and uncomfortable.

But she *had* said my name, in a breathy, decadent whisper... The sound replayed over and over in my head. The way my name had sounded like a prayer on her tongue, the way it slipped between her lips on a heated exhale—

I splashed a handful of water over my face.

We were just two folk, traveling together, who had to share a bed.

She needed my help. It was nothing more than that.

But I desperately wanted it to be...

When I finally wrangled my body into submission and got myself ready for the day, I slipped out of the room in search of a bright head of green hair. Kizzi had gotten herself ready before I did, and her hair had been twisted into a messy knot on top of her head.

I liked her hair up like that. It showed off her pretty ears, her soft-looking neck. And it kept her from hiding.

I spotted the witch quickly, seated on a fluffy chair in the inn's common room with her feet tucked under her. She was buried in a book that she must have pulled from the shelf on the far wall. She didn't notice me as I entered the room.

I took a detour to the kitchen to find some tea. It was my turn to repay the favor.

A shifter was working the kitchen with a bright white apron tied around his waist. He perked up when I entered. "Good morning, sir! Searching for something to eat?"

I smiled politely. "Good morning! Tea would be amazing, if you have it. And maybe a few pastries?"

He nodded and began pulling out glasses. "Of course. We have a new seasonal variety—apple and cinnamon. It's delightful." He poured the glasses only halfway full and then retreated to a large box in the corner of the kitchen. He returned with two handfuls of ice cubes. He plopped the ice into the tea and then smiled broadly, handing them to me.

I forgot that the folk of Sunhaven preferred their drinks cold. It felt entirely backwards to me—we always sipped on hot drinks in Moonvale to help fight off the constant chill. But it wasn't chilly here.

I accepted the drinks gratefully, along with a couple of sticky honey buns.

Kizzi was in the exact same spot when I returned, but I could tell she had made it a few pages further in her book. It was cute, how absorbed she was in the story. She was entirely oblivious to her surroundings.

I stopped to watch her for a moment, and a gentle warmth bloomed in my chest. I squashed it before it could become much more.

"Good morning, Kizzi!" I declared loudly as I stepped up beside her.

She jumped, almost dropping the book onto the floor. "Gods! You just scared a few years off my life."

"I wasn't quiet, you just weren't paying attention." I held out a glass of tea and a sticky bun. "Are you hungry?"

A smile stretched across her beautiful face. "Starving." She reached for the dishes greedily. I plopped down in the chair beside her, grateful that the common area wasn't as crowded as it had been yesterday evening.

I kicked my feet up on the low ottoman in front of me and examined the sticky honey bun. It was a little soft, but it was baked to a golden sheen. Perfectly cooked. The honey glaze sparkled in the firelight from the sconces, and a thick icing settled gracefully on top. The whole pastry was twisted into a swirl. I lifted it to my face and inhaled. The scent of warm, sweet bread with a sweet tang of honey flooded my senses. My mouth watered.

I took a slow bite, allowing my teeth to sink into the gooey center. Flavor exploded over my tongue. I had to swallow an indecent moan. The perfect balance of sweet, soft bread with a contrast from the honey. Incredible. I savored every morsel, careful to catch any dripping crumbs or icing with my tongue so they wouldn't be wasted on the grimy inn floor.

I glanced at Kizzi to find that she had already finished her bun. She was watching me with a glint in her eye. She licked her finger, pulling the last bit of icing into her mouth. My eyes traced the movement, latched onto her cute pink tongue.

"Good?" I asked. My voice came out rough.

"Delicious." Her eyes flicked to the rest of the bun in my hand.

Chuckling under my breath, I took another bite before I offered her the last of the honey bun. It was the center of the swirl—the softest part.

"Oh, no, you eat it." She argued.

I just held it aloft and quirked my eyebrow.

"Okay fine, if you insist. You don't have to twist my leg." She snatched the center of the bun and popped it into her mouth. She hummed happily as she chewed. A bit of icing lingered on her bottom lip. I waited for her to notice it, to wipe it away, to capture it with that pink tongue of hers.

She didn't.

"You've got a little..." I gestured to my own face.

"Huh?" She brushed her hands against her cheeks, looking confused.

I saw the opportunity in front of me. "I'll get it." I leaned forward, slowly reaching for her face. She held still.

I swiped the pad of my thumb along her plush lower lip. I lingered a moment longer than necessary, just enjoying the feel of her skin under my fingers.

And then I sat back. Slipped my thumb between my lips. Sucked the drop of icing from my skin.

A lovely flush crawled up her neck. I couldn't help it—I smiled in satisfaction.

Kizzi cleared her throat before slipping out a quiet, "Thanks."

I enjoyed watching the way her flush crept up her jaw, over her cheeks, to the tips of her ears. I watched her from the corner of my eye as we drank our apple cinnamon teas, long enough for the flush to fade from her skin.

"Ready to continue our journey, or would you like to linger in Sunhaven for a while longer?" I asked.

"I'd like to make a stop or two, and then I'm ready to move on if you are."

I nodded. "I was thinking the exact same thing—lead the way."

Later, after visiting three different shops and securing a few parcels, we returned to the inn to grab our bags and head on our way.

I had purchased a bundle of cinnamon sticks, a few jars of

honey, and a bag of dried mint leaves. All ingredients I was excited to introduce to my cider brews.

Kizzi had spoken with the shopkeepers in hushed tones, whispering into their ears as she asked for her ingredients. I wasn't quite sure what she purchased, but it looked like some sort of insect. As well as a vial of honey that was much thicker than the stuff I bought.

Witches.

The carriage was exactly where we had left it, and it looked even worse in the glaring bright light of Sunhaven.

Daisy neighed happily when she saw us. Her belly was full, and she was prepared for another journey. I stroked her mane, letting the coarse hairs slip through my fingers. "You ready for another journey, pretty lady?"

She whinnied quietly.

After tossing a few silvers at the stable keep, we were on our way.

CHAPTER 21
Kizzi

My shoulder bumped constantly against Tandor's side as the carriage rolled along the rough stone paths leading out of Sunhaven.

The carriage felt even more crowded than before, though the only change was the addition of a few parcels.

My skin hummed with awareness where it touched his tunic. I was achingly aware of how close he was. It took a valiant effort to keep my body still. I couldn't decide if I wanted to lean into the contact or escape from it.

The carriage continued to roll.

"Where to?" Tandor asked when we came to an intersection in the path. We hadn't discussed our next destination, simply continuing in the direction further away from Moonvale. "Left will take us toward the coast, and right will take us toward the grasslands, and eventually the mountains."

I hummed in contemplation. The shopkeepers at Sunhaven spoke of whispered rumors of a dragon egg being seen in Tidegrove many years ago, but I had heard of them historically originating from deep within the mountains of Rockward.

I made a leap.

"Let's go left."

Tandor glanced at me over his shoulder but tugged gently on the reins, guiding the horse toward the beach. "That's not the answer I expected," he said. "Are there a lot of smiths that way? I thought the largest cauldrons came from further inland."

I shrugged. "It's just a hunch."

He nodded thoughtfully. "Are you going to tell me what mysterious ingredient you're searching for?"

"Nope."

"Not even so I can help?" he pried.

I shook my head. "I can't. It's highly confidential."

If I told him I was searching for the mythical dragon eggs, he would think I was insane and abandon me, surely. And if I told him what I needed the dragon eggshells for... That I had drugged him and the entire town with a love potion and this was my only hope for a cure...

He would never forgive me.

Tandor sighed in exasperation. "Fair enough. Keep your secrets, I like unraveling them."

Daisy's hooves clopped against the stone in a steady rhythm, joining with the grinding whir of the carriage's wheels.

"Let's go to Tidegrove—you can visit your sister while we're there."

Tandor smiled at that, his eyes crinkling at the corners. "I like that idea."

The air thickened and warmed as our carriage neared the coast. The scent of brine and salt was heavy on the wind drifting past my face.

I was miserably hot under the weight of my clothes. Crammed in the small carriage next to Tandor, it was almost sweltering. Sweat beaded on my skin and dripped in tiny rivulets.

I had long since removed my cloak and corset to don my lightest tunic and skirt, but I was still uncomfortably warm, even with my hair pulled off my neck and fastened into a knot on top of my head. I scrunched my sleeves up as high as they would go and tied a knot in the length of my skirt, baring my shins to the flowing air. It helped, but only slightly.

Tandor was handling the heat much better than I was. He hardly broke a sweat—his forehead glistened with just a kiss of moisture. He made me look like a hot mess in comparison.

His short-sleeved tunic kept his muscled arms exposed. His forearm muscles flexed and bunched as he guided the horse by the reins. I resisted the urge to stare, to trace my finger down the veins I could see hidden below his skin.

The heat was clearly making me delusional.

Tandor flinched violently, rocking the carriage. "Woah!"

I grasped the wall with one hand, my other gripping onto his bicep for support. "What! Gods!"

"What is *that*?!" he asked, horrified. He was staring down at his feet, and his face blanched to a sickly pale color.

"What are you talking about? Fucking fates, is there

something in the carriage? Is it a spider?!" I leaned over, bracing myself, to catch a glimpse of the monstrosity that had made Tandor react with such horror. My heart thundered in my chest.

A startled chuckle burst out of me, which quickly turned into a full-blown belly laugh. I cackled wildly, the mixture of relief and adrenaline flooding my system and making me feel vaguely delirious.

Thank the Old Gods it wasn't a spider—I would've had to jump out of the moving carriage, damn the consequences.

"Kizzi!" he shouted. "Stop laughing and do something!"

Tears of mirth sprouted from the corners of my eyes and trickled down my cheeks. My stomach ached from the power of my laughter.

"This isn't funny!" the terrified orc shouted.

I tried to smother my laughter, but it persisted.

Tandor sat frozen, every muscle solidified to stone, with my cauldron sludge familiar slithering up the toe of his boot.

I bent to scoop them up with my hand, retrieving the jar from my bag. I kept the lid loose at their insistence, so they could come and go as they pleased. They resisted, clinging to my hand instead of sliding easily into the jar. I sighed. Giving up, I let my familiar curl up on my lap instead.

"It's just Hex!"

Tandor watched me with his jaw hanging open, the expression on his face somewhere between shock and horror. "Hex... is that what I think it is? Has that been in your bag this whole time?"

I nodded. "Of course. In my bag, in my pocket for a while, sometimes they leave their jar. I don't make a habit of telling them what to do—they don't appreciate it."

"Um... Why?"

"Why what?"

"Why is it *here*?"

"Oh, right. They insisted."

"Okay... the slime insisted on coming with you. And now it's... alive."

I nodded, glad he was understanding so easily. "Exactly."

"Okay..." He pulled the reins, bringing the horse and carriage to a slow stop on the side of the path. He let the reins fall slack and scrubbed his hands over his face. "Okay. This is completely normal."

I smiled in agreement. "It is! It's better if you don't question it. Thanks for understanding."

He peeked at me between his fingers. "I don't understand at all, if I'm being honest with you."

The smile dropped from my cheeks. "Oh."

"I just need a moment to process."

"Sure."

Hex gurgled gently, tiny bubbles rising to their surface and popping. I bent down to whisper to them, "it's okay. We can trust him."

Hex slumped, becoming more viscous. Slowly, tentatively, they slipped from my lap and crawled onto Tandor's knee. He watched, frozen in fear.

"Kizzi," he whispered urgently.

"Yeah?"

"It's on my leg."

"It is, yes."

"Can you tell it to get off?"

"They just want to be your friend," I insisted.

"Friend. Friend... this magical, moving slime wants to be my friend."

"They do, yes."

"And how do you know that?"

"They told me."

Tandor exhaled heavily, the air puffing out his cheeks and whooshing out of his pursed mouth. "They told you."

I nodded.

Long moments passed with Tandor blankly staring at Hex perched on his knee. Eventually, his tensed muscles started to soften. "Is it going to... bite me?"

"I don't know," I answered honestly. "They do bite sometimes. But if you don't piss them off, you should be fine."

He tensed again momentarily, but then seemed to convince himself that he was safe. That the handful of slime wasn't going to cause him irreparable harm.

He glanced at me with furrowed eyebrows. I smiled reassuringly.

Tandor tentatively reached for the reins again, being careful to avoid any quick movements. Slowly, with a gentleness I didn't expect from such a large, strong orc, he flicked the reins, urging the horse to move again. He kept his gaze on me for a few long moments and then flicked his eyes to the path in front of us.

He sat as still as possible, holding his spine ramrod straight and bracing his feet against the floor of the carriage.

It was funny how tense he was.

Sure, I had been absolutely horrified and almost dropped dead from shock when I found the living cauldron sludge in my bed, but that was different. This tiny amount of Hex was *much* more palatable than their full size.

Tandor was going to absolutely piss his trousers when he saw Hex in all their glory. I chuckled at the thought.

"Do I want to know why the slime, er, Hex is alive now?"

"I accidentally created a familiar," I answered simply.

He stared at me blankly. He had no response to that. *I think I finally broke his brain.*

The rest of the journey passed in a tense silence with Tandor holding himself perfectly still and refusing to look down at his lap, and me morbidly enjoying every single second.

Tandor

My muscles ached with a throbbing ferocity as I parked the carriage outside my sister's cottage. Kizzi had eventually coaxed Hex back into their jar, but she had allowed them to sit on my knee for what felt like days.

My shoulders twinged. I had held myself painfully still, refusing to allow my twitching to provoke the (slightly terrifying) magical slime. I bent and twisted, trying to relieve the stiffness.

Kizzi examined her surroundings with a brightness in her eyes and a look of awe on her face.

She was lovelier than the tides; I didn't want to look at anything but her.

But I forced myself to. I tore my gaze away.

Rune's beachside cottage was charming—spacious and warm, with a welcome breeziness. There were many windows letting in as much light as possible, and they were all thrown open to allow the salty air to drift through. The exterior was painted a light blue color that was closer to white than it was to cerulean, brighter even than the midday sky.

Daisy neighed with gusto as I let her free, allowing her to graze on the soft grasses sprouting from the sand. She stomped happily through the sand where water caressed the shore. I couldn't help but smile as I watched her playing in the shallow waves, allowing her hooves to sink into the sand over and over again while she pranced around.

A calm voice broke me from my reverie. "Tandor, is that you, little brother?"

I whirled around and my gaze landed on Rune—she looked the same as she had the last time I saw her. She was tall, lean but strong, with a skin tone the same green as my own, albeit more toasted and freckled from the brightness of Tidegrove's suns. She wore a sleeveless beige tunic and flowing trousers that cut off before they reached her ankles. One of her little ones was tucked on her hip, while the other clung to her knee, hiding behind her and peering out curiously. All three of them wore their smooth, shiny black hair loose and free.

A wide grin stretched across my sister's mouth. "I thought I recognized that big head of yours. What in the realms are you doing all the way over here?" She strode over and pulled me into a sideways hug, mindful of her daughter still perched on her hip. Her head tucked under my chin for a moment while we squeezed each other, and then she stepped back.

"I thought I'd surprise you," I said. "Where's that annoying mate of yours?"

She elbowed me in the side. "He's out fishing. It's the middle of the day, you know. But he should be back in time for dinner."

I groaned in mock dismay. "He's coming back? Damn!"

The little boy still creeping out from behind Rune's legs gasped. "Ma, he said a bad word!"

Whoops. "Sorry, Rune. It slipped."

Being an uncle had taught me many things, but one lesson stood out in particular—little ones were sponges and would repeat *absolutely everything* they heard. Especially if you told them not to, that would just make them repeat the word more often.

Little shits.

I bent down with a stiff groan and hoisted the little boy off his feet. He hardly weighed more than a pumpkin. I wrangled his squirming body until I had him clutched by his middle, dangling upside down. He giggled wildly the entire time. "Now you listen here, Ash. Bad words are for big folk only. Understood?"

"Damn! Damn damn damn!" The small orc mix shouted amongst his frenzied laughter. His arms dangled loosely above his head as he let his weight sink into my grasp. He didn't even bother trying to escape, instead choosing to flop around like a sack of grain.

"That's it! You're getting dunked!" I took two steps toward the ocean, and the boy squealed loudly.

"No!" He dragged the word out, pushing his lungs to the limit. "I already changed clothes today!"

"Fine, fine. You get off easy this time, but you better watch your back." I chuckled as I set the small boy back on his feet. He immediately trotted over to the horse to try to pet her.

"Soak any clothes, and I'll make you do the washing," Rune warned, but the threat had no bite to it. She was grinning too broadly.

"Point heard," I said. I caught a glimpse of Kizzi from the corner of my eye. She was still close to the carriage, watching us with a gentle but tight smile on her face. I beckoned her over with a wave of my hand. "Kizzi, come on over, Rune only bites sometimes!" To Rune, I said, "This is my... friend Kizzi. She's the best apothecary witch in the entire realm."

I hoped she didn't realize how I stumbled over the word *friend*. I supposed that's what Kizzi and I were now, friends. We had been neighbors before, perhaps acquaintances, but now I felt like we had forged something more. Something truer. I glanced at Kizzi's face to see if she was going to object, to insist we weren't really friends.

She didn't.

Kizzi walked over and shook Rune's outstretched hand. "It's lovely to meet you," she said.

Rune's smile turned downright devilish. "I've never met one of Tandor's lady friends before!"

"Don't even start. You've met plenty of my friends," I warned.

"Mmhmm. Not pretty ones."

I rolled my eyes. "We'll leave."

She snorted. "Fine! I'll behave. I am glad to meet you, Kizzi." Her gaze flicked between the two of us. "Are you just passing through or do you plan to stay a while?"

I glanced at Kizzi for confirmation.

"A little of both, I guess?" she said. "We just need to be back in Moonvale before Hallow's Eve, and we have at least one more town to visit. Maybe more."

Rune nodded thoughtfully. "Well, feel free to hang around as long as you please. We don't have any extra space in the cottage since we had the little ones, but there is an inn further down the beach. But we'd love to have you for meals, of course."

"Thanks, Runey Juney!" I tossed my arm around her neck. "You're the best, you know that?"

"I know I am," she grumbled good naturedly. "Now go get yourselves settled at the inn, explore town if you wish, and come back in a few hours for dinner."

"Yes ma'am!" I glanced at Daisy, still playfully splashing in the water. "Can I leave our horse here? Will she be safe? I'd hate to ruin her fun and make her pull the carriage again—we'll just walk while we're in the area."

Rune's gaze warmed as it zeroed in on the small brown horse. "She can stay for as long as you need her to. There are no predators here, and no folk would mess with her. Let her play."

"Thank you. She might eat all your grass, but I swear it'll grow back. See you later!" I waved at Rune, and then at her two littles in turn.

"Bye!" Kizzi called. I noticed that she also took the time to wave to the littles instead of ignoring them, even if they were too shy to wave back.

We grabbed our bags from the carriage and hoisted them onto our backs. I grunted with the effort, my muscles still feeling the strain from the carriage ride.

"Lead the way," Kizzi said, sweeping her arm broadly in front of her. I did, but I made sure to keep my pace slow so she would walk beside me instead of behind me.

"I love it here," I said wistfully as we walked along the beach, passing other cottages as we neared the center of town. The cottages were tucked back a stretch from the water to avoid being swept away by the tides, but they all had a similar architecture. Bright, open, and airy.

Kizzi hummed thoughtfully. "I have always loved visiting Tidegrove. It does have its charms."

I nodded in agreement. "The beach, for one."

She smiled and glanced up at my face. "Why don't you move here?"

I shrugged, not quite able to answer that question. I simply said, "It isn't home."

She gazed at me with an expression that said somehow, some way, she understood exactly what I meant.

We continued the rest of the walk in a warm, gentle silence, nothing but the sounds of our feet crunching in sand, water brushing against shore, and beach birds chirping in the distance.

Tidegrove's inn was more of a series of small cottages nestled together rather than a singular structure. There was a main, central room that housed the entryway, the check in desk, and the common areas and kitchen, but the rooms themselves were stretched in two straight lines with doors opening to the outside air instead of to a hallway.

It was almost like a tiny neighborhood. A small, charming neighborhood of single-room cottages.

Kizzi's attention was snagged by a vendor selling flowing, billowing palm trees beside the front door. Her eyes stuck to the plants like glue, and she actually faltered in her steps. The corner of my mouth lifted. "You stay here and look—I'll get us checked into some rooms," I said.

She glanced up at me for only a moment before her eyes returned to the foliage. "Are you sure? I can come with you. I just want to look for one second—"

"Stay," I interrupted her. "I'll take care of this. I'll be back. Watch my stuff."

I plopped my bag by her feet to give my back some momentary relief, grabbed my coin pouch, and strode inside. Her bright voice drifted to my ears as she happily chatted to the merchant.

A few folk lingered around the inn's common areas, but not many. Most of the folk here, like Sunhaven, had darker shades of skin, either naturally or toasted from the brighter rays of the suns. There were brightly colored and lighter folk as well, of course, but in general, everyone had been kissed by sunlight. They weren't shaded by near constant tree cover and clouds like Moonvale townsfolk were.

I caught a glimpse of a fluffy white tail rounding the corner of the inn, around back. *Was that a cat? Weird—it looks like that white one back in Moonvale.*

"Welcome! What can I do for you?" the smiley innkeeper asked. He appeared to be human, though there was an energy about him that suggested some magical heritage. His skin had the slightest blue tint to it, and perhaps a sparkle as well, if my eyes weren't deceiving me.

I smiled back. "Do you have any rooms available?"

The innkeeper flipped quickly through the leather-bound logbook in front of him. "Yes, we sure do! Just one?"

My smile froze on my face, turned to stone. I glanced in Kizzi's direction to find her still chatting with the merchant, holding up a tiny palm tree and examining its rich, shiny leaves. She appeared to be in no hurry, content to discuss every detail of the plant.

"How many rooms are available?" I asked. My voice came out tight. Strained.

"We have three, right now."

I gulped, my thoughts balanced somewhere between guilt and eagerness. I thought of the last time Kizzi and I shared a room—the way we had to slip around each other constantly, the way her apple scent filled the room and clung to my clothes. The way she gravitated toward me in the night...

All I knew was that I wanted to be as close to her as possible, for as long as I could.

"Sir?"

"How many beds in those rooms?" I asked around the tightness in my throat.

"Two of the rooms have one bed, the third is a larger room with two beds," he answered smoothly. "Would you like to have more space?"

I glanced at Kizzi again to be sure she wasn't within hearing distance. "And how much do they cost?"

He glanced at his logbook. "Two silvers for the smaller rooms, three for the larger."

I made up my mind. If my time on this journey with Kizzi was limited, I would make the most of it.

"One room, please. With one bed."

I placed the silvers into her open palm. She slid a silver key across the table. "One room it is. You'll be in the orange room closer to the water. Enjoy your stay, let us know if you need anything. Breakfast tomorrow is tomato fish tarts."

I snatched the key and glanced guiltily over my shoulder. "Fish tarts. Right. Thank you."

My heartbeat kicked up in my chest and my ears twitched with whatever tangled emotions I was feeling. I strode to where Kizzi stood, exchanging a few coins for the plant she was holding. I hoisted my bag over my shoulder and showed Kizzi the key. "Got us a room," I said nervously.

She tilted her head. "Only one? Are they full too?"

I nodded hastily. "They are, yes. Full. This is the last room left." My voice came out higher pitched than it should have. I cleared my throat.

The merchant furrowed his brows and started to speak but I interrupted him before he could get any words out. "Thank you for the plant, sir! I'm sure this lady here will take great care of it."

I grabbed Kizzi's elbow and gently guided her in the direction of the rooms. "Weird," she mused. "It doesn't look nearly as crowded here. And they only had one room?"

I coughed awkwardly. "Yes, they had an incident in some of the rooms. Very gross, very smelly. This is the only one available."

She just shrugged her shoulders, not seeming to mind too much. "Well, that's that then." She glanced at me guiltily. "I swear I won't attack you this time."

I laughed, but it didn't sound right. "I would be honored if you did."

She flushed, all the way to her ears.

CHAPTER 23
Kizzi

Rune's home was something straight out of a storybook. It was perched beside the water, with dunes and palm trees at its back, and it was as picturesque as a cottage could possibly be. Even scattered with signs of little ones, toys and art projects strewn about, it was adorable.

Rune's mate, too, was a pleasant eyeful. He was a fae, I thought, with a stocky build and pointed ears. Garren, his name was. He was draped in the light flowy style of clothing that was popular in the beach town. It was surprisingly comfortable—I had purchased myself a new outfit at the market after settling at the inn.

Tandor and I were seated at the family's dinner table as if we belonged there. Technically, Tandor did belong, but I was an outsider, and they accepted me with open arms. It was enough to tighten my throat and make the backsides of my eyes prickle.

Dishes were passed around the table. Some of the foods were familiar, things I had tried before, but some of them were new. The scent of herbs and broiled vegetables permeated the air, assuring me that whatever the foods were, they were sure to be delicious.

I loaded my plate up with a scoop of red rice, some grilled meat, and a healthy serving of the vegetable dish. Fresh baked bread was served on the side, still steaming from the oven. My mouth watered.

"So, Kizzi, do you have any plans for Hallow's Eve? It's right around the corner. Two weeks away, right?" Rune asked as she helped her little ones fill their plates.

I nodded as I swallowed a mouthful of rice. It was so delicious my toes nearly curled. "Yes, actually. Hallow's Eve is a big deal for the Moonvale witches. My coven performs quite a few rituals."

She looked intrigued. "I thought you were a witch, but I didn't want to assume. You radiate magical energy. I've had quite a few friends who were witches. What kind of rituals?"

I glanced at the little ones. "Some are hard to explain. But we celebrate the year, thank the Old Gods for blessing us with magic, ask for continued use of magic, that sort of thing. The veil is the thinnest on Hallow's Eve."

Garren chimed in, "The fae celebrate the year as well, but we do so a little differently. There's usually a feast, as well as a party."

Tandor nodded his head. "Same with orcs. We celebrate our wilder tendencies."

A tiny voice chimed in—Cely, Rune and Garren's daughter. "Are we making cookies?"

Garren snorted. "Of course we are, Cely bug. Cookies are essential for a successful Hallow's Eve."

"Almond and brown sugar?" Tandor asked.

Rune nodded with a smile. "Only the best cookie in the entire realm."

Tandor nodded with a dreamy look on his face. "I remember those. It's been ages since I've had one."

The evening passed quickly, full of calm conversation and warm laughs. My stomach was pleasantly full.

Little Ash squealed, and then giggled with glee. I glanced in his direction.

My stomach bottomed out. *Shit!*

Hex escaped from their jar, again, and was creeping over the edge of the tiny boy's plate, absorbing a few grains of left-over rice. The little one was absolutely thrilled, for some reason, clapping his hands and squealing again.

I stood up from as fast as possible, nearly knocking my chair over. I leaned over and tried to scoop Hex up, but they turned to liquid in my grasp, simply dripping back down onto the table. I tried to scoop again but had no luck.

Stubborn familiar.

I gave up and plopped down onto my seat while Hex solidified and continued their rice feast.

Tandor cleared his throat. "Um, that's Hex," he said by way of explanation.

"Oh, right," I said. "That's my familiar. I'm sorry, they're very stubborn. And hungry, apparently."

The parents stared at Hex with expressions somewhere between shock and awe. "Your familiar?" Rune choked out.

I sighed heavily. "Yep. I haven't really learned how to control them yet. They just sort of... do whatever they want. Just ignore them, that's what I usually do." And try to forget they exist, most of the time.

Hex gurgled.

"Huh... Okay then," Garren said. He clapped his hands together. They shook slightly. "Who's ready for dessert?"

For such a warm, sunny town, Tidegrove was frigid at night. I flexed my fingers and toes to ensure they hadn't turned into icicles. Wind howled with a vengeance outside the small cottage-like inn room, looking for a way inside. It pushed against the windows, rattled the walls, sought cracks and weaknesses.

The temperature fell rapidly as the suns slipped past the horizon and the moons took their place, and I was forced to throw my cloak on top of my nightgown as I huddled in the bed for warmth.

There was a tiny hearth in the corner of the room, but it was broken, collapsed from the previous guests. If there was another room to occupy, I would've jumped at the chance of a room with a hearth, but the fates were against me.

I shivered so violently my muscles ached—my teeth nearly snapped from their chattering.

Tandor laid on the floor beside the bed with just a pillow, looking annoyingly calm. He had tugged his cloak on as well, but he looked perfectly normal. Not a shiver to be seen.

I remembered how deliciously *warm* he had been when I'd woken up snuggled next to him in Sunhaven. How his skin radiated heat. *Lucky bastard.*

My chattering teeth clacked loudly in the relative quiet, echoed only by the whirling wind outside.

I had forgotten how horrendously cold the nights on the coast could be.

I shuddered to think of how cold it would be in the mountains—where snow was constantly on the brink of falling and ice crystals lingered in the air. I would need to purchase something warmer to sleep in or find us somewhere with a roaring fire in the hearth.

Clack clack clack.

Even Hex was curled up tightly in the bottom of their jar, cradled in the center of my bag. I had checked on them before crawling into bed to make sure they weren't frozen solid.

"You sound like a woodpecker." Tandor's rich voice drifted up from the floor.

"Sh-shut up," I stuttered. I clamped my jaw shut to fight the chattering. "I forgot how freezing the coast gets."

"It's not so bad." I heard rustling, like he had turned on his side.

"Th-that's easy for you to say. You radiate more heat than a fire."

He chuckled quietly. "It's an orc thing."

I pulled the lightweight blanket over my head to try to find more warmth. It didn't help.

Eventually, I couldn't take it anymore. "Tandor?" I asked.

"Hmm?"

"Will you... will you get up here?"

"Kizzi, are you asking me to come to bed with you? I'm honored."

I huffed out a breath. "Never mind."

Without another word, Tandor stood from the floor, removed his cloak, grabbed his pillow, and slid into the bed.

He slipped under the sheet and spread his cloak over the thin blanket, then he laid perfectly still.

I felt the difference immediately. Delicious warmth seeped from his skin, crawling through the space under the blanket and thawing my frozen body. I scooted as close as I possibly could without touching him. Mere inches separated us.

Slowly, my taut muscles relaxed as Tandor's warmth drifted over me. I ached to shove my face into his side, tuck my feet between his legs, and curl my body around his—and I was pretty sure he would let me, with the love potion still lurking in his system—but I resisted the urge.

This was enough.

"You know I won't bite unless you ask, right? You can come closer," Tandor murmured.

I ignored him.

I ignored him until I couldn't resist the temptation anymore. Slowly, I rolled so my back faced him, and then I scooted over. Inch by inch.

He stayed where he was, perfectly still.

When my back brushed against his side, his delicious heat sinking directly through our clothes and into my skin, I sighed. My heartbeat thudded heavily in my chest. Tandor stopped breathing entirely.

I was *much* warmer, but I still wanted more.

Like he could read my mind, Tandor gently lifted his arm and tucked it around me, allowing me to rest my cheek on his bicep.

I was achingly aware of every inch of contact between us. Every brush of skin. Every rustle of fabric against fabric. I wasn't quite so tired anymore.

It took ages, but eventually, sleep claimed me.

CHAPTER 24

Tandor

I watched Kizzi as she weaved through the town's central market, hastily examining the wares at each stall before moving onto the next.

I couldn't help but notice the way her hips swayed, the way her hair lifted in the gentle breeze.

I was still reeling from last night. She had asked me to lie in the bed next to her. Used me for warmth. We *cuddled*. My heart sped just thinking about it. She needed my body heat, sure, but I couldn't help but hope that it might have been more than that.

Tidegrove's central market was wonderful—full of fragile-looking colorful tented stalls sporting all sorts of things for sale. There were food and drinks, clothing, odds and ends, and even pets. I warily eyed the vendor selling small furry rodents in wire cages, determining if I wanted to set the critters free or go and get one for myself.

The stalls changed every morning and packed up again every night. Some vendors returned daily, but some only returned occasionally. It was like a treasure hunt, finding what you were searching for.

I knew Kizzi was on the lookout for a massive cauldron, but she wouldn't tell me what else she was hoping to find. It prickled at me, not knowing. It got under my skin. I couldn't tell if it was the genuine curiosity or the strange ache to help, but something about it bothered me.

I asked her over and over, of course. She never cracked.

I picked up a few items for myself as I wandered through the market, but I never let Kizzi too far out of my sights. I found a lovely herb basket, a few small taster glasses for my cider brews, and some aged peppercorns that would make a great spicy addition to some of my recipes.

Kizzi had her arms full as well. She struggled to hold her items as she browsed, constantly dropping the new pair of soft boots she had purchased.

I couldn't resist—I had to help her.

I purchased a satchel she could toss over her shoulder to free her hands. I made my way over to where she stood, chatting quietly with a witch selling powdered ingredients.

The market was noisy, but as I neared, I caught the tail end of the conversation.

"—eggs?" Kizzi asked. "I don't need the whole egg, really, just the shell. But I would love to have the whole egg."

"Hmm. I don't know. Come back in a few days, Starla will be working then, she might have some."

Eggs? Like... bird eggs? Reptile eggs? She had to come all the way to Tidegrove for eggs? That doesn't make any sense...

Kizzi sighed. "Thank you," she caught sight of me and startled. "Oh, Tandor! Hello!"

"Enjoying your shopping?"

She didn't answer—she had clearly not expected my interruption.

Slowly, I reached out and grabbed the bounty from her arms. She looked bewildered, but she didn't stop me. I dropped her items into the satchel and then reached over to tuck the satchel strap onto her shoulder. With two pats to her upper arm, I gave her a light smile. "There, that's better."

She stared at me wide-eyed.

With a wave in her direction, I left the witch at the stall to go find the metalsmith.

My mind kept circling back to the conversation I had overheard. Why in the realms would she be so secretive about needing eggs?

The metalsmith was tucked in the far back corner of the market, away from the main hustle and bustle. Heat radiated from a small makeshift forge set up in the middle of the stall.

The human woman working the forge had her hair tied back in a tight knot and sweat dripping down her temples. She held a small knife over the flame with care, heating the metal to a glowing red.

I saw a few cast iron cauldrons spread throughout the tables. I wandered over to take a look. The first one was tiny— hardly larger than my hand. The second was not much bigger. The third cauldron, on the ground, only reached the height of my knee. Larger, but not large enough. I kept looking.

Knives, swords, and mallets were laid out in a decorative

display. I admired them for a moment before moving on with a shrug. *Who needs swords these days? There hasn't been a war since long before the Old Gods left the realm.*

"Can I help you find something?" the human asked as she carefully lowered the knife into a pot of water. The water sizzled as the metal slipped below the surface. She brushed her hands off on her trousers and turned to face me.

"Do you have any large cauldrons?" I asked.

She held her hand out to gesture to the cauldrons I already examined. "We have these."

I smiled but shook my head. "I'm afraid I need a *huge* cauldron. Those are nice, but they are far too small."

She lifted an eyebrow and looked me up and down. "Wow. You're looking for the serious stuff. Okay, follow me." She led me around the back of the tent to where a makeshift workshop resided. We stepped inside. "I have these, as well, but I'll warn you—they're not cheap."

I stepped inside to examine the larger cauldrons. They were certainly bigger. One was short and wide, spanning almost my arms breadth. Not right. Another was the perfect depth, but was bizarrely narrow, shaped more like a cup than a bowl. The third was close but it was not *quite* big enough. It was also made of copper, which was bizarre for a cauldron. Kizzi would have hated it.

The human watched my face closely. "Not seeing what you're looking for, eh?"

I smiled at her, flashing my tusks. "Not quite. You don't happen to have any more lying around? Something this size?" I held my arms out in a vague bowl shape.

She shook her head. "I'm afraid not. We don't really make them that big here. Maybe try the mountains?"

I nodded. "Thank you for the tip." I waved as I left, and the human resumed her work over the forge.

I returned to the center of the market, feeling mildly discouraged but also strangely excited.

The journey was not yet coming to an end.

I found Kizzi purchasing a pouch of sugar-coated almonds. The satchel slung over her shoulder was now bulging to an impressive degree. My cheeks lifted into a smile.

"No large cauldrons here," I said as a way of introduction as I stepped up behind her. "Well, none large enough."

She glanced up at me and then popped an almond into her mouth. I could hear the crunch as her teeth broke through the sugary coating. "Fates," she cursed, lifting her hand to shield her mouth from view. "I thought they would have them."

"Afraid not," I said. "They suggested we try the mountains."

She nodded thoughtfully. "I had a feeling that would be the answer." She wordlessly stuck out her hand, placing a few sugared almonds into my palm. She tossed another into her mouth and crunched on it. "We should hang around here for a few more days, I need to try the market again when new stalls open up."

"Still not going to tell me what you're searching for?" I asked.

"Nope." The word popped from her lips with a flair.

I hummed thoughtfully. "Is it eggs?"

Her jaw slackened and the blood drained from her face. She gulped. "No."

I pointed at her in triumph, my finger inches from the tip of her nose. "Aha! I knew it!"

She shoved my hand away. "You don't know anything!"

"I still don't know what kind of eggs," I said thoughtfully.

"Exactly. Maybe I need... butterfly eggs."

"You're lying."

She said nothing, just gnawed on her lower lip.

I sighed. "Fine, fine. Keep your secrets. I'll figure it out eventually."

She mumbled under her breath, so quietly I could hardly hear her, "Gods, I hope not."

The next handful of days passed with a pleasant swiftness.

We split our time between Rune's cottage, the town market, and the beach, walking along the shore for hours and hours, just listening to the waves crash along the sand.

Daisy was having the time of her life. She grazed on beach grasses to her heart's content, trotted through shallow waves, and soaked up as much attention as possible from Rune's littles, as well as any passersby.

She loved it here. My heart squeezed at the thought of snatching her from so much happiness, of forcing her to journey back through the Barren Lands, and drag the heavy carriage all the way back to Moonvale. Unfortunately, there was no other option.

The market stalls exchanged, but Kizzi never found what she was looking for—whatever eggs she needed were elusive and hard to track down.

Every day, we tried again.

No luck.

I could see the way she withered as each day passed without finding what she was looking for, the hopeful gleam draining from her eyes.

When the fourth day rolled around and the witch Kizzi was waiting for had no eggs either, we decided to abandon Tidegrove and move on, toward the mountains.

CHAPTER 25

Kizzi

The carriage bustle was becoming strangely soothing. The rocking, bumping motions, once jarring, blurred into the background. My side pressed into Tandor became a familiar comfort, rather than an irritation. Something to lean into instead of move away from.

The horse walked slower than before, but it wasn't for lack of energy.

It seemed like a heavy sadness was weighing her down. Guilt had tugged at my stomach when we finally hooked her up to the carriage and tugged on her reins. She had let out the saddest whinny and her head drooped. She was certainly pouting.

We had no other option, though.

The air cooled as we ventured away from the breezy, beachy coast toward the more harsh and rugged climate of the mountains.

My breath fogged out in front of me.

The journey took two days, and we stopped at whatever inn we could find along the way.

And every time, we ended up in the same bed, Tandor helping me to stay warm. Somewhere along the way we stopped feeling embarrassed about it. It became normal. Tandor never pushed it any further than simply sharing body heat, even when I would have allowed him to. Would have begged him to. Would have done so myself.

The thought of the love potion nagged at me. Over and over, I wished that I had never dosed the entire town with the spiked chili. That I had never bent Tandor's will. That he was himself, still on the journey with me, but because he *chose* to be.

I didn't like having to wonder if his kindness, his helpfulness, his generosity, was real, or simply a product of a love-potion-addled mind.

Once I found the dragon eggs and cured Tandor, then I could take a closer look at... whatever was brewing between us. I could examine this strange warmth in my chest, and this bubbling sensation in my stomach.

I let my arm brush against Tandor's without pulling away. I let his warmth seep into me, let it thaw my frozen bones and soften my nerves.

Hex sat curled up on the orc's lap, soaking up his warmth as much as I was. Hex had softened to Tandor with annoying swiftness. They still hissed and snapped at me more often than not, but they curled up next to Tandor like a pampered pet. It was fucking ridiculous. *Damned familiar.*

The winding road to Rockward narrowed as we neared the mountains. The softly bending paths turned into rolling hills, which turned into spiking peaks.

The poor horse struggled with the incline—our journey slowed to a crawl.

We weren't the only ones entering the mountains, either. A handful of horse riders trotted the path in front of us. A beacon on the horizon. A target to aim for.

The air cooled even further.

I was accustomed to Moonvale's freeze season, to bundling up in a thick, fluffy cloak, and to hustling indoors as soon as possible to avoid frostbite. Luckily, Moonvale was small enough to walk from end to end rather quickly.

We weren't so lucky, here. This cold was another beast entirely.

I sank further and further into Tandor's side, desperate to absorb as much of his body heat as possible. His radiating warmth was delicious—I wanted to curl up and crawl inside his skin.

I settled for curling up against his side instead.

Eventually, when my chattering teeth became unbearable, Tandor released a deep, shuddering breath.

The orc scooped Hex up in one hand and, with the other, tugged me onto his lap. My pulse jumped in my chest. His arms cradled my sides, clutching the reins as his body surrounded me. He set Hex down on top of me, where they promptly settled back into a relaxed pile.

I could feel Tandor subtly shaking.

He was everywhere. His warmth, his smell. Even his cloak surrounded me like a blanket.

"Hang on, little witch. We're almost there." Tandor's smooth voice slid past my ear like a caress.

"If I turn into an icicle and die, please bring a cauldron back to the coven for me. They're counting on it." My clacking teeth made my words almost indecipherable.

His arms tightened on my sides. "Oh, hush. You're not going to freeze. It's not that cold."

"Are you j-joking?!" I exclaimed. "My fingers have been numb for hours!"

He released the reins with one hand and swept both of my hands in his grasp. The relief was instant. Tandor stiffened. "Gods almighty! Maybe you *are* going to freeze. Your fingers are *cold*."

"Told you."

We stayed that way for ages—with him clutching the reins with one hand, and my icy fingers in the other, the cauldron sludge curled up between us.

My numb fingers slowly regained sensation. It started with a pins-and-needles feeling, which faded into a mild burning, which eventually eased into blissful warmth.

I sighed in relief. "Oh Gods, that's so much better," I murmured.

He chuckled under his breath. "Stick with me, princess. I'll keep you warm."

I ignored the "princess" comment and leaned further into his embrace. The rock of the road and the comforting warmth lulled me into an unexpected sleep.

My eyes flew open when the carriage wheels dropped into a particularly jarring hole.

My heart rate rocketed in my chest for a moment before it settled and I realized where I was: in the cramped carriage, tucked in Tandor's embrace, rolling into the mountain city of Rockward.

Frost clung to my eyelashes in icy crystals.

Rockward sprawled in front of us like a painting—impossibly picturesque and beautiful. I scrubbed my eyes with my fists to make sure I wasn't dreaming.

Awe bled through me.

The town was nestled into a small mountain valley, cradled on all sides by snow-capped peaks. The road leading to the city was sloped, and the path overlooked everything.

The buildings looked as small as bugs from a distance. Tiny log cabins were dotted sporadically. Some clustered in groups, some seemed to be miles away. The central town was more packed together. Lingering snow dusted every surface— I could tell it hardly melted here.

The dual suns sank toward the horizon, preparing to slip away for the night. The sky was painted a mesmerizing red color.

Tandor's body heat kept me from feeling the brunt of the cold, but as soon as I straightened and leaned away from him to get a better look, the cold seeped straight into my bones. I immediately leaned back into the orc again, uncaring of whether I should or shouldn't. His arms grasping the reins tightened around me.

"Holy fucking shit," I mumbled through chattering teeth, staring at the scene spread out in front of us.

Tandor snorted. His head dipped slightly so his chin settled on top of my head. "You have such a way with words."

I nudged him in the stomach. "I'm just saying. It's stunning."

"Yeah. It really is," he murmured appreciatively. He

tugged on the reins, bringing the carriage to a halt so we could enjoy the scene for a moment longer.

It really was breathtaking. The way light glinted off the ice, fracturing into tiny rainbows. The way the mountain peaks stretched so high, so far off into the distance that I couldn't tell where they ended.

Even the air smelled icy and cold, in a pleasant sort of way. It stung my nose but settled with a crisp almost sweetness. Like snow and fresh hay, with a hint of pine.

Hex crawled up onto my shoulder and stretched. They might have been nearly frozen, but they wanted a peek at the scenery too. I curled my hand around them to offer some warmth. I knew how much it sucked being cold, and being a liquid (sort of), they would probably freeze solid if we weren't careful. Even if they were made of magic.

Hex snapped at me for a moment, but then softened, leaning into my touch.

For some reason, that made me feel strangely accomplished. Almost... warm.

Damn familiar was making me go soft.

An owl hooted in the distance. I wondered what it was trying to communicate. Was it hunting, claiming its territory, or simply calling out to see if another would respond?

After long, peaceful moments, the carriage descended into Rockward. Daisy moved as slow as a snail—every step was a massive effort. The carriage creaked and rattled.

Rockward didn't have a central inn. Instead, visiting guests could rent a cottage to stay in, or a tent. The portable tented structures were extremely popular due to their ease and convenience. The structures could be placed on top of the rock without the need for any digging into the mountain surface. They were set on wooden platforms, with tarped walls and large central fireplaces.

Heating enchantments were particularly popular in the mountain regions, for obvious reasons. I brewed many of them for my traveling customers.

We left the carriage at the stables and ushered the horse into the surprisingly warm barn. She wandered in slowly, her head drooping in relief, almost low enough to brush the ground. I patted her on the rump as she passed. "Cheer up, girl. We'll be heading home soon." I could've sworn that her head sank even lower as she neighed quietly.

It was becoming normal, settling my things into a new space with Tandor. Comfortable. We left our newly purchased items in the carriage (after bribing the stableboy to protect them) and dragged our packs into a surprisingly roomy tent.

We hadn't even bothered asking for two separate rooms—we told each other it was to save silvers, because we already shared a room together for multiple nights, a few more wouldn't hurt anyone.

And secretly, I just liked being around him.

I glanced surreptitiously over my shoulder to find Tandor leaning his hands onto the bed, testing the strength of it. He nodded to himself, looking satisfied as the fluffy surface bounced back under his weight. I suppressed a smile.

The room was tallest in the center, the tarped ceiling opening at a point to let the smoke from the fire drift to the skies. Embers smoldered in a brick fire pit, crackling and popping, whispering secrets. We would have to start a better fire before night swept in, chasing away any lingering warmth, but for now it was bearable.

I knelt and placed Hex's jar on the ground, close enough to the fire pit to feel the warmth but not close enough to burn. It didn't matter where I placed the jar, really. Hex would simply escape and find a new place to settle. I tried not to think about that too closely.

Hex still made me nervous. Scary, magical bitch. Er, familiar.

"I still can't believe your slime friend is just... traveling with us," Tandor mused as he tucked his bag into the chest in the corner and tightened his cloak across his throat.

My eyes caught the movement of his hands, fumbling with the cloak's clasp. His fingers were strong and sure, but he struggled with the fabric, being too hasty with it. Too hurried.

My own cloak was tied securely over my shoulders over top of my thickest layers of clothing. The hood was even yanked up to protect my ears—my ears were always more susceptible to the cold.

I shrugged. "I couldn't just leave them behind." I glanced at the jar of sludge with a strange surge of affection. "Believe me, I tried."

He hummed in contemplation. "I believe you. I wouldn't want to be on the bad side of the magical concoction."

Hex simmered at that. I couldn't tell if that was a bad reaction... or a pleased one. I had the strange sense that they were feeling prideful. Glad to be feared.

My stomach growled, the sound echoing through the quiet room. I patted at it. Embarrassing.

The corner of Tandor's mouth lifted. "I think it's about time we wander out into the cold and find something to eat. What do you say?"

I grimaced and tugged my hood tighter around my face. "Are you sure you don't want to just let me curl up by the fire? You can bring me back something." I cracked my sweetest smile.

He barked out a laugh. "Not a chance. We're in this together, princess." He nodded to the jar on the floor. "Bring Hex too. I think it's about time you tell me some of your stories."

I groaned. "Fine. But you're paying."

A massive fireplace crackled in the corner of the brick building, casting a warm orange glow over the dining patrons. Large sconces were dotted along the walls, with more fires dancing in invisible winds. The flames were not enough to overpower the intense darkness, and shadows crept along the floors. Instead of being eerie, the effect was cozy. Snug. It made the room feel protected and private.

Dim light danced over the skin of Kizzi's face, creating shadows. Under her eye, below her cheek. Carving out the shape of her bones. I ached to reach a hand out and run my fingers over her smooth skin. To see if I could feel the shadows, if they would cling to my skin the way they slipped over hers.

She was art, this little witch. A beauty that made my stomach ache.

If she noticed me staring, she did nothing to stop me.

Her eyes flitted around the room. She took in every detail, never lingering long in one place before glancing to the next folk, the next movement. She was easily distractible. It amused me—watching her be herself. Watching her sit and relax and observe a room.

When her gaze finally made it back to mine, she startled slightly, as though she had forgotten I was there. A blush crept into her cheeks and a shy smile tugged at her mouth, but she held my eyes. We stared at each other for long moments, and even my own face began to feel warm.

"Another mulled wine?" a voice interrupted our moment.

Reluctantly, I dragged my eyes away from the witch and toward the vampire woman that had spoken. "Yes, please. Extra cinnamon."

She nodded politely. "And you?" she asked Kizzi with a warm smile.

"What? Oh, more wine, sure. Yes. Please." She cleared her throat and sat up straighter in her chair.

I quirked an eyebrow at her as the vampire flitted off toward the kitchen. "Is the wine getting to you, little witch?" I tsked. "You usually hold your alcohol much better than this." I raised the nearly empty mug to my mouth and took a sip, draining it to its dregs. Bits of cinnamon followed the wine as it dripped into my mouth, and I held it there to catch every morsel. The perfect spice to counteract the rich fruity taste. The drink was no longer hot, having cooled to a mild warmth, but it was still delicious.

"I don't know what you're talking about," Kizzi mumbled. She picked up a piece of bread and tore a chunk off. She didn't eat it—she merely squished it between her fingers.

"Sure," I laughed under my breath. "I can always carry you home, if you're too unsteady on your feet."

The blush that crept to her ears was extremely satisfying. I couldn't fight the smile that forced its way onto my face.

"That won't be necessary. Like I said, I'm fine."

The vampire returned with two fresh, steaming mugs and placed them on the table next to our nearly empty plates. Kizzi grabbed her mug immediately, tossing the bit of bread she had balled up in Hex's direction and instead wrapping her delicate fingers around the drink.

Hex slithered out of the jar to snatch up the bit of bread and absorb it. It was slightly terrifying—I tried not to wonder what else they were capable of engulfing. I glanced around the room to see if anyone had witnessed the ordeal, but the room was too dim, and the nearest patrons were paces away. Just us, then.

We sipped our drinks in charged silence as the noise of the diner flowed around us. We pretended like we weren't watching each other.

Our eyes played a game of cat and mouse, and I wasn't sure if I was the predator or the prey.

Eventually, I forced myself to speak. I cleared my throat. "So, Kizzi. Do you think we're going to find what you're looking for tomorrow?"

She contemplated this as she ran her tongue slowly over her upper lip. I tracked the movement. A hunger bit at my insides.

"I hope so," she said finally. "I have a good feeling."

This intrigued me. "Oh? What do you mean?"

She shrugged noncommittally. "I'm not sure, really." She glanced around the room as though looking for something. Eventually, her gaze settled onto Hex, where they sat on the edge of the table, resting contently in their jar. "It's just this...

feeling. A knowing, almost. A slight charge to the air, a bit of a pull. It's on the wind, maybe."

This made absolutely no sense to me, but I found it fascinating, nonetheless. I knew witches were more in tune with magic than other folk. Of course. Orcs were generally not very magically inclined at all—even less so than humans. I had heard magic described, I had read about it once or twice, but I would never actually get to know it. To *feel* it.

Back before the Old Gods abandoned the realm, they say magic was so prevalent that most folk could sense it. Use it, even. Access it and manipulate it. What a wondrous time that must have been.

"Well, I hope you're right," I mused. "Any other towns to try if you have no luck here?"

She shook her head. "Not anywhere we'll reach before Hallow's Eve, I don't think. We're going to be cutting it close as it is."

I held out my mug. "Well, here's to good feelings, then."

She tapped her mug to mine with a small smile. "To good feelings."

My hand crept to the small of Kizzi's back as we wandered back to our tent for the night. She didn't need me to guide her, but I couldn't help myself. I simply wanted to touch her.

Surprisingly, she let me. I could almost feel the warmth of her through the fabric of her cloak. My fingertips pressed in just a bit harder.

The moons were high in the sky, shockingly bright from our valley in the mountains. Fireflies sparkled all around us. If I reached out, I could surely catch one, but I preferred to leave my hand right where it was.

We walked slowly in the direction of the tent. My breath fogged out in cloud-like puffs in front of me. If I was this cold, surely Kizzi would be freezing. I glanced at her with concern. She looked tense, but she didn't speed up her pace.

"Sure you don't need me to carry you?" I asked.

She shot me a glare. "Very funny. My feet work just fine, thank you."

I slid my hand around to her hip and tugged her closer to me, ever so slightly. "I know they do."

She simply rolled her eyes, but she let her body brush against mine for the rest of the chilly walk.

The tent was disappointingly warm when we tucked ourselves inside. I fastened the tarp closed with the provided straps.

I was hoping the cold would drive Kizzi into my arms again and force her to wrap her body around mine. To cuddle up against me, and to tuck herself perfectly under my chin.

I considered tugging the tarp open, just a crack, but dismissed the idea almost immediately. Her comfort was more important than my sordid fantasies.

I double knotted the straps.

A small fire crackled steadily in the fire pit. A metal grate covered the pit. The light was dim, but the warmth radiated well enough.

"Turn around," Kizzi said quietly. "I need to change into my nightclothes."

With a start, I realized that there was nowhere to go for

privacy in this tent. A small partition separated the main room from the washbasin, but the rest of the space was open.

Heat suddenly flooded my veins at the thought of Kizzi removing her clothes. I cleared my throat. "Of course." My voice was gravel.

I turned and stared at the canvas wall. My ears perked at every sound, every rustle of fabric, every brush of skin against skin. It was torture, being here, *knowing* she was undressing, but not being able to do anything about it.

My cock swelled painfully in my trousers, and I was suddenly thankful that I was facing the other direction and she wouldn't be able to see it.

I was frozen, barely breathing.

Eventually, her soft feet padded across the floor, and she slipped into bed. I remained where I was, rooted in place.

My heart thundered in my chest. I silently begged it to slow.

She laughed quietly, and my cock hardened even further. "You can move now. It's safe."

It took long moments for her words to break through my haze of lust, but eventually, I forced myself to move. I cleared my throat twice before I could speak. "Right. Yes. I guess I'll just—" I let the half-formed thought drift away as I shuffled to my bag in the corner. I kept my back facing the bed as I unfastened my cloak and let it drop from my shoulders. I tossed it onto the floor.

I glanced toward the bed to find Kizzi watching me, her eyes gleaming in the darkness. She had the blanket pulled up so high that it was covering her nose, and only the top half of her face was peeking out. Her witch eyes were not as keen as mine, but she still had decent vision. She could see me perfectly fine. I smiled wickedly.

"You can watch, if you'd like," I murmured as I slowly reached for the laces of my tunic.

"I would never," she said quietly, but her eyes never closed. Never looked away.

I untied the neck of my tunic and tugged on the laces to loosen them. Slowly, trying my best to look sensual and not awkward, I grabbed the hem and tugged the garment over my head. It was a bit chilly with so much skin exposed, but not uncomfortable. The blanket on the bed would keep me plenty warm.

I tossed the tunic aside, not caring where it landed. I shucked my boots off and kicked them aside too.

Next, I reached for my trousers, relieved to find that my cock had softened enough to not jut vulgarly from my body. I tried not to think about Kizzi's eyes feasting on my flesh— that thought threatened to send my blood racing again.

I unfastened the button and let my trousers slip down my thighs. They pooled around my feet.

A quiet inhale of breath from the bed let me know that the little witch was still watching.

I stood for a moment in just my undershorts, debating if I wanted to don my sleep pants. I would be uncomfortably warm if I did, but they would add an extra layer between Kizzi and me.

Did I want an extra layer between us? Absolutely the fuck not. But did she?

I could still feel her eyes boring into my back, nearly burning me with their intensity.

I decided to take a risk.

I kicked the trousers aside and strode to the washbasin, quickly washing my hands and mouth. When I turned to the bed, Kizzi's eyes were closed, but she was breathing too quickly. Her lids were clenched too tightly.

She was faking.

I cracked a grin. Sneaky witch.

I poked the fire and slid the grate aside until the flames were low but steady, and most of the light was blocked out. Darkness ascended. There was enough glow to see by, but only just.

I made my way to my side of the bed and slipped under the covers.

Kizzi didn't move a muscle. She remained perfectly still as though she were made of stone. Tense, rapidly breathing stone practically vibrating with restrained energy.

I turned on my side to face her. The bed was warm from her body heat, and her sweet apple scent delicately perfumed the air.

For long moments I just watched her. The side of her face, the slope of her nose, the way her upper lip flicked out just slightly. Her eyelashes draped across her cheek like feathers.

I began to feel drowsy, but the desire to stare at her pretty profile overrode my desire for sleep.

After a long time, she sighed and rolled to face me. Her eyes flicked open and narrowed slightly. Accusatorily. She tucked one of her hands under the pillow to rest below her cheek. I was jealous of that hand.

Beneath the blanket, her foot crept forward and brushed against my shin. Barely, just a butterfly's wing against my skin. But it was more than nothing.

The bed was large enough that we wouldn't touch accidentally.

Hesitantly, I let my hand drift toward her. The rustle of the blanket was quiet, only rivaled by the sound of crackling embers, critters chirping in the distance, and our breathing.

Her breaths halted when my fingertips made contact. They danced along the curve of her hip, where it dipped into her waist. I froze for a moment to see if she would push me away. If she would retreat.

She didn't.

I let the weight of my hand settle onto her hip. The fabric of her nightshirt was soft and smooth, but I ached for the feel of her skin.

Our eyes bored into each other in the darkness. Her gaze smoldered.

When Kizzi breathed again, it was on a sharp inhale as my hand sought the hem of her nightshirt and slid beneath it. Her skin was warm and even silkier than I imagined. I let my hand rest there on her hip, content to just feel her skin on mine. I allowed my fingertips to wander only slightly, drifting around her hip to the small of her back.

I ached to grab onto her, to yank her into me, to shove my face against her soft flesh, but I resisted. If this was all she allowed, it would be enough.

My fingertips tingled where they touched her.

I let my eyes drift closed as my fingertips continued their gentle stroke over Kizzi's hip.

I wouldn't push the witch any further. I didn't want her to flee.

A frog croaked somewhere in the distance, a soothing, distracting rhythm.

The blankets rustled quietly as Kizzi moved. I was sure she would pull away, would roll away from me, but my heart jumped in my chest when I realized that wasn't the case.

She inched toward me. Only slightly. The space between us was shrinking—she was close enough that I could feel her breath drifting across my face. My hand slipped lower, spanning the width of her lower back. I gently dug my fingertips into the muscle there, but I didn't pull her closer. Not yet.

Her foot snaked out again, brushing my shin. A teasing stroke. When I shifted slightly, she slipped her foot over my leg and hooked her heel around my calf. She tugged, just a bit.

A low, quiet laugh rumbled from my chest.

I kept my eyes closed, content to let her torture me in the darkness. Using my hand on her back, I dragged her closer, but not all the way. Precious inches still separated our bodies.

She would have to be the one to make the move. This push and pull between us was addictive, but it was fragile, and I didn't want to shatter it.

I could almost feel her pulse thumping beneath her skin. Or perhaps that was mine, thundering so hard it was throbbing in my fingertips.

Something soft and delicate brushed over my collarbone. Her fingers, I realized. A smile pulled at my mouth. I allowed her to explore for a moment, her touch drifting over my shoulder, down my arm where it bent at the elbow, and back again, to the divot on top of my collarbone. A shiver worked down my spine.

"Nice outfit," she whispered, her words caressing me in the darkness.

"You like this one, huh?" I asked, teasing. "It's one of my best."

"Mhm," she hummed in response. "Looks good on you."

"I thought you liked it, the way you were practically stroking me with your eyes."

She snorted in mock outrage, grasping a lock of my hair and tugging on it. "I did no such thing!" She allowed her leg to slip further, her knee sliding up to rest on the side of my thigh as her calf curled around the back of my leg.

"I know what I saw, princess."

My eyes flipped open as I slid my hand up her spine to the center of her back. Her skin was so smooth, it begged to be caressed. Every inch deserved to be stroked, kissed, worshipped.

I wondered, idly, if she would ever let me. I was surely getting ahead of myself.

Her eyes followed her fingers as they lazily drifted over my skin and traced invisible patterns. Her cheeks were flushed, her lips swollen as though she had been biting on them.

I had to swallow a groan at the sight of her flushed face. Maybe, miraculously, she was as affected by this as I was.

With a tug, I pulled her to me, closing the space between our bodies.

She gasped and gripped my shoulder as her front plastered to mine, as her knee slipped from my leg to settle back on the bed, and as my bulging erection pressed into her stomach. I ignored it, and I prayed to the Old Gods that she would too. There was no avoiding it—I ached to press my skin to hers.

Her gaze snapped to mine and held, her lips dropping open to form a silent O. Her eyebrows lifted slightly.

Our faces were mere inches apart. We breathed each other's air as our hearts thundered in battling rhythms and her heat seared my skin.

On a sweet exhale, she tilted her face and closed her eyes, her mouth softening to an inviting pout.

It was all the invitation I needed.

I softly pressed my lips to hers. I braced myself for her to pull away, but to my immense relief, she didn't. Miraculously, she kissed me back. Her lips were impossibly soft as they stroked against mine. The smell of her was everywhere, apples and honey and perfection. I inhaled it greedily as I deepened the kiss.

My left hand remained on her back, while I slipped my right one beneath us to cradle her head. Her hair flowed over my fingers in soft curls as I hooked my thumb under her jaw, angling her face for better access. She fit in my hands perfectly, like she was made for me.

Her lips parted on an exhale that was somewhere between a sigh and a groan. The sound was *everything*. I wanted to hear that sound again and again.

I stroked my tongue against her lower lip. She shivered, and I relished the way I could feel it as it traveled down her body.

Her tongue met mine, tentatively at first, but then urgently. Passionately. Our tongues danced together in a delicious rhythm as we devoured each other. My cock throbbed where it was pressed to Kizzi's stomach, begging for friction, but I ignored it. I forced the lower half of my body to remain still so I could enjoy the taste of the little witch for as long as possible.

Kizzi snaked her arm around my neck, pulling her body closer to mine, smashing her breasts against my chest. I growled in appreciation.

I rolled our bodies, pressing her into the bed as I loomed

over her, careful to hold my weight up with my knees on either side of her hips and a hand above her head. My other hand was free to roam.

Her hair was a wild sprawl beneath her, her green curls tangling.

I dragged my mouth from her lips, across her jaw, to her small, pointed ear. I ran my mouth over her ear and allowed my teeth to drag over the edge. A sharp exhale escaped her lips. I smiled and laughed quietly when she dug her nails into my skin. I kissed her ear a few more times before moving my ministrations to her throat, scraping my teeth over her impossibly soft skin. I lingered when she squirmed, paying attention to the spots that evoked the strongest reaction.

Her hands left my shoulders and slipped to the collar of her nightshirt, fumbling with the buttons. When I realized what she was doing, wicked glee flooded me.

I batted her hands away. "No. Let me."

"Okay," she breathed, her exhales heavy and panting.

Slowly, fumbling with only one hand, I unbuttoned the soft shirt. I ran my fingers over each new inch of skin I exposed. I ached to kiss it. With a relish, I realized that I could.

So I did.

As I unbuttoned her shirt, I dragged my lips over her skin, allowing my small tusks to scratch lightly. I kissed a path over her sternum, between her breasts, over her stomach. Inch by decadent inch, I descended. She squirmed beneath me, her hands fluttering over my shoulders, my chest, my head.

When I got to the last button, I hesitated, taking a deep breath and glancing up at her face. She was watching me with hooded eyes, her lips parted. She nodded frantically.

I allowed the fabric to open, sliding off her body to reveal her torso to me.

I groaned in appreciation at the goddess sprawled on the bed below me.

Her skin sloped in perfect curves. Her stomach was beautifully soft, and I ached to sink my teeth into it. She crossed her arms over her chest to cover herself, but when I shot her a heated glare, she dropped her arms back to the bed.

"Let me look at you," I begged.

And look I did. My eyes feasted upon her body, upon her full breasts that settled onto her chest and her gorgeous, pert nipples that tightened in the cool night air.

"Tandor," she said quietly, lifting her hands to grasp her breasts, covering herself from my view.

"You are stunning," I groaned, shoving her hands away and lowering my face to her throat. I kissed her neck again, letting my hand drift to her breast. I kneaded the soft flesh in my hand and she moaned, arching her back. She grasped my shoulders tightly.

"So soft," I murmured. I kissed her neck again. Her collarbone. Her sternum. "So pretty."

A soft, wordless sigh escaped her mouth.

I grasped her breasts with both hands, the full weight of them perfect in my palms. "So pretty," I repeated. I kissed the curve of breast and slid my thumbs over her taut nipples. She writhed beneath me. "And so sweet," I murmured as I lowered my mouth to one of her nipples, rolling it with my tongue as I continued to tease the other with my thumb.

"Tandor," she said again, a plea this time. I relished the sound of my name on her mouth. Nothing sounded better than my name drenched in her pleasure.

I hummed against her skin, lightly biting at her. I repeated my ministrations on her other breast, dragging my teeth over her nipple and enjoying the way it made her squirm.

"Tandor," she sighed.

"Yes, princess. Say my name again."

I shifted my weight, kissing the underside of her breasts as I ran my hands down her sides. I gripped her hips as I kissed a trail down her stomach.

I tossed the blanket off the bed to get it out of the way.

I was dying to taste her. To *really* taste her. To lavish my tongue between her legs and make her scream. Make her shatter.

Her legs fell open, parting slightly as I settled my knees on the floor beside the bed. I kissed her stomach again, biting at the soft flesh there. She squeaked with a jolt.

I continued my path, kissing my way onto her hips, where her bones were hard beneath her skin, onto the softly rounded flesh of her lower stomach. I slipped my fingers under the waistband of her sleep pants. I tugged on the fabric.

She lifted her hips to help me.

The pants slid down an inch. Two.

An owl cooed from outside, startlingly loud in the quiet of the tent.

"Tandor," she said again, more clearly this time.

I glanced up at her face. "I'll take care of you," I breathed. "I've got you. Let me make you feel good."

She groaned and clenched her eyes shut tight. "Wait."

I froze, my muscles turning to stone. "What is it, Kiz?"

"Just wait." She scrubbed her hands over her face and ran them through her hair. With a grumbling sigh, she reached down and tugged her pants back into place.

I slowly rose to my feet. "What's going on? Are you okay?"

Kizzi met my eyes, and her face was conflicted. Tormented. "You don't want this," she said.

What the fuck? My eyebrows shot to my hairline, and I glanced down at my crotch, where my cock was painfully hard and nearly oozing with pre cum. "I want this."

"Trust me, you don't." She buttoned her nightshirt back up with her face screwed into a pained scowl.

I stepped forward and gently grasped her hands, stilling her motions. "You have no idea how much I want this, Kizzi." I fought the urge to spill my guts to her—to let her know just how much I wanted her. How long I had wanted her. How deeply, how soul-achingly I wanted her. I was sure that confession would scare her away.

Her expression cracked and her eyes watered. "You don't."

"What are you talking about? I want this. I want *you*. If *you* don't want this, it's okay. We can stop. We can back up. We can slow down. Whatever you need." I was practically begging her, pleading with her not to withdraw from me. I could sense her slipping away, building up her walls.

She shook her head furiously and grabbed the blanket from the floor, pulling it over her as she flopped on her side and curled up into a ball.

"It's not that," she choked out with a watery voice. "It's not that, Tandor."

I stood at the foot of the bed, confused and vaguely hurt. "Talk to me, Kiz. What's going on?"

"I can't." She sniffled quietly and her voice quivered. "I can't explain right now."

"Please," I begged. "You can talk to me. Whatever it is, I'll listen."

My heart felt cold, and my hands felt even colder. The immediate loss of her warmth was jarring.

I slowly climbed back into the bed, staying on the far edge so I wouldn't crowd her. She stayed where she was. The distance was small, but it might as well have been miles.

Long moments passed while our breathing settled, and she sniffled quietly in the dark.

"I'm sorry," she whispered.

"You don't have to be sorry," I insisted. "Whatever it is, I just want to know what you're thinking."

"I'm so sorry," she repeated.

My mind whirled at the swift change. My thoughts churned. Had I done something wrong? Had I pushed her too far? Had she never wanted this in the first place? Lead settled into my gut. I felt sick.

We fell asleep like that, sharing a bed with a chasm between us.

<h1 style="text-align:center">CHAPTER 27
Kizzi</h1>

Guilt gnawed at my stomach like acid. I couldn't even enjoy the cocoa coffee beverage that Tandor had brought me, tentatively leaving it beside the bed when I refused to get up while he was watching me.

I didn't know how to face him.

I had gotten carried away last night, lost in the enjoyment of the evening, the warmth of his presence, the comfortable familiarity.

I had almost let him have his way with me. Gods, how I wanted him to have his way with me. I would have let that orc do whatever he wanted; I was putty in his hands.

And then I remembered the love potion.

I yanked the blanket over my head to wallow in my misery.

For a split second, I almost fucked him anyway. Did that make me a monster? Maybe. But *Gods.*

Guilt and pleasure fought for dominance as I remembered the way Tandor had kissed me, the way he dragged his hands over my skin, the way he...

I scrubbed my hands over my face with a groan.

Monster. Definitely a monster.

He didn't *actually* want to be with me. It was just the love potion warping his mind, influencing his free will, taking away his choices. And I couldn't even tell him about it. Because if I admitted that I accidentally drugged him, he would never forgive me.

And I wanted him to forgive me. Oh, how I wanted him to forgive me. A secret, sick part of me hoped that once Tandor was cured, and was no longer influenced by the love potion, that he would want me anyway.

That he would still be sweet to me, and kind to me, and flirty to me.

And would still want to toss me around and drag his teeth over my skin.

Maybe... just maybe...

And if not, I would shove the feelings down, go back to being his friend, and accept the fact that I was the dumbest bitch in the entire realm.

After long miserable minutes, I dragged myself out of bed. The cool air punched me immediately. I picked up the mug of cocoa coffee and gave it a sniff. It smelled incredible, bitter and sweet in a perfect harmony. It was still a bit warm.

I drank the beverage greedily, enjoying every single swallow, ignoring the way it churned in my stomach.

My heart twinged when I thought about the orc that had brought it to me.

Did he want to bring it to me, or did the love potion make him do it?

The cocoa roiled, threatening to reappear.

I dragged myself to my bag to change clothes. I took advantage of the washbasin in the corner, getting myself in order, trying to look presentable even though darkness ringed my eyes from my fitful night of sleep. I fastened a chain around my neck, a new necklace I bought myself in Tidegrove.

I glanced around the room. Tandor hadn't returned, but the fire was stoked. He had tended to it that morning, even though I knew he wasn't cold.

Love potion? Real kindness? I wanted to throw up. I couldn't take the uncertainty anymore.

Hex sat in their jar, curled up in the bottom. They looked almost as sad as I was. I picked up the jar. "Hi," I said quietly. I pulled the lid off and set it aside.

Hex stirred and let a bubble pop.

I sighed. "I know, buddy."

Hex slowly slid out of the jar and onto my hand.

"You really think so? I'm not sure..."

I placed them onto my shoulder where they nestled into my hair. I briefly worried that they would get stuck in the curly strands.

That would be a future problem.

I slipped out of the tent and into the bright, cold air. I missed the tent's warmth immediately.

I missed Tandor's warmth even more.

Speaking of Tandor, the orc was perched on the corner of the tent platform, braiding together strands of grass. There was a small pile of braids on the platform next to him, as though he had been waiting for ages.

Nausea churned in my gut.

He stood up slowly, quickly brushing the grass aside and

dusting his hands on his trousers. He gave me a tentative wave. "Good morning," he said.

I tried to force a smile onto my cheeks, but my face felt like plaster. "Good morning."

He nodded curtly. "Want to talk about it?" he asked. Hope lifted his brows.

I grimaced and shook my head. "I'm sorry," I said simply. I couldn't string any other words together to depict my tattered thoughts.

His face fell. "Whenever you're ready to speak, I'm ready to listen."

I swallowed tightly. "Thank you."

He nodded, sticking his hand out to gesture in front of him. The same hands that had trailed over my skin last night. I yanked my gaze away.

"After you," he said. "Let's go find some cauldrons and secret ingredients."

An ember of hope burned in my chest. A cure. If I could find a cure, I could know for sure.

"Let's," I agreed. I strode in front of him into town, following the flow of folk into the market.

My fingers danced over sparkling stones and crystals, admiring their unique shine.

The mountain mines surrounding Rockward produced the most beautiful stones and the rarest gems. Folk traveled from the far reaches of the realm for the chance to mine their own sparkling treasures alongside the reclusive mining gnomes.

I knew the ironwork shop down the road should have been my first target, but I could admit it—I was stalling.

And I was a sucker for a pretty crystal.

My attention caught on a particularly lovely geodite sphere. I picked it up, tossing it between my palms. The stone radiated a strange magical energy. Something that felt wise and ancient. Like if I held it long enough, a few strands of my hair would turn silver.

The shopkeeper noticed my attention. "A good choice," the old man murmured. He nodded sagely. "I see it has chosen you as much as you have chosen it."

I glanced at him warily. He could sense that? Perhaps he was a wizard—it was hard to be certain. I couldn't tell if he oozed magic, or if the shop was overwhelming my senses. "I thought it was pretty."

His wrinkled cheeks lifted into a smile. "Of course. Usually, this one would cost four silvers, but you're special. Two silvers, please."

"Oh, I'll pay four," I insisted. I fumbled around in my satchel and placed the coins on the counter. "I like to support my fellow businessfolk."

He simply tilted his head before turning around and returning to his rearrangement of the shelves.

What a peculiar interaction.

As I left the shop, my satchel heavier, I tucked my hands in the pocket of my cloak.

Something cold and metallic met my fingertips.

The two silver coins.

I sighed. When I tried to turn, the door had a "Closed" sign on it, and the lights were dim.

I fumbled with the two silver coins as I made my way to the ironwork shop. I had spent an alarming number of silvers in the recent weeks. I wasn't one to turn down a bargain, but I liked to pay my dues. I didn't want to owe anyone anything.

I felt strangely off kilter.

I spotted Tandor's glossy black hair at the end of the road as I slipped into the shop that I was pretty sure would have a cauldron large enough to suit my needs. He was perched on a bench, bent over, feeding cookie crumbs to a small fluffy squirrel. I huffed out a snort at the sight.

A rush of warm air blanketed me as I stepped into the ironwork shop. The heat was almost stifling after adjusting to the cold, dry air outside. Something brushed against my ankle, exiting at the same time I was entering. I caught a flash of white fur.

Damn, why does everyone get to have a cat friend except me?

Hex shuffled, slipping out from my hair and onto my shoulder. I batted them back under the cover of my curls. I didn't need anyone spotting them and asking questions. "No," I whispered. "You have to stay hidden."

Hex yanked on a strand of my hair.

"Bitch," I hissed.

They pulled out two more hairs.

I let that slide, rubbing my fingers against my now-sore scalp. I knew when to admit defeat.

A fire roared in the back of the shop. Clanking sounded from the forge, but I couldn't see anyone.

I caught a glimpse of a telltale blur of vision from the

corner of my eye. Sprites. With a surge, I missed my shop sprites. Somewhere along the line, I had started considering them *my* sprites. My little buddies. My little pests.

The thought was as nauseating as it was heartwarming. Whoever ran this shop must have been dealing with them too. Poor sap.

I spotted promising cauldrons immediately. The right wall was lined with them in varying sizes. Some were even a shining gold color. I wandered over, trailing my fingers over the gorgeous gold material.

The price tag made my eyes pop out of my skull. I immediately moved to the less flashy black cauldrons.

A short witch emerged from the back. "Got your eye on a cauldron, huh?" she asked.

I nodded with a smile. "I sure do. The biggest one you've got."

She raised her eyebrows, pulling a cloth from her apron to dab at her damp forehead. "The biggest? You sure? That's a lot of cauldron to work with."

I nodded again. "The biggest. Huge. I run an apothecary over by the Greenwood Forest," I said by way of explanation. "Moonvale."

That jogged her memory. "You're Kizzi, ain't ya? I've heard of ya. Good brews, you make. The witches talk about how crisp they are. How effective." She looked at me through slightly squinted eyes. "I think I've got something that'll get the job done."

The air rushed out of my lungs in a huff. "Thank you."

She ushered me to the back corner of the shop, where boxes and crates were stacked up. She shoved some of them aside.

An involuntary gasp escaped my lips. Even Hex stirred where they were tucked in my hair, slipping forward for a peek.

The cauldron was glorious. It was massive, maybe even bigger than what I had before. The material was a smooth, luxurious coated cast iron. I could feel the magic humming off it in gentle waves, as though it had been made with great care and intention.

It was perched on a wooden slab that protected the four short feet from touching the ground. And it probably weighed as much as five adult witches.

It was perfect.

"I can see the light glimmering in your eyes," the witch laughed. "I take it this'll do?"

I schooled my expression into something less embarrassing. I didn't want to drool all over myself. "This'll do. How much?"

She tilted her head. "Five hundred silvers."

My joy quelled. That many silvers could buy an entire cottage in Moonvale. It would entirely drain my coffers.

But I had to do it. I gulped down the bile rising in my throat. "Five hundred it is. Can I come pick it up in a bit?"

"Sure, hon. You going to be able to get that thing back to the Greenwood? That's across the realm." She skeptically eyed my arms, which clearly weren't laden with muscle.

"I brought a friend." I pulled my coin pouch from my satchel and counted out the coins. By the luck of the fates, I had exactly five hundred. After this purchase, I would only have two silvers left—the two that were still resting in my cloak pocket.

I silently prayed to the Old Gods that the dried dragon

eggshells wouldn't be too expensive. If they were, I would have to figure out a backup plan. Returning to Moonvale without them was not an option. Perhaps I could get a loan of some sort.

I felt nauseous as I handed the pouch to the witch. "Don't spend it all in one place," I joked.

She gave me a tight smile. "Just come back to pick it up before dark—I lock up when the suns start to sink."

"I'll make that happen. Thank you!"

As I turned to flee, the witch held a hand up. "Oh, miss, you've got a little—" she gestured to her neck, indicating I had something there. I reached toward my throat. My fingers brushed against Hex, in their more solid form, where they were entirely visible. And looked like... like purple slime. Stuck in my hair, sitting on my shoulder. This witch probably thought I was nuts.

"Ah, right. I'll take care of... this situation." I slipped out of the shop without another word, letting the cold mountain air shock me back to my senses.

CHAPTER 28
Tandor

The critters in Rockward were entirely different from the ones in Moonvale. They were different species, of course, with completely different appearances and lifestyles. But their attitudes were different, too.

In Moonvale, they scurried around without a care in the realm. They weren't necessarily brave, they still spooked easily, but they were carefree. They didn't notice the folk much.

Here, they were slyer. Savvier. They were certainly harder to catch.

The small fluffy squirrels seemed to warm up to me as I continued to feed them. I had snagged a cookie for myself, and had grabbed an extra for Kizzi, but she clearly needed her space today. And I would give it to her, no matter how much it bothered me.

So, half of her cookie ended up being a bribe to lure the critters closer. And the other half was about to become a bribe as well.

I still hadn't been able to pet the sneaky critters, no matter how close they darted to my boots to snatch the crumbs.

They always scurried away before I was able to scratch their soft-looking backs.

My attention was snagged when a figure drifted into my line of sight. I glanced up, and then immediately straightened, surreptitiously dusting my hands off. "Oh, hey," I said lamely. Kizzi looked greener than usual, her usually olive toned skin more of a pale sickly shade. "Having any luck?"

She nodded her head grimly. "I found a cauldron."

"That's great!" I stood awkwardly. "Why don't you look happy? This is a good thing, right?"

She lifted her hand to her neck and rubbed. Hex was sitting there, and they liquified for a moment to avoid being squashed. It really was jarring, watching the living sludge move on its own. "It is a good thing. I am happy. It was just... expensive. I need to process for a moment."

I grimaced. "How expensive?"

She shook her head.

Sympathy pinched my brows together. "That bad?" I asked.

"That bad."

"Over fifty silvers?"

She winced. "Ten times that."

I puffed my cheeks before letting the air rush out. "Fuck." That much money would keep Ginger's Pub operating for weeks. Months, maybe.

"Fuck," she agreed.

"And you—you paid that?"

"I sure did," she said solemnly.

I was impressed. I glanced from her messy, curly green hair tucked back behind her shoulders all the way down to her tidy black laced boots. For such a tiny witch, she sure was a savvy businesswoman. "Atta girl. Need a drink?"

She nodded quickly. "Or five. I need to save my last silvers, though. For... the other thing."

I gestured in front of me to where Rockward's pub could be seen further down the street. "I'll buy you a cider, princess. It won't be as good as mine, though. You'll have to make do with something mediocre."

Her cheek lifted at the corner. "I think I'll survive with mediocre. Thank you."

After two decent ciders and a few slices of cheesy bread, Kizzi was looking more like herself. The healthy color returned to her cheeks, and she looked less haunted. Less like she was seconds away from vomiting on the rock beneath our feet.

She drifted toward a witchy shop on the corner. I followed behind her. I had scanned the shops already, buying myself a few items, but not many—my desire to shop was dying out the longer I was away from home.

I had already secured a few pumpkins from a mountain farmer. I was giddy about them—I had already loaded them into the carriage. It was going to be a tight fit on the return journey.

Now, I just wanted to follow Kizzi around and watch her eyes light up as she spotted things that piqued her interest.

Much to my dismay, she was still being standoffish—still acting strange after our *incident* last night. And we still hadn't talked about it. It pained me to lose the easy comfort that we built over the recent weeks. The closeness. The friendship.

Now she could hardly look me in the eye.

I couldn't decide if it was worth it. The kiss had blown my mind, but if it was going to ruin the closeness between us... I wasn't sure if I would take it back or not.

I missed her, even though she was standing right in front of me.

When we approached the shop, Kizzi turned, tilting her head back but not quite meeting my gaze. "You okay?" she asked.

"Of course," I said, confused.

"Do you need to go look at anything else?"

I admired her pretty green eyes, the way they glimmered in the sunlight. "Are you trying to get rid of me, little witch?"

Her eyebrows pinched in a small wince. "I am. I'm sorry."

"Is it that big of a secret?"

"It really is."

My heart squeezed. "Are you going to keep it hidden the entire ride back to Moonvale?"

This seemed to stop her short. She stared at a spot over my shoulder. "I—I guess I must."

I sighed. "Alright, do what you have to do."

I wandered to a new bench while Kizzi slipped into the shop. The critters would surely appreciate another snack.

This time, a small bird took notice. It was a light gray color, about the size of an apple, with a shiny black beak. It gobbled up my cookie crumbs with no fear. It chomped its beak at me when I first attempted to stroke its feathers.

"Hey!" I admonished. "I just want to be your friend."

I dropped a few more crumbs onto the ground. This

time, the bird let me trace a gentle finger down the back of its head. A tiny wave of triumph lightened my spirits.

There was nothing better than befriending a new critter.

As I continued feeding the bird crumbs, my thoughts wandered home—back to Moonvale. Was Ginger doing alright without me? Was she handling the crowds? Suddenly, I missed the pub fiercely, along with the faun that owned it. She would have many colorful words for the situation I had gotten myself into with Kizzi. I would never hear the end of it.

I sat for what felt like a long time. Eventually, hunger began to gnaw at my stomach again. I decided it was time for another snack, and maybe a warm drink.

I wandered into a bakery.

I couldn't help myself—I bought a treat for Kizzi as well. I knew she was low on silvers, and I knew she couldn't resist a pastry. With two hot cocoas and a pouch full of mini pumpkin muffins, I strolled toward the witchy shop.

I would simply drop off the snack and then retreat, keeping my eyes to the floor to let her maintain her privacy. That was my plan.

The door was propped open. I stepped inside, determined to be swift.

But her words drifted to my ears.

"They're so... *shiny*," her smooth voice uttered.

"You've got to be careful with them," an unfamiliar voice said. "They can break enchantments, but they can also be used to *create* enchantments. Dangerous ones."

"Believe me, I know. I'm trying to correct a mistake I made."

The voice hummed. "Mind if I ask what happened?"

"It was a love potion," she murmured.

The other folk gasped. "No!"

"Unfortunately, yes. Believe me, it was an accident."

My mind whirled. She was trying to break... a love enchantment? That didn't make any sense.

I cleared my throat to announce my presence, stomping my feet a little so it sounded like I just walked in. Kizzi whirled and slapped a hand over her chest. "Oh, Tandor! Hi!"

"Hi." I smiled tightly. "Just brought you a snack."

I thrust the mug and pouch of pastries at her. She accepted them tentatively, her face pulling into a strange frown. "Oh, that's lovely. Thank you."

The other witch shot Kizzi a pointed look. Her mouth dropped open in something that looked like disbelief.

The gears in my brain started turning.

I retreated to the front of the shop quickly, taking a sip of my own cocoa.

"Oh, by the way," I cleared my throat awkwardly. "Do you need to borrow any silvers? For... whatever you need to purchase? I know that cauldron really drained you dry." I shifted to the balls of my feet and then settled back on my heels again.

Kizzi dragged a hand through her scalp, yanking her fingers through any tangles she encountered. She sighed heavily. "I do, actually."

I fished my coin pouch from my pocket. "How much do you need?"

She looked at the shopkeeper. "How much do I need? For the herbs... and also for the second thing." She leaned over the counter to glance at something I couldn't see from where I stood.

The shopkeeper looked worried. "I am really not supposed to—"

"Please. You can trust me. How much?" Kizzi insisted.

A deep sigh echoed through the shop. "A hundred silvers."

I nearly choked on my cocoa. "A hundred?" That wouldn't drain my savings... but it would make a large dent.

Kizzi fluttered her hands nervously. "I'll pay you back. With interest! I'll pay you back two hundred!"

I examined her face for a moment. I knew she was good for it—her business slowed during some seasons, but it was always consistent. Someone always needed her brews.

And I simply couldn't deny her.

I would buy the little witch anything she wanted.

"Sure. Of course." I tossed the coin pouch onto the counter near the two women and dropped my gaze to my feet, careful not to appear too nosey. "Just bring back whatever's left. I'll be outside."

"Thank you! Two hundred, I swear to the Old Gods!"

I flapped my hand at her. "I believe you."

I slipped out of the shop and into the cold.

Puzzle pieces slowly clicked together in my mind as I decided to take a stroll along the base of the mountains. There were trails here, some leading up into the peaks, some weaving through the valley. I chose a simple-looking path, careful not to venture too far so I wouldn't get lost.

Kizzi was trying to break a love potion enchantment.

I hadn't caught a glimpse of whatever was lying on the counter, too shocked from the information that was revealed. Was there an ingredient that could counteract a love potion?

Who had she enchanted?

I knew love potions were outlawed, of course. Everyone did. The fact that Kizzi had cast one was cause for concern.

I considered how strange things were in Moonvale before our swift departure.

I thought about Linc, with his strange behavior and his vacant stare. Was he her target? Did Kizzi have feelings for the human? The thought wasn't unbelievable—Linc was handsome, if a little strange. But she didn't seem to appreciate his presence. I remembered how she had sighed and rolled her eyes when he had shown up.

My thighs burned as I picked up my pace, trudging the rugged terrain mindlessly, letting my thoughts wander as the path swept me away. A knee-height-tall critter crossed my path, but I paid it no mind. I didn't even bother looking at it directly.

And then I remembered the other folk. How they had been acting... The strange behavior and vacant stares in the pub...

And it all clicked. I understood.

I barked out a humorless laugh that echoed off the rocky bluffs.

"Gods be damned, Kizzi."

The tent was dark when Tandor and I finally slipped inside for the night. Embers were simmering in the fire pit, the light dim.

Tandor had hauled the cauldron to the carriage with a surprising amount of effort. We had almost considered borrowing a wheelbarrow, but his pride had gotten in the way. His muscles had heaved and strained as he hoisted the massive bowl across town.

It had certainly been a sight. I shivered as I thought about it. His raw strength. His power. His muscles and tendons gliding beneath his skin.

A tension simmered through the air, low and hot. I couldn't quite figure out where it came from. Neither of us broke the silence.

Memories of last night flashed through my mind as I wandered over to my bag, letting my cloak drop from my shoulders.

I glanced at Tandor to find him sitting on the edge of the bed, his chin propped up on his hand. He was staring at a point on the canvas wall so fixedly I swore it would burst into flames.

I murmured a warning anyway. "Don't look."

It wasn't like it mattered. He had seen most of my goods already anyway. *And he liked what he saw.*

I swatted the thought away like a fly.

He didn't respond, simply continuing his strange stare. His eyebrows were pursed. I ached to know what internal battle he was fighting.

He couldn't know... could he? He hadn't walked into the shop early enough to overhear anything particularly damning.

He was thinking about something, though.

I hastily changed into my nightclothes.

As I tossed more logs into the firepit, Tandor finally snapped out of his concentration. He rose to his feet, pulled his cloak off, and planted his hands on his hips. He looked at me with a strange, twisted smile on his mouth.

My eyebrows pulled together. "...What?"

"I know what you did," he said mischievously.

My stomach bottomed out. My pulse kicked up in my chest and a sweat broke out on my forehead.

This was it. Somehow, he had figured out the truth. This was the moment that Tandor would scream at me, and report me for outlawed witchcraft, and get me thrown in the dungeon.

But... he was smiling.

I gulped. "And what did I do, exactly?"

His smile grew into a triumphant grin. "You tried to ensnare me with a love potion, didn't you? If you wanted me so badly, princess, you could've just asked."

I choked out something between a gasp and a laugh. "I did what?"

He stepped toward me, still smiling in a way that wrinkled his eyes at the corners. Mirth lit up his features in an endearing way. My stomach pinched.

"You could've just asked," he said again. "I'm afraid I'm already yours."

My jaw dropped open completely. "Tandor, what in the realms are you talking about?"

He laughed heartily. "I'm just joking, I had to. You can't blame me." He grasped my shoulder and squeezed for a moment before letting his hand drop away. "But I know about the love potion. I overheard a few things at the witchy shop, and then I figured it out."

All the air whooshed out of me in a hot exhale. "You overheard."

He nodded. "I sure did. It took me a while to put it all together, though. And then I had to decide if I would keep my mouth shut. But I hate secrets. I really, truly do. I would've burst on the journey home trying to pretend that I didn't know anything."

I walked over to the bed, dropping down onto the edge and letting my knees give out. I breathed in deep, pulling air all the way to the base of my lungs. I held it there for long moments before letting the air rush out. My voice was shaky when I spoke. "Are you going to turn me in?"

"Turn you in? Why the fuck would I do that?"

My gaze caught his. "You're not going to get me thrown in the dungeon?"

He stared at me blankly, a "what the fuck" expression on his face. "Pardon?"

"I drugged everyone! I drugged *you*! I took away your free will! I—I took advantage of you!"

He dropped onto the bed next to me. He gently gathered my hands into his, squeezing them firmly. The warmth was more comforting than I had expected.

"You didn't drug me, Kizzi."

I sighed in exasperation. I thought he had figured it out, but apparently, he was still missing some important details. "I did. I drugged everyone."

He squeezed my fingers. "Not me," he said gently.

"At the potluck?"

"No."

"Yes. Yes, I did—"

He winced, looking abashed. "I didn't eat your chili."

It took a moment for his words to sink in. First, I felt a brief flash of outrage. How *dare* he? And then the shock was washed away by a heavy, overwhelming wave of relief. "You didn't eat my chili?" I was repeating his words, I knew it, but my mind was whirling too fast to care.

"I—I couldn't bring myself to eat it." He pulled my hands to his chest. "But I didn't want to offend you! I knew how proud you were of your dish. I just... I have a weak stomach. And I... saw a feather in it."

I stared at him for a moment, slack jawed. His pulse thundered against the backs of my fingers where they were pressed to his heart. "You didn't eat the chili."

"I didn't eat the chili."

"You're not enchanted with the love potion."

"I'm not. No love potions. Just..." His sentence trailed off.

His eyes burned into mine hot enough to bring my blood

to a simmer. The reality of what he'd confessed sank in. My stomach flipped a somersault. "You've had free will this whole time."

He scooted closer, keeping my hands cradled to his chest like a treasure. "I have. I was never under any magical thrall. Only yours, little witch."

I pulled my hands from his grasp and ran them through my hair, tugging on the strands. "If you would have told me you didn't eat the chili, we could've avoided this entire misunderstanding!"

"If you would've told me what you were looking for and *why* you were looking for it, I could've let you know! We were on completely different pages." He hesitated for a moment, tilting his head. "What eggs are you looking for, by the way? I heard you mention eggs back in Tidegrove, but I never figured that part out."

I brushed the comment off. "Oh, just some dragon eggs."

His eyes nearly popped out of his head. "Dragon eggs! You can't just say that like it's something casual."

I shrugged. I slid my hands up over his shoulders, letting them rest there. "They're just eggs."

"The rare, mythical, extinct creatures?" He looked like he wanted to continue arguing but was having a hard time keeping his concentration.

"Mhm. They have some."

"They have dragon eggs?"

"Mhm."

"We are discussing this later. I have so many questions." He brought his hands to my hips, tentatively scooting me toward him on the edge of the bed.

"Sure. Later." I let my hands wander behind his neck, tugging slightly on the hair at his nape.

"Kizzi," he said haltingly.

"Yes?"

"Last night, you—"

"I thought it was the love potion," I interrupted.

The tension slowly melted from his face, replaced with something warmer. "Ah."

"I didn't think... I didn't think you actually wanted me."

"I tried to tell you," he said teasingly, "just how much I wanted you. So much."

I tugged harder on his neck. "Shut up and kiss me."

His laugh was a low, hot rumble. "Whatever you want, princess."

As he leaned toward me, closing the gap between our faces, a rattle from the floor caught my attention.

Hex was rocking their jar back and forth, waves of irritation pulsing from them.

I snorted. "One moment," I said to Tandor.

I extracted myself from the orc's grip and scooped the small jar from the floor. I hastily untied the tarp, set the jar outside, and then sealed it up again, leaving a small gap so they could come back inside later if they chose to.

I didn't care where they went, but they would have to entertain themselves for a while. I knew they wanted to flee just as badly.

Tandor was stifling laughter as I skipped back to the bed, hopping up onto his lap. His arms circled me easily. Naturally. "Kicking the familiar out?"

I nodded. "I'm not into voyeurism."

"Bummer," he joked.

"Maybe next time."

His laughter died out when I pressed my mouth to his.

His lips were smooth and firm as they slid against mine in an intoxicating caress. My blood heated and my pulse pounded. His hands wandered up my back, my sides, my hair, as if he wanted to touch me everywhere at once.

And then he took over the kiss.

Tandor grabbed my waist, hoisting me up and shifting me on his body until I straddled him. My thighs stretched to the point of discomfort to accommodate his broad hips, but they fit.

He devoured my mouth, his lips stroking, his tongue tasting.

His hand fisted my hair, tilting my head back with a gentle tug. He groaned as I settled my weight onto his lap. His cock was hot and hard in his trousers, and I rolled my hips, reveling in the delicious friction.

My head dropped back as I let out a breathy sigh. I rolled my hips again, rubbing myself against him. He grabbed my ass and squeezed. "Kizzi," he groaned.

His mouth dropped to my throat, kissing, nibbling, sucking. Arousal pooled in my stomach.

"Yes," I breathed.

His hands moved to my nightshirt, tugging at the hem. I leaned back, allowing him to peel the shirt from my body. A shiver worked down my spine when the cool air of the room kissed my skin, but Tandor was on me immediately, his hot hands warming me.

His calloused palms slid over my back as he pulled me back into a kiss, more frantic this time. More heated. My hands roamed over his chest, his shoulders, hooked around the back of his neck. His skin just felt so *good* against mine, I wanted to keep exploring.

A shiver shot down my spine when he pulled my lower lip between his teeth, hard enough to sting.

I broke the kiss. I wanted *more*. He grumbled in complaint, but only for a moment. My mouth drifted toward his ear—hot and flushed, and so smooth under my lips. I kissed the delicate skin, dragging my mouth to the very tip, where I bit down lightly.

A garbled sound escaped his mouth, his hips bucking wildly. "Gods, woman. Are you trying to kill me?"

I laughed. "Are you into that sort of thing?"

"With you, I'd be into anything."

"Fucking Gods." My core clenched, sending a wave of hot need through me.

I continued my exploration, kissing his neck, his collarbones. I slid off his lap and yanked his tunic, aching for more of his skin on mine.

I had to stop for a moment to admire the orc in front of me. I had seen him shirtless, sure, but not like *this*. He was gorgeous. All smooth, green skin, and bulging muscle softened at the edges.

I let my eyes feast on his body—from the erection bulging in his trousers, past the curves and valleys of his strong torso, to his face, where he was grinning devilishly.

"Careful, little witch. I think you're drooling."

I grinned back. I couldn't help it. "Shut up. Can't I just admire you for a moment?"

He leaned back where he was perched on the edge of the bed, elongating his frame and letting his knees drop open.

"Admire as much as you wish. The fates know I've been admiring you for ages, it's your turn."

My mouth went dry. Gods almighty, what a *man*.

"Trousers off," I commanded. If I was going to look, I wanted to see the entire image.

He lifted a brow. "You first."

I took that as a challenge. Slowly, maintaining eye contact, I unbuttoned my trousers, shoving them down over my hips, my ass, my thighs. The fabric pooled around my feet, and I stepped out of them, kicking them aside.

Tandor's eyes nearly popped out of his head. He brought his fist to his mouth to bite on his knuckles.

I spun in a circle, achingly aware that the only piece of fabric on my body was my undergarments. I didn't feel exposed, like I thought I would. With the way his eyes were devouring me, I felt sexy. Powerful.

He tried to reach for me, but I flicked a tiny spark of magic at him, just enough to sting where it connected with his palm. He jumped, his forehead creasing in an expression somewhere between disbelief and pride. His arms dropped back to his sides. "Bossy."

"Don't touch. I said trousers off."

Finally, he obeyed. He lifted his hips and slid his trousers onto the floor, leaving his undershorts on.

I tsked. I stepped forward, trailing my fingers over the waistband. I slipped my fingers under the fabric, just a bit. His erection bulged obscenely under the thin material, begging to be released. I tugged lightly. "These too, please." I smiled my sweetest smile.

His chest rose and fell in a rapid rhythm. "When you ask so sweetly..."

The orc lifted his hips again, and I pulled the undershorts down, letting them drop to the floor.

His cock sprang free, rock hard and throbbing and impossibly *huge*. I knew it would be big, but seeing it at attention like this, I briefly feared for my own safety.

The size wasn't the most shocking part. Through the head of his cock, silver and gleaming, was a shiny bar. He was pierced.

The slickness of my own arousal soaked through my undergarments.

I raised my gaze to find Tandor looking tense and nervous, his tusks biting into his upper lip. Was he afraid I would see him and find him inadequate?

He was *wrong*.

I dropped to my knees between his spread thighs, desperate to put my mouth on him. Desperate to make him lose control.

He tensed when my hands slid up his muscled thighs. "Kizzi."

"Yes?" I glanced at his face for confirmation.

"You don't have to..." His words trailed off to a groan when I reached his impressive cock, circling it with my fingers. My hand couldn't close around his girth. I wasn't sure if I would be able to fit him inside me, but I was excited to try.

I stroked experimentally, sliding my hand from root to tip and back down again. His skin was burning hot and so, so smooth.

A choked sound escaped Tandor's mouth. I stroked again with more confidence, tightening my fingers around him, desperate for more of those reactions. I wanted to drive him wild. I glanced up to find his head rolled back, the veins in his neck bulging.

I leaned forward to drag my tongue up the underside of his cock. His thighs clenched. His hands found my hair, weaving into the strands and fisting.

I slid my tongue over the piercing, swirling in teasing, coaxing motions, letting saliva collect on my tongue. I tortured him for a few more moments, stroking and licking, before I took him into my mouth.

A pained groan escaped him. "Kizzi, yes, holy fuck. That's—that's so good."

I preened at the praise and simply hummed in response. My jaw strained to open further and I struggled to shield my teeth, but I did my best. I bobbed my head, stroking whatever I couldn't fit in my mouth with my hands.

His thighs practically vibrated with tension. His hands in my hair pulled tighter. "Ah! Stop—if you don't slow down, I'm going to—"

He pushed me back and immediately hauled me off the floor, tossing my body onto the bed. "You shouldn't have stopped me," I complained.

He crawled over top of me, laughing lowly in his throat. "You will be coming first, little witch. It's my turn."

Tandor planted a searing kiss on my mouth before trailing lower, yanking my undergarments off and dragging his hands and mouth down my body.

With a heated glance at my face, he settled between my thighs. My heart pounded in my chest.

His voice was gravel. "Gods, I've wanted to do this for ages." He leaned forward, swiping his tongue over my slick flesh. He groaned in appreciation.

Hot pleasure simmered in my veins. I writhed under his ministrations, unable to hold still. He grabbed my thighs, pushing them up to my chest and spreading me open wider. My muscles strained in protest, but I didn't care—I was putty in his hands.

His tongue swirled over my clit. Once. Twice. I gasped, bliss shooting up my spine. "Yes. Yes—keep doing that."

He did—his tongue moving over my body expertly. When the waves of pleasure finally peaked, I screwed my eyes shut, holding back a scream. Shivers worked down my spine, through my limbs, curling my toes.

When the waves settled and the sensation became overwhelming, I grabbed Tandor's hair, tugging him up.

He crawled up my body like a beast on the prowl, eyes gleaming.

He hovered over me, holding his weight up with an elbow. His head dropped to my neck. I ran my hands up his broad back, letting my nails graze his skin. I felt the goosebumps as they formed.

His cock notched at my entrance, swollen and throbbing. The shock of cool metal against my hot flesh made me shiver. A sudden wave of apprehension made me hesitate.

"Still want to do this?" he murmured against the skin of my throat.

Did I still want this? Absolutely. With every fiber of my being. But was I nervous? Definitely.

I took a deep breath, letting the fresh air calm my worries. I shifted my hips, rubbing myself against him. "Yes."

He pushed forward, just an inch, enough to stretch my entrance. My breath hitched.

He lifted his head to meet my eyes. "Breathe. You can take it."

I nodded, lost in his dark gaze. I could drown in the depths of his eyes. His dark brows were furrowed. He pushed forward another inch. Two. It stung, an uncomfortable stretching sensation, but I dug my nails into his shoulders, desperate for him to continue.

He pulled back before shifting forward again in a tiny thrust, and then he pushed further. Tingles of pleasure worked up my spine, slowly breaking through the pain. "You look so pretty like this, taking my cock. You're doing so well."

He continued, pulling out and pushing in shallow thrusts until he was bottomed out, seated to the hilt.

I was full—impossibly so, uncomfortably so, but his cock was fully seated inside me. I released a deep breath, trying to force myself to relax.

Tandor's eyes burned into mine. His cheeks were flushed, his teeth were bared, and he was trembling with tension. He lifted his hand to stroke my cheek. "Are you okay?"

Was I okay? I was crammed full, underneath my favorite man who was staring at me like I hung the moons. I was more than okay. "Yes. I'm good. You can move."

He pulled back, all the way to the tip, and slowly thrust forward, watching my face closely. My body stretched to accommodate his massive size.

His piercing stroked a tender spot deep inside of me, igniting a flame in my belly. I nodded frantically. "More."

Pain drifted away, a mere memory as he thrust into me again and again. I tugged him down into a kiss as he fucked me into oblivion.

His tongue stroked against mine in a delicious rhythm.

Pleasure pooled in my stomach, insistent and all-encompassing. My body ached for another release, desperate to explode again.

I threaded my fingers into Tandor's silky hair, anchoring myself against the onslaught of sensations. I was drowning, and I never wanted to come up for air.

"Come, little witch," he murmured against my mouth. "I have you."

I whimpered. I was so close, I could practically taste it.

He picked up the pace, the bed shaking as he pounded me into it. I couldn't breathe. His piercing stroked that tender spot perfectly. It was the push I needed. I shattered, falling over the edge as an orgasm tore through me. My head dropped back. My lungs struggled for air.

Over the roaring in my ears, I heard Tandor's strangled grunt as he found his own release. He pulled out of my body and collapsed, careful to let most of his weight fall onto the bed beside me.

We stayed like that for long moments as we caught our breath—both of us entwined and sprawled on the bed. Sweat slicked my skin.

Eventually, my heart rate slowed.

"Holy shit," I whispered in the darkness.

He pressed a kiss to the side of my head. "I couldn't have said it better myself."

CHAPTER 30

Kizzi

I slipped into the witchy shop, hot cocoa in hand, a smile permanently etched onto my mouth.

It was time to haggle for some dragon eggs. I would do whatever it took to bring those treasures home with me, lest Fiella skin me alive.

Tandor drifted in the door behind me, close enough that I could feel his breath rustling my hair. I enjoyed his proximity. I had gotten used to him being around during our travels, but the newness of him being so *close* was invigorating.

I feared I was becoming addicted to him.

Hex curled up on my shoulder, tucked under my hair in a manner that was becoming their favorite way to travel. They liked their jar fine, but they preferred to look around. To see things.

They were nosey just like me.

I had briefly described the dragon situation to Tandor as we laid in bed together in the dark. I hadn't explained much, but I hadn't needed to. He was on board with my plan immediately.

262

I was going to bring a live dragon egg home to Moonvale.

The witch brightened as I entered. "Kizzi—back so soon! Did you need something else?"

I donned my friendliest, sweetest smile. "I'm back to talk about the eggs."

She looked puzzled. "The eggs? You already bought all the dragon eggshell powder I have."

I shook my head, still smiling. "The eggs. The *whole* eggs."

Her eyes rounded. "Oh! Oh. I'm afraid those aren't for sale."

Tandor stepped up behind me, placing a supportive hand on my shoulder. "The price isn't an issue," he insisted. "We can pay."

I grabbed his fingers and squeezed for a moment, grateful for the backup. I was stone cold broke, and his coffers would be funding this purchase.

She shook her head. "That's not it. They're fossilized. Practically relics. They've been sitting in a Rockward mine for hundreds of years. If they're going to hatch, they've always hatched in the warm lagoons deep below the mountains." She glanced between me and Tandor with a pained look on her face. "They're not supposed to leave the town."

I clasped my hands under my chin in a pleading gesture. "Please? It's been hundreds of years. Thousands. They'll probably never hatch. What's the harm? If they don't hatch before next Hallow's Eve, I'll bring them back."

She considered this. "I'd have to discuss this with the coven."

I nodded quickly. That wasn't a hard no. "Of course! I expected as much. That's no problem at all!"

Tandor's hand on my shoulder squeezed. "We have to hit

the road soon—we need to make it back to Moonvale by Hallow's Eve."

The witch sighed. "Come back when the suns start to set. I'll see what I can do."

I held down a squeal and cleared my throat. "Of course! Thank you!"

After a stroll around the perimeter of town to kill some time, Tandor and I settled into a pub for a late lunch of mulled wine, fluffy pretzels, and dippable cheese.

Tandor popped a cheese-loaded bite of pretzel into his mouth, chewed, and swallowed. I watched his throat as it worked, entranced by the muscles. I shifted in my seat.

"So," he started as he dabbed at his mouth with a napkin. "Dragons, huh?"

I nodded. "Dragons." I brought my mug to my mouth, letting the hot mulled wine pour over my tongue.

"What if they actually hatch?"

I smiled at this. "That's the goal. Fiella made me swear that I would bring her an egg—she's convinced that her presence will crack the fossilized shell."

He snorted out a laugh. "She thinks that, huh?"

"Could you imagine—a tiny dragon running around Moonvale? Frolicking in the trees, splashing in the river, playing with the local cats."

He tilted his head. "That would definitely keep things interesting."

"Maybe the coven will have some ideas. It's been ages

since anyone has tried to hatch a shell—the rest of us assumed they were completely extinct. Gone. Poofed out of existence when the Old Gods abandoned us."

"I had always assumed they were gone. Just stories in fairytales."

"Exactly! I'm sure if we really put our minds to it, we can figure something out."

Hex stirred on my shoulder, reminding me they were there. I pointed at them.

"Like Hex! Familiars are supposed to be a thing of the past. But somehow, some way, they exist." I stroked a finger over Hex's slimy surface. I only cringed a little at the off-putting texture.

Tandor hummed in contemplation. "Good point. That is peculiar. Maybe it's you—maybe you're the secret ingredient that will finally crack those eggs open."

I snorted out a laugh. "Funny."

He smiled broadly. "I'm serious! There's something special about you."

A flush rose in my cheeks. "You're just saying that because you like me."

"I've been thinking that for years, actually."

"Oh?"

He nodded sagely. "The first time I used one of your potions, a headache reducing blend, I knew you were special. You are a rare talent."

Warmth bloomed in my chest. "I just practiced. Anyone can do that."

He allowed me to dodge the compliment. "If you think that's all it is. We'll just have to see. What do you think Mayor Tommins is going to say?"

My smile dropped. "I hadn't considered that."

"You traveled the entire realm to find a dragon egg and didn't consider if you would actually be allowed to have it?"

"I had bigger concerns!"

"Right," he snorted. "Does he know about the love potion?"

"Gods, no!" I couldn't imagine how angry he would be if he found out my plan. It didn't deter me from it, not even close. But it did make me apprehensive. An angry gryphon was not something I wanted to deal with any time soon.

"He was influenced by the love potion too, wasn't he? I remember how weird he looked when he dropped into your apothecary."

I slumped in my seat. "He might've been."

Tandor barked out a loud laugh. "That's incredible."

I slapped him on the shoulder. "It's not incredible! It's awful!"

"It's funny," he insisted.

I grumbled, "Fine. It's a little funny,"

"How are you going to cure them all? Convince them to eat another batch of chili?"

I considered this. "That's actually not a terrible idea." My chili hadn't been the most delicious item at the potluck, but folk hadn't gagged when they ate it, and I considered that a win.

"I was joking!"

"I know, but it's not the worst idea." And then a better idea came to me. I gasped, turning to grasp his wrist. "I know what we can do!"

He looked suspicious. "I don't like that look on your face. You're up to something."

"No, I'm not!"

"Spit it out, little witch," he sighed in resignation.

"Put it in your cider! We'll only need to use a tiny pinch, there should be enough powder in that jar to cure the entire town."

He grimaced. "My recipes are exact, Kizzi. They've been perfected. I can't just toss powder into the barrel. What if it alters the taste? I don't want the entire town thinking I'd willingly serve them gross cider."

I shook his wrist. "You big baby. I would never ruin your precious brews. What if we just sprinkle a little bit into the bottom of the goblets as you serve drinks? That way, it'll get to every folk."

He looked like he was going to protest, but then he considered. "That might actually work."

I grinned in triumph. "Of course it'll work! Everyone loves your drinks. We can catch them before Hallow's Eve."

"You're full of ideas, aren't you?"

I nodded, releasing his wrist to pick up my warm mug. "Stick around and you might find out."

He smiled warmly. "I certainly plan to."

The witchy shop was dark when we returned, the enchanted lights extinguished. A "closed" sign was hung on the front door.

I knocked anyway. "Hello?"

The door slowly creeped open with a resounding creak.

Tandor looked at me questioningly. "After you?"

"Sure, let the lady enter first after the creepy door opened by itself."

He smiled. "You're the one with the magic. You can protect us if there are any monsters in there."

I stepped forward to enter, but Tandor slipped an arm around my waist and tucked me behind him. "I'm joking, I would never send you first into danger, imagined or not."

That warmed my insides.

We entered.

There were no monsters.

The shop was dark, all curtains drawn tight to keep the light of the setting suns out, but a small candle in the back allowed me to see.

"Hello?" I asked.

Hushed whispers sounded somewhere in the back of the shop. A quiet, nervous muttering.

"...Oh, protect us, Old Gods, keep us safe from the wrath of the dragon flame. Let these eggs remain whole..."

The witch was crouched on the floor, praying. That couldn't be a good sign. I glanced at Tandor to find him looking as nervous as I felt. His dark brows were furrowed, his mouth a taut line.

I cleared my throat. "Did your coven come to the decision? Can I buy the egg?"

The witch rose to her feet, glancing at me nervously. "The coven has decided. You can take the eggs, yes. But you must be careful with them. There are three, and they must stick together. You must dedicate your life to protecting them."

I gulped. A little more intense than what I was expecting, but I respected the passion. "Okay, sure. Done. I'll protect the eggs. How much do we owe you?"

Her eyes widened. "With your life, you must protect them with your *life*. Your essence, your very being. You will be The Hand of the Dragons."

Hex shuffled on my shoulder, slinking closer to my neck. I glanced at Tandor, but he simply shrugged, leaving the decision up to me. He slipped a hand over my other shoulder and squeezed reassuringly.

The Hand of the Dragons was a pretty badass title—it did the opposite of discouraging me.

I straightened my spine in an attempt to look more powerful. "I will protect the dragon eggs with my life."

"Do you swear it to the Old Gods?"

"I swear it to the Old Gods."

This seemed to satisfy the witch—her strange intensity eased, and a smile stretched across her face. "Great. Glad we got that settled. That'll be three hundred silvers."

Tandor coughed. Twice. And then he composed himself. "Three hundred silvers. For eggs that might never hatch. Great. Of course." He pulled out his coin pouch with trembling fingers.

The witch grabbed the pouch from his hand, deftly sorting out the appropriate payment before tossing the pouch back to Tandor, almost empty. He missed it—the pouch smacked his chest before dropping to the floor. He fumbled as he bent to pick it up.

The witch drifted to the back corner of the shop, grabbing a large woven basket lined with blankets. She dropped it on the counter in front of us.

"Well, here you are. Three dragon eggs."

Nervously, I approached to take a peek.

Three shiny, scaled eggs sat nestled in the blanket. They

were about the length of my forearm and perfectly ovoid. Magic radiated from the eggs in sweet, eye-watering waves.

I had the sudden strange desire to drop to my knees. They were the most beautiful things I had ever seen.

Fiella was going to lose her mind.

CHAPTER 31
Tandor

Kizzi and I stood in the Rockward stables, perplexed. We found ourselves in a sticky situation.

She stood with her arms crossed, her foot tappingly rapidly against the ground. Her head was tilted, and her brow was furrowed in concentration.

The carriage, the ugly wooden thing we had dragged from Moonvale, was completely full. To the brim. It had slowly filled up throughout the weeks of the journey, becoming more cramped with every purchase, but now it was ridiculous.

The cauldron took up almost the entire bench, and our bags and parcels filled every remaining gap.

There was no way we would be able to fit in it to journey home. Kizzi might have been able to squeeze, but no way in Hell's Realm was my frame fitting in there.

I ran my hand over Daisy's back, scratching at her smooth mane and digging my fingertips into her taut muscles. "We'll get you home soon, girl," I said to the horse quietly. "You'll be back home with your friends!"

Instead of perking up, the horse seemed to slump slightly, as though she could understand my words and wasn't happy to hear them.

I thought about how lively she had been in Tidegrove. How she happily stomped through the waves, grazed along the shore, accepted pets from any folk passing by.

I knew we were supposed to bring her back to Moonvale, but what if we found her a new home?

Rockward's stables were full of horses; there were at least twenty. The beasts were large, strong, and powerful, built for hiking mountains instead of strolling through forests and fields.

They looked like they could easily carry an orc or two.

The solution solidified in my mind.

We needed to rent a horse from Rockward to carry us and help drag the carriage. I glanced at Daisy's thin legs. She had pulled the carriage here just fine but, with any additional weight...

And if we needed to drop her off along the way...

We needed to rent two horses. One to haul the carriage, and one to carry Kizzi and me. I glanced at Kizzi from the corner of my eye. We could each rent a horse—there were plenty, of course—but I wasn't going to let that happen.

I was looking forward to journeying home with the little witch in my arms.

After some rearranging, reattaching of saddles and harnesses, and some finessing, we were on our way. Our traveling party was certainly a sight.

Two folk, three horses, a hideous carriage, and a living pile of purple slime.

Hallow's Eve was days away. If we kept a brisk pace, we would make it with a sleep or two to spare, even accounting for the detour through Tidegrove.

I was looking forward to getting home—to getting back to the pub, seeing the local folk, sleeping in my own bed. But I was going to soak up every single moment of this journey.

Kizzi and I had been getting along, and we had connected irrevocably last night, but I wasn't sure how things would be when we returned home. When things went back to normal.

Would she forget about me? Was this just a casual thing for her? It certainly didn't feel casual.

Kizzi was bundled in front of me on the giant black horse (alarmingly named Nightmare). Her cloak was tucked tightly around her body to fight off the wind, and she clutched my arms with quivering fingers.

Her hair tickled my nose, smelling of apples and honey. I brought my elbows in, squeezing her tighter. She was always so cold, the little witch. It was a wonder she was able to regulate her own body heat at all.

There was probably a potion she could brew for that. But I would never make that suggestion. I liked being her personal heat source.

When night eventually fell and the moons were high in the sky, we pulled aside to make camp. We set up a small tent we had purchased from a supply shop, along with a small mat to lay on. Our bodies barely fit inside, but I wouldn't have it any other way.

Hex was left in the carriage, tucked inside the cauldron with the dragon eggs. They spent a lot of time around the eggs—squishing around them, poking at them, simply sitting near them. It was strangely endearing.

Kizzi and I laid there, face to face, legs entwined. Our faces were close enough to share breaths, but neither of us moved.

Our eyes locked in the dark. I reached out a hand, brushing an errant lock of hair from her face. I allowed my fingers to linger there, tracing idly over the pointed shell of her ear.

I just wanted to touch her.

"Your eyes are so pretty," I murmured. "Like fresh grass."

She cracked a smile. "Are you flirting with me?"

"I've been flirting with you for years."

"Really?" She looked perplexed. After a long moment, she snorted out a laugh. "You're not very good at it. I thought you were just being nice."

"I'm nice to everyone," I agreed.

"Exactly!"

"But I'm *extra* nice to you."

"Are you?"

"You never noticed?" I fought the urge to roll my eyes. I hadn't thought I was being subtle.

"Well... no I didn't."

I picked up another curl, rolling her soft hair between my fingers. "Would it have made a difference? If you had known?"

She considered this. "I don't know. It's hard to tell."

I hummed in contemplation. "The fates have a way of pulling our strings," I mused.

Her eyes dipped to my mouth, and then bounced back up to my eyes. "They do," she agreed.

My blood warmed. "I'm glad you invited me on this trip with you." I flexed my arm obnoxiously. "Thank the Old Gods you needed my muscles so badly."

Her mouth spread in a wide, sweet grin. "I'm glad too," she agreed. "It would've been a drag by myself."

I slid my hand down to her waist, tugging her closer. "Admit it. You like having me around."

Her smile became shy, her cheeks warming. "Fine. I like having you around."

Warmth flooded my chest. "I knew it," I joked.

"You like me more, though," she insisted.

"I'm not going to argue with you there."

And then I pulled her into a kiss, pressing my mouth to her impossibly soft lips.

Waves crashed against shore in a soothing rhythm, spraying a fine mist of salty water into the air.

My boots crunched against sand as I dropped from Nightmare's back. Kizzi was already wandering to the shore, yanking off her boots and pulling up her trousers so she could dip her toes in the water.

Rune looked confused when she emerged from her cottage to find me, but she definitely wasn't upset.

"Tandor! Kizzi!" she called out as she pulled me into a

hug. "What are you doing here? I thought you were headed back to Moonvale?"

She gripped me by the shoulders and examined my face. I wasn't sure what she was looking for, but apparently, she found it. A sly smile spread across her cheeks. "How was Rockward?"

I fought to quell the warmth that seeped into my cheeks, but I couldn't hide the way my ears twitched. Her smile grew.

"It was fine." I coughed once. Twice. "It was nice."

She laughed. "I'm sure it was. What are you doing back here?"

I extracted myself from her grip to turn back to Daisy. She was trotting in place, practically buzzing with excitement. I grabbed her reins and led her over to Rune.

"I thought you might be open to another family member?" I suggested hopefully.

My sister crossed her arms over her chest. "Oh?"

"She just loves it here so much... I can't stand the thought of dragging her back to Moonvale."

Rune considered this. "And will we get in trouble for stealing a horse?"

I shrugged. "Probably."

She barked out a laugh. "Fine. You're right, she's got sea legs, she should get to live where she's happy." She took Daisy's reins from me and stroked the horse's broad cheek.

"You want to stay here with us, pretty girl?" she cooed.

Daisy let out a high-pitched trill, stomping her hooves.

"I thought so. Here, let me get this off you." Rune pulled the reins from the horse and gave her a gentle nudge. "Go play. I'll find a spot for you in a barn to sleep."

Daisy glanced at me for a moment, as though seeking

approval. I held my hand out in invitation. She wandered over to me for one more scratch on the neck before she neighed and plodded off toward the water's edge. She passed Kizzi on the way, splashing the witch with sandy water.

Kizzi squealed, but she didn't seem to mind. Her face was stretched in a gleaming smile.

Rune followed my gaze.

"Be good to her. She seems like a great match for you."

I started to argue. "Oh no, we're not, that's not—"

"You don't need to explain. I have eyeballs." She pulled me into another hug. "But I hope you bring her with you next time you visit."

I squeezed her back. "I hope so too," I mumbled under my breath.

CHAPTER 32
Kizzi

It was strange, waking up in my own bed.

It was comfortable, of course, with my collection of fluffy pillows and the gentle pulse of familiar magic. But it was cold. And lonely.

I missed waking up with Tandor next to me.

The sprites were a flurry of activity when I returned last night while the rest of the town was asleep, and they had clearly wreaked havoc on my shop while I was away.

I couldn't even be mad—I had expected nothing but shenanigans from them.

I was happy to be back in their presence, though. Even if they were annoying little bitches. They were *my* annoying little bitches.

Hex was also happy to be back, even more so than me. The larger portion of their mass was curled up in the broken cauldron, exactly where we had left it when we departed on our journey. Hex had leaped from my shoulder, absorbed into the remaining slime, and reanimated in their hefty, intimidating form.

I tried to remind myself that I had sort of bonded with my familiar over the journey. I wouldn't call us friends, but we weren't necessarily enemies anymore.

They still made me squirmy, though.

And they had tried to sleep curled up in my bed again.

I attempted to scoop them up, banishing them to the cracked cauldron that had become their new home base, but the effort was futile. My threats didn't even work, nor did my curse attempts. For being my familiar, Hex didn't follow my instructions very well.

So, there they slumbered, curled up under the covers at the bottom corner of the bed.

I did warn them that if they touched my toes during the night, I would set fire to the entire shop. I sort of meant it.

The brave blue water sprite also tried to sleep in by bed, perched on the pillow next to my head. It felt like a fucking slumber party.

A thundering knock at my door yanked me to my feet, forcing me to finally get out of bed.

"Hang on! Gods!" I called out grumpily. The suns were high in the sky, and it was probably around lunch time, but I still needed more sleep. It had been a long night.

"Open the door, bitch!" a familiar voice called out. "There's a pile of letters out here, by the way! And a few gifts! Can I take some of these?"

A grin split my face. Fiella.

She pounded on the door, wiggling the handle relentlessly.

"Hold your unicorns, I'm coming," I grumbled, but there was no heat to it.

I yanked the door open to find her standing there, two mugs of tea in hand, smiling devilishly. "Tell me everything."

And I did.

Well, *almost* everything. I left out the juiciest bits about me and Tandor, deciding I wanted to keep some of those memories private.

The vampire leaned back, propping her feet up on the counter with a satisfied smirk on her face. "So, it sounds like you had a nice time with our friend Tandor?"

I shrugged noncommittally. "He was decent company."

A snort escaped her. "Right. Decent company." Her eyebrows bounced mischievously. "And was he good in bed?"

I threw a rag at her.

"Fiella! That's none of your Gods damned business."

"Considering the blush on your face right now, I'm going to assume he's pretty *decent*."

"Well... I'm certainly not complaining."

"I knew it!"

"But don't get too excited—I still don't know what exactly is going on between us."

Disbelief clouded her face. "What's going on is you finally secured yourself a man, Kiz."

Had I? Secured myself a man? "I don't think—we didn't talk about—"

She interrupted me. "It's about time. The poor orc has been crushing on you for ages."

I snorted. "He said the same thing."

"He admitted that? Wow. You would've had to waterboard that information out of me," Fiella mused.

"Some of us are able to talk about our feelings."

She raised an eyebrow. "Like you're one of them? Sounds like you haven't told Tandor about *your* feelings."

I sighed in resignation. "I know. I know. I've been avoiding it. Everything is just so new and so fun. I don't want to ruin it by making things serious."

"So don't."

"Huh?"

She sipped her tea casually. "If you're enjoying how things are going, just let them keep going. You don't have to go and get mated right this instant. You should tell him how you feel, though. Just to make sure you're on the same page."

Her words sank in. She was right, and I knew it. I was just being a little pansy. "I will," I mumbled.

A few folk knocked on my door, but I refused to let them in, insisting they come back later. Soon, they would be cured of the annoying love enchantment. Soon, everyone would quit bothering me. Hopefully.

After a few minutes of companionable silence watching the sprites whir around the shop while we sipped our teas and ate our pastries, Fiella sat upright. Tension tightened her frame.

"Kizzi," she said cautiously.

"What's up, Fi?"

"Is that... is that what I think it is?" She gestured to the corner where Hex was hanging out in their cracked cauldron, half slumped over the side in a position that looked extremely uncomfortable but they refused to shift from.

I took another sip. "Yep."

"Holy fates."

I nodded in agreement. "They're my familiar. Hex." I spoke up a little louder. "Hex, this is my best friend Fiella.

Don't mess with her or I'll... do something bad to you." No suitable threats came to mind, but I was sure Hex could sense my intentions.

Fiella's gaze snapped to mine. "Are you kidding?"

I shook my head. "No," I lowered my voice to a whisper. "I accidentally brought them to life and now they're my magical sidekick. Forever."

Her complexion paled. "That's—I mean good for you, badass witch lady, but that's horrifying."

"You're telling me."

Hex hissed for a moment, but it didn't have as much bite to it as it used to. Our love-hate (mostly hate) relationship was complicated like that.

Fiella continued her examination of the shop. When she spotted the new cauldron in the corner, filled with a pile of blankets, she jumped to her feet. "Oh! This must be the new one—wow it's gorgeous!" She approached, gently running a finger over the cauldron's rim. She had spent enough time around me and other witches to appreciate a well-crafted caldron.

"It sure is. You don't even want to know how much it cost me; it'll make you sick. Look inside." I smiled behind the rim of my mug.

She tossed me a suspicious glance before she tentatively reached inside, removing one of the blankets. She stared blankly for a few moments.

And then she let out an ear-shattering screech. "Kizziah Cedarton! Is this what I think it is?"

I nodded smugly. "It sure is."

Three shiny, scaled eggs sat in the cauldron, nestled snugly together.

"You smuggled dragon eggs into Moonvale! Actual dragon eggs!" she shouted.

"Yep," I let the word pop from my lips with a flair. "And they weren't cheap, either."

Fiella bolted to my side, pulling me into a bone-bending hug. Her chin rested on top of my head. "You're crazy, did you know that?"

I patted her back. "It'll be a nightmare when Mayor Tommins finds out. And they might not even hatch. But still —you owe me one."

She released me and wandered back to the cauldron to admire the eggs. "I always do. This is going to be so much fun."

CHAPTER 33

Tandor

allow's Eve was only a day away, and with that came hours and hours of preparation at Ginger's Pub.

I had unloaded all my purchases from the journey—some for the pub and some for my personal collection—before dropping into a deep, dreamless sleep the night before, and my treasures were waiting for me when I woke.

I needed a wheelbarrow to haul everything to the pub. I could carry a lot, but the pile of pumpkins exceeded my limit.

The pub was lively when I entered.

Ginger set down a goblet with a thunk, letting out a deep sigh of relief when I walked into the kitchen with my wheelbarrow in tow. "Tandor!" she called out. "Thank the Old Gods! I thought I was going to have to handle the Hallow's Eve morning rush without you!"

"I would never do that to you, Ginny."

The faun fluttered into the kitchen behind me, eager to sneak a peek at my bounty. Her hoofed feet hardly made a sound as they clacked against the stone. "How was the trip?"

she asked. "New stuff?" She stretched out a hand to examine a bag of spices, but I swatted her away.

"It was great! And yes—but don't touch, I'll share but I've got to sort everything out first."

She rolled her eyes, but a smile spread across her face. "Rude. So, the trip was *great* huh?"

I glanced at her sidelong. "Mhm. It was nice to get away for a while."

"Sure. Because you love getting away so much. And your witchy companion?"

"She's good. Got what she needed." My ears twitched. She tracked the movement with her eyes. I shoved my wheelbarrow back to the corner of the kitchen—I would sort through everything and put it away properly later, when I had time to spare.

"Very ominous. I'm dying for more information here."

I steered the conversation into safer territory. "How have things been? Falling apart at the seams? Missing me dearly? Can hardly function without me?"

She gave my shoulder a shove. "We've been hanging in there. Linc over there is pretty useless, but he's a body in the room, so at least the folk *think* he might be able to help them."

I glanced at Linc to see him idly running a rag over a table that was clearly already clean. The rag wasn't even wet. He stood there, wiping the table for a few moments before he walked up to a table, grabbing an empty goblet and bringing it to the bar counter. And then he started running the rag over the counter. I stifled a laugh. "At least he's collecting the dishes."

She snorted. "You should see what he does when he washes them."

"I'm not sure I want to know what that means."

A family chose that moment to enter the pub. I snagged an apron, hastily tying it around my waist as I strode to the bar. I called out to Ginger over my shoulder, "I've got this one."

She flapped a hand in my direction. "Glad to have you back."

I slipped back into my pub routine easily, like slipping into my favorite pair of trousers. I served patrons, washed goblets, and checked on my cider barrels in the cellar.

Luckily, the brews I started before the journey were perfect.

And I now had more ingredients to toy with. Excitement hummed in my blood at the possibilities. Ginger was going to be *so* jealous.

When nobody was looking, I retrieved the jar of dragon eggshell powder, sprinkling tiny amounts into the bottoms of every single goblet, mug, flask, cup in the pub.

Evening came around before I knew it. Ginger and I had decided to close the pub early so we could prepare for the Hallow's Eve festival—I wasn't sure exactly what she would be doing, but every folk honored the holiday in their own way.

I was meeting up with other folk who preferred to take a wilder approach to celebrating Hallow's Eve. We would gather, acknowledge the holiday together, and then we would let ourselves be free. Free to run, free to prowl the woods, free to let our inner beasts out.

We had decided to meet deep in the Greenwood Forest, in a spot where spongy moss padded the ground and cushioned every step. It was far enough from town that the more mild-mannered folk wouldn't hear any suspicious sounds, but close enough that the walk home wouldn't be too strenuous.

The perfect spot for what we had planned.

I was one of the last to arrive. Fae, orcs, shifters, vampires, and other folk were milling about, chatting excitedly. Some I knew personally, some I had only seen a few times. We welcomed anyone who wanted to participate.

I noticed Redd and Fiella among the crowd—the two vampires had decided to join us in the woods this year. I tried not to think too hard about what they would be doing to celebrate. Blood made me queasy. I drifted over to them. Fiella greeted me with a cheery smile and wave, while Redd simply nodded.

The group of folk began our discussion when the first of the dual suns kissed the horizon. Mayor Tommins kicked us off. "So, everyone, we'll meet here again tomorrow, at this time. Come prepared. Eat beforehand, nurture your bodies, and bring anything you'd like." He glanced sharply at a shifter man. "But no sacrifices this year. That's barbaric."

"Lame!" a voice called out.

"We don't need to end another life to honor Hollow's Eve," Tommins argued. "We will light a bonfire—you can bring something to toss in. Incense, letters, herbs, whatever calls to you. And then we will run."

An excited chatter kicked up throughout the small crowd.

This was what we did—we gathered, we paid mind to the holiday, and then we let our instincts run free. We prowled the forests, we ran, we screamed, we let the wildness take over our bodies. Most of us chose to don masks and cloaks, hiding our identities so we could be our truest and most free selves.

"Behave yourselves. Or if you're going to damage something, at least repair it before morning, so I don't have to deal with it."

I stifled a laugh.

"No violence of any kind. Keep your wildness away from anyone who is not privy to it. And don't be an idiot. Now—is everyone clear on the rules?"

Murmurs of assent echoed through the forest. Most of us knew better, but occasionally someone got carried away and took things a bit too far.

"Great. Now, go get some sleep, and we will be back tomorrow."

Magic hummed in my veins as I milled about my apothecary, gathering ingredients and making my Hallow's Eve preparations.

Magic always felt stronger on Hallow's Eve—richer, more saturated—and today it felt galvanizing. The hairs on my arms stood on end.

It wasn't an unpleasant feeling, but it was overwhelming. It took up too much of my attention. I could normally tune out magical sensations with minor effort, but it demanded to be noticed today.

The sprites were one edge, too.

They flitted around, lifting strands of my hair, jostling papers, nudging jar lids. They usually kept their mischief contained where I couldn't see it, but they were especially rambunctious.

I had given up on trying to control them. I would simply clean the mess up later.

I packed a basket with the essentials. Dried onion skins, swan feathers, a rose quartz crystal, berries from an ancient bush, ever-tree bark, royal honey, and a few potions, tonics, and poultices.

A breeze caught my attention. I glanced up to find the front door drifting open.

"Hello?" I called out. "I'm closed for Hallow's Eve. Sorry. If you need anything, I can grab it for you later."

No voices answered. Nobody entered, either.

"Hello? Anyone there?"

Nothing. The door (newly repaired, thanks to Redd) creaked quietly on its hinges.

Huh. Maybe I had left it open?

I drifted toward the door, only to be stopped short. A squeal escaped my mouth.

A fluffy white cat was sitting gracefully on the floor just inside the open door. Her tail swished slowly behind her. She gazed at me with striking green eyes that peered all the way to my soul.

"No fucking way," I whispered. "Hello!" I reined in my excitement. I reached out to the cat to pet her. She allowed me to scratch the top of her head one time before she ducked away and hopped onto a stool.

That one scratch felt like a prize.

"Is it finally my turn to get chosen by a cat? I've been waiting for this day!"

The cat's ears shrank back to her head at my volume. I lowered my voice. "Sorry. I'm just excited."

For long moments, we just stared at each other.

"Do you... want to just hang out here?" I asked the cat.

Her whiskers twitched. Her fluffy tail swished twice. I took that as an answer.

"Right. Cool. Okay. What do I do now?"

The cat curled up on the stool and closed her eyes.

"Do you have a name?" I asked, suddenly nervous. "Am I supposed to give you a name?" I thought about it for a second. For some reason, I had the feeling that I already knew her name. Like it was undeniable. "Casper?" I asked.

Her eyes flicked open. She blinked at me slowly. And then she closed her eyes again, looking quite comfortable.

I smiled. "Casper," I said quietly to myself. What a fitting name for such a cute but intimidating little critter.

Sprites, cauldron sludge, dragon eggs, and now a cat—this place was beginning to feel like a zoo.

I secretly loved it.

Moonvale's streets were bustling as I met with Fiella and Redd for morning tea and pastries. Lemon ginger tea with berry tarts today. Scrumptious.

The air was crisp and smelled like icy apples and leaves, a telltale sign that the mild season was firmly in the past. We sat on crunchy grass in town square park as we ate. Leaves were beginning to fall, clustering in small piles as gusts of wind brushed them aside.

"So," I said to the two vampires. "Ready for tonight's festivities?" I wasn't exactly sure what they would be getting up to—and I certainly didn't want any of the blood-sucking details—but I was nosey enough to want to hear *some* information.

Redd nodded as he swallowed a large gulp of tea. "We're ready. It's going to be fun." He glanced at Fiella from the corner of his eye as she smiled smugly. I held down a gag.

"I'll try not to be grossed out by that."

"Shut up, Kiz," Fiella laughed. "We saw Tandor in the woods last night. He's going too."

This piqued my interest. "Oh?"

She gave me a knowing look. "Yep. He'll be running with the wild folk while you witches do... whatever it is you do. What are you doing?"

I waved a hand. "Oh, rituals and stuff. Nothing crazy."

It was pretty crazy, actually. We performed the biggest rituals on Hallow's Eve. Anything that required an abundance of magic, a pooling of power, would be performed. We would ask the Old Gods to continue supplying magic to Moonvale's lands, we would banish evil spirits, we would seek health and longevity for any folk of ailing strength. Whatever needed to be done. We would chant and toss offerings into the cauldron until our throats went raw, if necessary.

Fiella interrupted my thoughts. "Have you talked to him?"

I quirked an eyebrow. "Have I *talked* to him?"

"Since you returned."

"No." I tried not to let my unease show on my face. "But I'm about to."

Fiella pumped her fist in the air. "That's my girl. Go get your man."

I shakily rose to my feet. My sweating palms made my grip on my mug tenuous. "Wish me luck."

"Good luck, Kiz." Redd said with a slight smile lifting his cheek. "Knock 'em dead. Not actually, of course. Unless you need to."

"To the moons!" Fiella shouted at my back.

I rolled my eyes and waved at them over my shoulder. "Suns!"

I made my way to Ginny's Pub, walking as fast as I could without breaking into a run.

Crowds of folk were lined up outside of both the pub and the diner, everyone trying to squeeze in a hearty lunch before the Hallow's Eve celebrations kicked off in the evening. It was common Moonvale knowledge that both establishments would be closing in the early afternoon, with the two suns still high in the sky. Food available later in the day would be scarce. Mitz would be serving some delicious pastries, surely. But now was the time to fill up.

Only a few folk cast me longing glances as I passed, and almost nobody attempted to speak to me. The dragon eggshell powder must have been working. I silently thanked Tandor in my head (and myself, for coming up with the genius powder-in-drink plan).

I waited in line for a moment before I felt my nerves start to fizzle out. Drastic measures needed to be taken.

I shouldered my way through the crowd, ducking my head and pulling my cloak up so maybe folk wouldn't notice me as I jammed my way in front of them.

Hex perched on my shoulder, bubbling in satisfaction as I weaved through the line. They were more vindictive than I was.

Damn supportive familiar. I made the slime sit as far back on my shoulder as possible, almost entirely shielded by my hair. Unless someone looked *really* closely, we were safe.

I wasn't sure I wanted the entire town knowing about my "not supposed to be possible" familiar. It wasn't that I was ashamed of them, I just felt... protective. I shivered at that. Since when was I protective of the cauldron mishap?

I was growing soft.

I spotted Tandor behind the bar as I squeezed my way through the door. I ignored any protests as I passed. I was a woman on a mission.

I slipped up to the bar counter and laid my forearms on the surface, pressing to my toes and leaning forward. Tandor hadn't noticed me yet.

"Boo!" I shouted when he drifted closer.

He jumped, his entire body flinching as the mug he had been carrying clattered to the floor. He slapped a hand over his chest. "Gods almighty! You almost killed me, little witch."

Manic laughter escaped my mouth. He was entirely too easy. "Hi," I said between giggles.

"Hi," he answered as he calmed himself. He retrieved the mug from the ground (not broken, luckily) and returned to filling glasses. He poured a goblet and slid it in my direction.

I smelled it before I took a sip. Spiced pumpkin cider. A grin split my face.

"You made more?" I asked.

"Mhm," he answered. "It felt right for Hallow's Eve. I started it before we left."

I couldn't help but agree. The rich pumpkin flavor was perfect for the turning of the seasons. I almost wished it was hot, like the mulled wine back in Rockward.

The orc drifted away for a few minutes to serve other patrons. I helped myself to one of the barstools.

When he returned, he leaned forward over the bar counter, grabbed my chin between his thumb and forefinger and tilted my head back. He planted a quick kiss on my lips before grinning, releasing me, and casually grabbing another goblet.

My cheeks flamed. I didn't know what to say. I glanced around to see if anyone else had noticed—if any other lives had been irrevocably changed by that very sweet, very public kiss.

Nobody was staring. Just my life, then.

Tandor filled a few other drinks before returning to my end of the bar.

"Ready for tonight?" he asked.

My mind was still whirling from the chaste kiss. "I—I hope so," I stuttered. "The cauldron will certainly do the trick."

He glanced up, catching my eye. "I'm glad." He smiled gently. "It sure was a lot of effort, it better be worth it."

"It's worth it." Everything about the trip had been worth it.

His gaze softened. Warmed. His smile grew. It was almost like he could read my mind. "Is it?"

I nodded urgently. I braced myself, finally ready to confess my feelings. "Tandor, I—"

He interrupted me. "Kizzi, you are the most breathtaking, impatient, nosey, kind-hearted woman I have ever met. You could brew a potion to shatter the realm, if you set your mind to it." His voice was quiet, only for my ears. He gathered my hands in his. "I will be grateful every day that you invited me on that journey with you. Now, go ahead—" He pressed my knuckles to his lips, "—I just had to get that out."

I gaped at him. My cheeks were burning hot—the tips of my ears absolutely flaming. "I don't know what to say. I can't believe you just stole my moment like that."

The corners of his eyes wrinkled in glee. "You were about to confess your undying love for me?"

Impossibly, my cheeks heated even further. My lips refused to form words.

His eyes widened. "You were, weren't you? In front of the entire town? Kizzi, I didn't realize you were such a romantic!" He kissed my knuckles again. "I think this is the best day of my life."

I laughed, any lingering tension draining away. "I was just going to tell you, since we're back home, and things will be going back to normal—"

"That you love me?"

"That being around you makes me feel alive. I've never been happier. I want to keep doing this." I paused, gathering my thoughts. "I want to be with you, if you'll have me."

"Kizzi, you've held my heart in the palm of your hand for longer than you know."

I melted. "I'll take good care of it. I promise."

I gazed into his liquid onyx eyes, getting lost in them. His smile was beautiful. I saw countless happy days in the twinkle of his eyes, the creases in his cheeks.

Somewhere behind me, someone cleared their throat.

Pulling my eyes away from Tandor's magnetic stare, I remembered where I was—leaning over the bar in Ginger's crowded pub.

I couldn't muster any embarrassment. All I felt was sweet, heartwarming, soul-tingling happiness.

I straightened. "I better get out of your hair—you've got a line here."

Someone muttered a bratty thank you, but I ignored it, too giddy to come up with any retorts.

Tandor released my hands, returning to his customers. "Have a happy Hallow's Eve, little witch."

"Happy Hallow's Eve to you too, orc."

"I'll see you later," he called out as I stood from my barstool. He drifted away.

Later? What did he mean by that?

When the suns began their descent, I returned to my shop to gather my supplies and don my traditional cloak and pointed witch hat.

The witches were gathering in a small clearing just inside the perimeter of the Greenwood Forest. We didn't go in very far, only far enough to be surrounded by trees. Most of us didn't want to hike any further, and the clearing worked perfectly.

This would be the ninth Hallow's Eve ritual that I got to participate in. Young witches not yet to adulthood were welcome to watch, to observe the rituals, but only the adults could participate. It was safer that way.

I wasn't the only witch hauling supplies to the clearing in the woods. Hyacinth was, too. And a few others—Giada and Giselle, the red-haired rust-complected twins and Rayna, a younger witch with hair and eyes the color of sunflower petals, all carried baskets.

We marched to the clearing like bees returning to a hive.

"Can you ladies help me with something?" I asked when every basket was placed in the clearing.

Hyacinth groaned. "What? Please tell me we don't have to carry anything else."

I squinted at her. "You don't have a deep desire to help me for a reason you can't quite put a finger on?"

She looked at me like I had two heads. "No. Not all. No offense."

Relief flowed over me in a wave. "You don't think I look pretty today?"

"You look fine, I guess. Your tunic is nice. I like your hat. Why are you being weird?"

"I'm just making sure." The love potion enchantment clearly wasn't impacting her anymore.

"Do you actually need help with something or was that some sort of theoretical question too?"

I cleared my throat. "I do need help. With carrying something."

The black-haired witch tensed. "Carrying what?"

"Only the most important part of the entire ritual."

"You're joking."

"Unfortunately, I'm not. The cauldron is in my apothecary. If we all carry it together, it won't be that bad!"

The witches whined and complained as I corralled them into my shop. The cauldron was heavy, ridiculously so, and Tandor wasn't around to help me move it this time.

So, five witches would have to do the trick.

We surrounded the cauldron (sans dragon eggs—those were now tucked under the covers in my bed), everyone grasping the bowl with white-knuckled fingers. On the count of three, we heaved, hardly lifting it off the ground.

"Gods! This thing is a fucking boulder!" Hyacinth complained.

I gritted my teeth. My shoulders screamed in protest. "We can do this. Just don't let go. Let's move."

"My hands are going to fall off," Giada grumbled. "Ouch."

"Oh hush, we'll make it. Just keep going. Okay there we go, through the door. Yep—I'll close that later. Careful, now."

Grunting and groaning, sweating and swearing, shuffling our feet in tiny, careful steps, we slowly carried the cauldron to the clearing in the woods. My fingertips were blistered and raw by the time we finally dropped the hunk of cast iron onto the leaf-littered ground.

Other witches were in the clearing—some faces familiar, some new. I could feel the magic dripping from them all. Warm, bubbling magic from the witches with an affinity for water. Sharp and hot magic from the witches of the flames. Nurturing magic from the witches more closely tied to nature.

If I closed my eyes and breathed in deep, I could feel remnants of other magic, too. Older magic. Stronger magic.

And when the first of the moons began to rise in the sky, my blood began to simmer. Magic thrummed in the air, tickling my skin, tightening my muscles, hardening my bones.

I braced myself for the night ahead.

CHAPTER 35
Tandor

My arms ached as I rinsed my last goblet, setting it on a towel to dry.

I lost count of how many drinks I served, but it felt like I had given something to every folk in town. And thank the fates for that, because I was almost out of dragon eggshell powder. Luckily, it seemed that everyone had gotten their dose.

And that meant nobody would be prowling after Kizzi tonight.

Well, except for me, of course.

"Alright, I think we're good!" I shouted to Ginger. She was back in the kitchen, washing up the last of the dishes.

She peeked her head out for a moment. "Go ahead and head out, I've got a few more bowls to wash and then I'll lock up for the evening."

I removed my apron, draping it over the bar counter. "Pretty successful morning, I'd say."

"Certainly busy," she mused. "But we did it. Now we can enjoy the evening and whatever shenanigans it brings."

I wasn't sure what Ginger would be getting up to, and she never told me anyway, so I didn't bother to ask. It was personal for some folk.

"Be safe tonight!" I called as I strolled out the door.

"You too!" Her voice drifted to me on a brisk wind as the door knocked shut.

My cottage was a mess. I hadn't bothered tidying or putting away any of my newly purchased items. I washed myself quickly and pulled on a black tunic and trousers, along with my black cloak.

I wanted to blend into the night—to become the darkness.

My heart had been thumping heavily all day. The air was heavy, like the heavens were sinking too close to the surface. Hallow's Eve was looming. I could practically feel the hours as they passed.

I smeared some charcoal on any exposed skin to mask my green hue and I tugged a mask over my face. I brought the charcoal around my eyes, too.

I stared in the mirror at the stranger in front of me.

I was darkness incarnate. The mask was shaped to my face and tied behind my head with a strip of fabric to keep it secure. It was painted to resemble the skull of a beast. The only holes were for my eyes. My hair was slicked back to keep it out of the way.

The whites of my sclera seemed to glow, surrounded by so much shadow. The effect was eerie.

I was ready.

My pulse thudded in my ears as I ventured back into the Greenwood Forest. The suns were long gone, and the moons were beginning their ascent in the sky.

The other wild folk vibrated with the same energy that charged me. It was contagious. Most were masked, cloaked, disguised as I was.

I couldn't distinguish friend from stranger, but that was the entire point. Tonight, we were simply wild. We were free.

Cloaked figures gathered deep in the woods, surrounding a roaring bonfire.

Tommins was nowhere to be seen, blending into the crowd instead of standing in front of it. Tonight, he wasn't the mayor. Tonight, he was simply another folk.

My breathing was noisy to my own ears. Air sawed in and out of my lungs.

A figure stepped forward, tossing a tunic into the bonfire. The flames surged and crackled. Another figure stepped forward. This one carried a bundle of herbs. The flames flared again. The cycle repeated—everyone stepping forward to drop an offering into the fire.

When it was my turn, I set my offering aflame—a small bundle of dried roses.

We remained still for what felt like hours, absorbing the sounds of the forest, watching the bonfire engulf every offering—turn them to nothing but embers and ash.

And then we began.

CHAPTER 36

Kizzi

Magic. All I could feel, hear, smell, *taste* was magic. It saturated the air so heavily I was practically swimming in it.

It was impossible. Magic was always easier to feel, easier to manipulate, easier to gather on Hallow's Eve, but this was different. This was *more*.

And I reveled in it.

I never felt more alive.

The witches stood in a circle in the clearing, all of us joining hands around the cauldron. I could tell the others were feeling the magic too. There was a charge to the air, an expectation. A readiness.

Hex, about a gallon of them, was bundled into a backpack slung over my shoulders. They were heavier than I expected, weighing more than a sack of grain.

My familiar was a roiling mass of energy as they gurgled in the sack. I was tempted to set them down, to let them be free, but I worried about where they would run off to out in the woods with so much magic charging the air.

303

Losing them would be an inconvenience. I might miss them a little.

The main ritual commenced.

Ani, the coven leader, led the ritual. As the oldest witch in Moonvale, she was the expert.

"Witches!" she shouted. "One by one, bring your offerings to the cauldron."

We did.

Herbs, gems, metals, spices, flowers, leaves—the cauldron held the most magical mixture.

When it was my turn, I stepped forward with my offering. Rose quartz. For healing, for compassion, for love. Unconditional love.

I clutched the crystal tightly in my palm. The rigid material bit into my flesh.

My foot landed on something soft as I strode forward. On a reflex, I immediately yanked it back.

An unholy screech echoed throughout the clearing. My gaze darted down to see Casper in front of me, her tail angrily swishing back and forth. It was covered in dirt and leaves.

I had stepped on the damned cat's tail.

I frantically bent down to assess the cat, to pet her, to make sure she was okay. "Oh, Gods! Sorry Casper! Why were you sitting right under my boots?"

The cat batted my hand away with angry paws, claws bared.

She barely swiped my finger, the one clutching the crystal. The flesh split and blood welled.

Just a drop or two.

Guilt flooded me. I hastily dropped my crystal into the

cauldron, murmuring apologies to the cat under my breath the entire time. I deserved that one.

Luckily, Casper seemed to forgive me quickly. She rubbed her head against my boot and then sat quietly beside me, licking her paws and grooming herself.

The other witches completed their offerings, and then we began to chant. The chant for the main ritual was the same every year—it never failed to chill my blood.

Hallow's Eve! Hallow's Eve! Old Gods, hear our pleas! We bring our offerings to you, to keep the magic free. Hallow's Eve! Hallow's Eve! Old Gods, hear our pleas! We dedicate ourselves to you, so magic may be free.

The trees surrounding the witch circle began to shiver. Leaves rained down around the clearing, blanketing us in drops of yellow, red, orange.

And then the ground began to shake. It vibrated my bones. Chattered my teeth.

"What's going on?" someone shouted. "Is this supposed to happen?"

"Stay calm," Ani insisted. "The fates will forge the path. All is as it should be."

A vicious wind whipped through the clearing. Leaves lifted off the ground, carried in a spiral. They whirled around us as though they were alive.

Hex leapt from the backpack, landing with a splat on the ground. They split into two, one half of them wrapping around my ankle, the other half darting toward the cauldron. I didn't even have time to stop them. They crawled up the edge of the cauldron to sneak a peek.

The cauldron bubbled up and spilled over. A plume of smoke, a rich purple color, drifted free. Instead of drifting straight up to the skies, it drifted outwards, toward the witches, and then beyond. It crept through the forest like a fog.

The smoke smelled of ice and ashes, of magic in its purest form.

Sweat beaded on my hairline. My hands began to shake. Acid burned up my throat.

And then darkness swallowed me whole.

"Kizziah," a voice called, near and far, loud but soft. I couldn't see anything. Couldn't smell anything. Couldn't feel the air on my skin or the ground beneath my feet.

The only thing I could feel was Hex's solid weight curled against my ankle. I almost cried at how relieved I was to feel them there.

"Kizziah."

I didn't know what happened to the ritual. Had I fallen asleep? Was this some sort of dream? The beginnings of panic fluttered in my stomach.

"Kizziah Cedarton. Answer." The voice was haughty now. Impatient.

I swallowed the lump in my throat. "Y–yes?"

"You have summoned us," the voice boomed.

"I what?"

"You have summoned us," the voice repeated. "We have been waiting for one of our ancestors to call us back to the realm. Waiting and waiting and waiting. The time has finally come."

"What are you talking about?" I asked, dumbfounded.

"We are on our way." The voice was further now, slipping away. Sinking underwater.

"What? Who? Huh?" My mind fought to piece together what was going on.

What the fuck had I done?

I felt their presence drift away, and some of the overwhelming magic went with it.

And then I could finally pull my eyes open.

I was still standing in the circle, still holding the hands of two witches, and Hex was still perched on my foot with Casper leaning against the other.

What the fuck was that?

My bed had never felt so comfortable. I was exhausted, the kind of tired that sank into my bones and made them feel malleable.

I didn't even have the energy to brush off the sprites as they settled on my shoulders, on my hair.

I readied myself for bed and sank into one of the deepest sleeps of my life, surrounded by Casper, Hex, and countless sprites.

CHAPTER 37
Tandor

Wind whipped by my ears as I ran through the Greenwood Forest. I wasn't nearly as fast as some of the other folk, but I didn't care. I pumped my arms, pushing myself as fast as I could go.

My thighs burned with the effort. It was a pleasant agony. I didn't know where I was going, and I didn't care. I just let my body carry me away. Deeper into the forest, farther from the familiarity of Moonvale.

A strange purple fog cloaked the forest, blurring the edges of trees, camouflaging the leaf-covered ground. It seeped into my skin, snaked up my nostrils. The ice and ash scent of it was pleasant—it made my blood feel thick and sticky in my veins.

A product of the witches, surely.

I had only one witch on my mind. Kizzi. Kizzi with her sass, her obliviousness, her contagious laugh. Her long flowy skirts and her delicate pointed ears.

Kizzi, who cared for me too. Impossibly. Miraculously.

I wanted to go to her. To be with her. To finish out Hallow's Eve with her by my side.

I pushed myself harder. Leaves whipped my skin as I passed.

My thoughts strayed to the journey, to the hours spent in the carriage with the witch pressed to my side. To the shared meals, the traded snacks. To the nights spent sharing warmth. To the nights spent sharing *more* than just warmth.

I brought myself to a stop. I clutched the trunk of a tree for support as I caught my breath.

I couldn't resist anymore.

Turning in the other direction, I set my targets on Kizzi's apothecary.

I slipped through the forest like a ghost, avoiding the critters and folk alike. My blood thrummed in my veins—my muscles surged with renewed energy.

Mind full of green hair and greener eyes, the run passed quickly.

The apothecary lights were off, the front door locked. But I knew she was inside.

My breaths sawed in and out of my lungs, fogging behind the mask strapped to my face.

I knocked on the door. Nobody answered. I knew better than to try to break in—she surely had enchantments set up to prevent that—so I knocked again.

And again.

And again.

Eventually, I heard the telltale creak of wood. The soft pad of feet. The sound of Kizzi approaching.

My pulse thudded in my ears.

When Kizzi pulled the door open, her hair was mussed with interrupted sleep, pulled up into a loose knot on top of her head. She was wearing a thin nightgown that clung to her in all the right places. Her feet were bare. She looked soft, warm, *delicious*. I ached to taste her. To tease her. To touch her.

She rubbed her eyes sleepily. "What's going on?" she asked. Her voice was rough, and so unbelievably sexy. My cock hardened at the sight of her.

I didn't say anything. I simply stepped forward, pushing her inside and slamming the door shut behind me. She gasped in surprise.

I grabbed her by the waist and pushed her back against the door. I crowded her, dropping my face into her neck, enjoying her proximity. I traced one of my hands up her throat, curling my fingers around her neck, lifting her chin with my thumb.

She was so small, my little witch. So delicate. I could snap her bones beneath my hands if I wished.

Or I could shatter the skulls of anyone who tried to harm her.

The thought brought a rumble to the back of my throat.

She trembled in my grasp, her breaths picking up speed. "What's happening?" Kizzi breathed. "Tandor?"

I didn't answer.

I gripped her around the waist and tossed her body over my shoulder. I held her carefully but firmly, making sure her soft stomach didn't bruise.

She protested weakly.

I wanted her in my space. My home. And I wanted to keep her there.

I opened the door with one hand and carried Kizzi across town to my cottage.

She peppered me with questions the entire way. "Tandor? Hello? Where are we going? I have legs, you know."

I didn't respond. I had one goal in mind—to get her into my bed.

My focus homed in on the witch slung over my shoulder and nothing else. I didn't know if we passed any other folk, if there were critters in my path. I wouldn't have even noticed if the streets were on fire.

My cottage came into view quickly.

"Isn't this your home? Tandor?"

I shoved the door open and kicked it shut behind me.

CHAPTER 38
Kizzi

My heart pounded in my chest, my body awake and thrumming. I was achingly aware of Tandor, his muscled shoulder I was slung over, the ease with which he tossed me around.

His strength was intoxicating. I was not a thin witch, I enjoyed sweets too much for that, but he handled me like I weighed nothing.

The orc dropped me onto a soft surface—his bed, I realized, saturated in his warm rain scent—and prowled over me.

He still didn't speak. His face was obscured except for his eyes, coal rimmed and gleaming.

He was another beast entirely. I relaxed, meeting his gaze, letting my eyes tell him that I was here. That I would take whatever he decided to throw at me.

His gaze turned wicked.

He started with my hands, running his palms along my fingers, my wrists, my forearms. He stroked my skin tenderly, but the heat in his dark eyes promised something feral. Something wicked.

When he reached the fabric of my nightclothes he paused. His gaze flicked down, and he tilted his head to the side.

And then he grasped the fabric in both hands and tore my nightclothes from my body. The sound of snapping threads was deafening in the quiet of the cottage, setting my pulse racing. The fabric gave easily under his strong hands.

Soon, I was bare on his bed, naked and wanting. Air heaved in and out of my lungs in a frantic rhythm.

He leaned back to gaze at me, his eyes hot on my skin. I could practically feel his eyes tracing over me, my breasts, my stomach, the vee between my legs. I squirmed, antsy.

I reached for his cloak, tugging at it, begging him to remove it. To free his skin so I could run my hands over it.

Tandor snatched my wrists, pressing them to the bed above my head. "No," he growled.

I gulped. "I want to touch you."

He visibly shuddered. His eyes shut for a long moment before he dragged them open again. "No. You don't get to touch me, little witch. I'm going to run my hands over every single inch of your delicious body. And if you're good, maybe I'll let you touch me. But until then—" he trailed off, snatching my wrists and binding them to the posts at the head of the bed with a swath of fabric. "You're mine to play with."

I didn't resist, too shocked to put up a fight. Arousal pooled in my stomach. I didn't know what had gotten into Tandor, but I *loved* it. This feral side of him made my mouth water.

Satisfied with the knot at my wrists, he slid his hands over my arms, across my collarbones, and settled them at my breasts. "Are you going to be good?" He kneaded my flesh in his hands, sending shivers down my spine.

I nodded, my hair rasping against the sheets.

"I didn't hear you. I said, are you going to be good?"

My core clenched. "Yes."

His eyes wrinkled at the corners. "Good little witch." He stroked his thumbs over my nipples, massaging the taut skin. My back arched. A quiet whimper escaped my parted lips.

He watched my face closely, monitoring my reactions. Something about the mask on his face, the covering of his expression, made his eyes feel impossibly intense. Intimate, like he could see all the way down to my soul.

He continued his torment on my nipples until I was writhing beneath him, panting, ready to beg for more.

Tandor released me for just a moment, long enough to pull his cloak off and toss it somewhere behind him. And then he was back, his hands on my skin.

He trailed lower, dragging his fingers over my sternum, my stomach, my hips. He stopped there, allowing his fingertips to dance over my hip bones, mapping their shape.

And then he dipped even lower, his hands tracing my thighs. My shins. My ankles. I spread my legs in invitation.

His eyes flicked to mine for a moment before returning to my pussy. "Impatient, are we?"

"Please," I begged.

"Please what, little witch?"

"Please touch me."

His hands stroked over my thighs again, stopping just short of where I wanted them to be.

I whined. "Please, Tandor. *Please.*"

He tilted his head. "When you ask so sweetly..." Finally, his hand slid over my center.

I cried out in relief. I pulled against my restraints,

desperate to touch him, but I was trapped, completely at his mercy.

His fingers slid over my slick folds, parting me, igniting waves of pleasure. He found my clit, stroking it in smooth circular motions.

"Yes," I breathed. My stomach tightened.

His fingers continued their delicious torture, pulling me closer and closer to the edge. I bucked beneath him.

When I thought I couldn't take it anymore, he slid his fingers lower, teasing at my entrance. With a glance at my face, he pressed a finger into me.

My hips churned, begging for more friction. Begging for *more*.

He pressed another finger into me, fucking me slowly. My head dropped back onto the bed. My blood absolutely boiled, release threatening to pull me under.

Tandor leaned over me. His other hand slipped up to my throat, my jaw, forcing me to meet his gaze. His eyes bored into mine, only inches away.

I was suddenly desperate for his mouth, his tongue, his lips on mine. I tugged at the restraints, but the effort was useless.

He kept fucking me with his fingers, slow and languid. "Do you want something, little witch?"

I panted. "I want your cock. I want you to kiss me."

He tilted his head, his fingers continuing their torment.

"Please," I added.

He pulled his body off me and stripped, removing his tunic, his trousers, his undershorts.

He lined his body up with mine, his cock replacing his fingers and teasing at my entrance. The metal of his piercing cooled my hot flesh. Slowly, he pressed in. I was so wet, he slid in easily, all the way to the hilt.

I would never tire of how perfectly he filled me. I was so *full*.

He shifted his hips, thrusting into me. I gasped and wrapped my legs around his waist. I couldn't hook my ankles together, he was too broad, but I dug my heels into his ass, urging him on.

He pumped his hips, fucking me in a punishing rhythm. I wriggled beneath him.

"Let me touch you. Please. Untie my hands."

He watched my face as he thrust into me, his cock stretching me to my absolute limit. "You want to touch me?"

"*Yes*," I cried. I wanted to run my hands over his chest, his shoulders, his hair. I wanted to anchor myself against his onslaught.

He relented, leaning forward to untie the fabric around my wrists.

My shoulders twinged when my arms were finally free, blood flow returning to my fingers.

I dug my fingers into his hair, untying his mask, yanking it from his face. I tossed it across the room. It was a relief to see his face again. He was smiling wickedly at me.

I yanked his mouth down to mine. His lips were hot and soft, and his tongue was even softer. He devoured my mouth as he pounded into my pussy, overwhelming my senses and filling me with nothing but him.

I threw my arms around his neck, desperate to hold him close. My breasts pressed against his chest.

After long blissful moments, when I felt the release creeping up on me again, he rolled, flipping us over and pulling me on top of him. My knees settled on either side of his hips as he sprawled beneath me. I braced my hands on his stomach.

This new position changed the angle of our bodies in a *very* interesting way. His piercing stroked that perfect spot deep inside of me, sending jolts down my spine. I shifted experimentally.

Pleasure churned in my belly.

Tandor spoke. "Even better than I imagined." He grabbed my ass, lifting me on his cock before pulling me back down again, helping me ride him.

I threw my head back and groaned. "What are you talking about?" My thighs worked as I established a rhythm that made my bones feel malleable.

His fingers clenched on my ass. "I've been thinking about you like this since that night at the inn."

Surprised, I laughed. "I thought we were never speaking about that again."

He bucked his hips, hitting me impossibly deeper. "It's all I've been able to think about."

"I've been thinking about it too," I admitted on a breathy exhale.

Tandor growled, grasping me by the hips and taking over, holding me still while he thrust his hips up into me. His pace was brutal. Wild.

I was boneless, unable to move, unable to breathe. My mouth fell open on a silent scream.

Finally, agonizingly, I fell over the edge. The orgasm ripped the air from my lungs and shattered me into a million pieces as Tandor continued to fuck me, muttering praises under his breath.

As I came back to my body, Tandor's muscles clenched, a strangled shout escaping his throat. He released into me, his cock pulsating as he continued his shallow thrusts. His fingers dug into my hips hard enough to bruise.

I hoped they would bruise—I wanted the reminder for later.

When my body stopped twitching and Tandor finally caught his breath, I lifted myself off him and settled into the bed beside his massive form. His bed was so much bigger than mine. We fit perfectly.

I rolled to face him to find him already looking at me. The coal lining his eyes was smeared.

I grinned. "Happy Hallow's Eve."

He smiled back. He reached out to brush my hair from my forehead. "Happy Hallow's Eve, little witch." He leaned forward and pressed a sweet, lingering kiss to my lips. My mouth felt swollen.

I wriggled closer, pressing my face into his chest. He engulfed me in an embrace. His body curled around mine.

His heart beat loud and strong against my cheek.

After long, comfortable moments, I spoke again. My voice was quiet and sleepy. "You kidnapped me."

A laugh rumbled in his chest. "I couldn't help myself."

"I'm flattered," I mumbled. "But you could have just asked."

He shook with silent laughter. His hand stroked over my snarled hair. He took a deep inhale, held it for a moment, and then let it out. "I love you, little witch."

My heart nearly stopped. I smiled, hidden in the safety of his chest. I had never felt so comfortable. So warm. So protected. "I love you, Tandor."

<h1 style="text-align:center">CHAPTER 39
Kizzi</h1>

I awoke with Tandor curled around me, my back pressed to his front, our legs entwined, his chin tucked on top of my head.

My muscles had never felt so languid. I never wanted to move.

I soaked in the comfort for long minutes, but eventually Tandor began to stir.

"Good morning. You snore, by the way."

He snorted. "No, I don't." He snaked his arms around my waist, tugged me even closer.

I snuggled into his embrace. "No, you don't."

A laugh rumbled in his chest. "I like this."

"This?" I shifted, rubbing my ass against his crotch.

His laugh turned into a growl. His arms tightened around me. "I'm trying to be sweet."

"Nobody's stopping you."

"I was trying to say that I like this. You. In my bed. In my cottage."

I rolled to face him. His eyes were half lidded, still sleepy. "I like this too."

Tandor tucked a stray lock of hair behind my ear before he let his fingers stroke over my cheek, petting the skin there. "You should stay."

I smiled. "I would, but I need to get to the shop. I've got orders to catch up on."

His cheek twitched, and he met my gaze. His eyes burned into mine. "I'm serious."

I remembered our quiet confessions the night before. Nerves fluttered in my belly. "You want me to move into your cottage?"

He nodded. His eyes scanned over my face before meeting my stare again. "Yes. At least part of the time. You've got your room in your shop, but whenever you want to spend time with me..." He trailed off, either distracted or nervous, I couldn't tell.

I grinned. He was adorable. "I think that's a great idea."

His eyes lit up. "You do?"

"I do."

I leaned forward, tossing my arm around his neck and pulling his lips to mine.

It wasn't until I returned to my apothecary that I noticed some of the repercussions of the ritual last night.

My shop, usually simmering with magic, was at the point of boiling. I stepped outside.

If I paid attention, I could sense the magic everywhere. It coated the cobblestones, soaked the folk, clung to the breeze.

It was *everywhere*. I inhaled deeply, pulling magic into my lungs and huffing it out on a sigh. It was delightful, so much magic. Euphoric. I glanced around to see other folk doing the same thing, looking bewildered, looking stunned.

The Hallow's Eve rituals could strengthen magic, sure, could pull more to the area. But *this?* This was something different entirely.

I had never been so entirely drenched in magic.

I took a moment to stand there in awe, breathing in the magic, letting it soak into my pores and drift out on my exhales.

And then it all clicked into place. And I knew what was happening.

Fiella's voice called out from down the street, shouting the same thoughts. "Kizzi! What's going on? Has magic finally returned to the realm?"

Tandor and I sat, legs intertwined, curled up on the couch in his cottage. Casper was seated on my lap, purring gently as I ran my fingers through her smooth fur.

We passed a roll of mirthroot back and forth, taking turns inhaling the enchanted smoke.

"Did I tell you I had a vision?" I asked as wispy smoke drifted past my lips. "During Hallow's Eve."

"Oh? Did it involve me?"

I shoved his shoulder. "Oh, of course. But there was another one. Without you in it."

"What about?"

I shrugged. "Some voice. Deep but soft, far but close, it was hard to pinpoint."

"Just a voice? How is that a vision?"

"Do you want to know what they said or not?"

He gestured for me to continue. "Go ahead, princess. Tell me."

"They thanked me for inviting them back."

"Huh. Who was it?"

I took another puff, exhaling slowly through my teeth. "I have no idea."

"What do you think it means?" he asked.

"Your guess is as good as mine."

"Were you smoking mirthroot that night?"

I laughed. "No. But nobody will believe me, will they?"

"I believe you."

I reached out to pat his hand. "You have to believe me. I'm the one sharing your bed."

His smile was roguish. "I would believe you regardless."

"Whatever you say, orc."

"I believe you too, Godsblood" a tiny voice chimed in. I nearly jumped out of my skin. I whirled, seeking the source of the intrusion. Did someone sneak into the cottage? The drugs were getting to me.

A tiny sprite, blue and wispy, perched on the arm of the couch beside me. It was the brave water sprite, I realized. She must have followed me here.

And she was *speaking*.

"Tandor, am I hallucinating right now?"

Tandor coughed, pounding a fist on his chest. "Nope. I see it too."

The sprite froze, turning to ice. Actually. Frost crystals clung to her hair. "You can hear me?" her squeaky voice asked.

I nodded, dazed. "I sure can."

The sprite jumped up and down, fluttering her tiny wings and waving her arms. "She can hear us! The Godsblood can finally hear us!"

I glanced at Tandor to find him looking just as frazzled as

I felt. He slowly set the roll of mirthroot aside, extinguishing the flame on the end.

"You guys have been... trying to speak to me?" I asked.

"Yes! For ages! We have *so much* to catch up on."

"What should we try next?" Fiella asked, arms crossed. We stared at the three scaled dragon eggs where they sat in a basket on my worktable.

We had tried countless methods to get the eggs to hatch.

We'd tried potions. Spells. Immersing them in boiling water. We'd even tried using brute force and cracking them open with a hammer.

Fiella and I wrote letters to folk across the realm, begging and pleading for suggestions. For answers. For ideas.

We tried everything. Nothing worked.

"Let's just toss them in the broken cauldron and let them rest for a while. I'm fresh out of ideas."

Fiella sighed. "That's not the right attitude to have, Miss Hand of the Dragons."

I snorted at her use of my new title. "I'll think of something tomorrow. I just need a break. If we don't figure it out by Merry Day, we'll take them back to the mountains and see if anyone has any ideas."

"Merry Day! How could I have forgotten about Merry Day! I need to start preparing my gifts!"

Just like that, Fiella had moved on to a new mission.

I needed to prepare my gifts, too. I had no idea what to get for Tandor. I would probably make some sort of potion for him, or maybe a fancy mug for his ales, but I wanted it to be *perfect*.

Fiella and I left the dragon eggs in the broken cauldron as we left the shop, heading to the bakery for teas and pastries. Hex curled up around them like some sort of sludge cushion.

We didn't notice the hairline crack beginning to form on one of the eggs.

Also by Hailey Blackwood

The Moonvale Matches Series

#1: Love Letters and Thirst Tonics

#2: Cauldrons and Cat Tails

#2.5: Merry in Moonvale

#3: Shadows and Ciders

#4: Coming soon! (Late 2025)

Acknowledgments

THANK YOU, reader, for coming back to read the 2nd installment in the Moonvale Matches series. I appreciate you more than you will ever know. Moonvale has become a comfort for me, and I hope it's become a comfort for some of you too.

Thank you to my family and friends, for letting me shut down and focus on this book for the past few months. For letting me cancel plans to sit in my office for hours, days, weeks on end, sipping on pumpkin spice ciders and giggling about orcs. And for listening to me talk about it endlessly.

Once again, Mom, Emily, Laura, I couldn't do it without you. You ladies are my backbone and my motivation, my biggest cheerleaders and my strongest supporters. Thank you.

And Žana, my artist, thank you for helping me catch readers' eyes before they've even read a single word. You've changed the game for me.

If you're hoping for another venture into the magical town of Moonvale, don't worry, there is more to come (:

XOXO,
Hailey Blackwood

About the Author

Hailey Blackwood is a lover of all things fantasy—from cozy to dark and everywhere in between. She has always been an avid reader, but she has stepped into the author world with her debut novel, Love Letters and Thirst Tonics, and now the sequel, Cauldrons and Cat Tails. When Hailey is not reading or writing, you will probably find her drinking tea (or wine) at home surrounded by her four cats and multitude of house-plants. She loves witches, golden-retriever MMCs, and cozy fantasy worlds that you feel like you can step right into.

www.authorhaileyblackwood.com

instagram.com/authorhaileyblackwood

tiktok.com/@authorhaileyblackwood

amazon.com/author/haileyblackwood